THE
MEDUSA
DEEP

ALSO BY DAVID NEIL LEE

Young Adult
The Midnight Games

Fiction
Commander Zero

Non-fiction
*The Battle of the Five Spot: Ornette Coleman and the New York
    Jazz Field*
Chainsaws: A History
Four-Wheeling on Southern Vancouver Island
Stopping Time: Paul Bley and the Transformation of Jazz

THE
MEDUSA
DEEP

DAVID NEIL LEE

– a sequel to *The Midnight Games* –

POPLAR
PRESS

Poplar Press is an imprint of Wolsak and Wynn Publishers.

Editor: Noelle Allen | Copy editor: Ashley Hisson
Cover design: Rachel Rosen
Cover image: Rachel Rosen; airship image from San Diego Air & Space Museum Archives on Flickr; ostrich skeleton photo by Hans van der Lubbe from Pexels; bat wings from photo by Jeremy Bishop on Unsplash
Interior design: Jennifer Rawlinson
Author photograph: Maureen Cochrane
Typeset in Headline One and Garamond
Printed by Brant Service Press Ltd., Brantford, Canada

Printed on certified 100% post-consumer Rolland Enviro Paper.

10 9 8 7 6 5 4 3 2 1

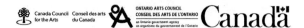

The publisher gratefully acknowledges the support of the Ontario Arts Council, the Canada Council for the Arts and the Government of Canada.

Poplar Press
280 James Street North
Hamilton, ON
Canada L8R L23

Library and Archives Canada Cataloguing in Publication

Title: The Medusa deep / David Neil Lee.
Names: Lee, David, 1952- author.
Description: Series statement: The midnight games ; 2 | Sequel to: The midnight games.
Identifiers: Canadiana 20210117419 | ISBN 9781989496312 (softcover)
Classification: LCC PS8623.E436 M44 2021 | DDC jC813/.6—dc23

To Cal and Ian
It's an incredible world out there.
You never know what's going to happen.

PROLOGUE
THE PRIME MINISTER
OF EVERYTHING

Even if you just glimpse it for a second, it stays with you forever. That's what it's like for people who witness an act of war, a violent crime, a natural disaster, a fatal car crash. The same can be said, I guess, if you've seen a sasquatch, lake monster, angel, UFO, et cetera. You've got an idea about how the world works, and in the space of a few seconds something chews up that idea and spits it out, and you never see things the same way again. It's been true for me since the night I saw *Sorcerer*.

It was at the last of the nighttime ceremonies, the "midnight games," in Ivor Wynne Stadium. The Resurrection Church of the Ancient Gods had conjured up a continuum threshold strong enough to bring through Yog-Sothoth, the giant extraterrestrial being they worshipped; the alien they called a god. Yog-Sothoth, in fact, was halfway through already, its tentacled bulk billowing up like a thunderhead in the night sky, and if that wasn't bad enough, all hell was breaking loose in the stadium itself. Creatures called the Hounds of Tindalos had been summoned – to kill my father – and they swarmed the playing field, tearing through anyone who got in their way. Giant centipedes called *dritches*, attracted by the energy field generated by the expanding threshold, were digging their way up through the Astroturf.

Then something appeared against the boiling clouds and expanding void of the threshold. A blast of blue flame drove Yog-Sothoth back from the brink, and something else, just as huge and alien, emerged in the sky above the stadium as the continuum threshold shimmered and shredded and faded out of existence.

That "something" was an enormous airship – not one of the new shiny ones I've been checking out online, but one as old as the *Hindenburg*. Everything about it looked ancient – the flaking rubber of its mountain-sized gasbag, the yellow incandescence that glowed from the windows of the gondola, the official ID numbers – R102 G-FAAX – painted on its side along with the vessel's name: SORCERER.

Like I said, this took a matter of seconds. Then *Sorcerer* flickered into translucency, and vanished altogether into the stormy sky north of the stadium. I remember a few other details – there seemed to be some kind of shiny hood covering the nose and spine of the bag – but a lot of things were happening at once. One of the Hounds had slashed me across the right side, its talons ripping through my shoulder and down my chest, and I was losing blood. In fact, if Mr. Shirazi hadn't happened along, the Hound's next blow would have torn me to bits. But Mr. Shirazi, with that device he called a Delphic scythe, sent that Hound back to the pound. What I took away that night is mainly scars.

There have been changes, mind you, in day-to-day life. My dad is still alive, though he squeaked through by an even narrower margin than me. We are still in our house on Somerset Avenue, though it has been invaded by dad's brother, Don, and his family. (I've stopped complaining to Dad about them because I'm sick of him saying, "We're lucky they're here.") Even with these upsets, my life has excellent prospects if not to remain unchanged, then at least to settle into some kind of stable, boring routine. That is, if it weren't for the scars.

At night the scars come alive, tingling and throbbing from my right shoulder blade to my chest, and I rise from my bed and sulk around the house, reading books, shuffling through the rows of videotapes I know by heart, watching old movies online or on late-night TV, or checking for messages (there are usually none) on my new smartphone.

I have to tiptoe not to wake up the new family that I am — yes, I know — lucky, so lucky to have. Not just Dad, but Don and Melanie, and their kids, Brittany and Austin. I thought we were doing just fine without them, but if Dad says . . .

Anyway, one night nothing seemed to help, so I got dressed and went out.

Sulking, skulking, lurking — I was better off out on the street. It was a couple of weeks before Christmas. There was still no snow, but the leaves were off the trees, and gusts of wind spattered me with drizzle. Tuesday night, before garbage pickup, so everyone's green bags and blue boxes were out on the curb.

I stood for a moment in our front yard and then went left, toward the construction site that would become the new Prince of Wales Elementary School (we all called it "PoW"). Beyond that was Ivor Wynne Stadium, now fenced off and dark, where the "games" had made a hell of a mess: at least one light tower knocked over by Yog-Sothoth; sinkholes in the field and foundations dug up by excited dritches; blood and bullet holes all over the bleachers.

There had already been a movement underway to tear down the old stadium and build a new one, so after the scandal of that final midnight game, things moved pretty fast. Ivor Wynne was quickly being reduced to mountains of fractured concrete, elephant-sized chunks with twists of rebar jutting out like fossils of Paleozoic worms. But I thought I'd head straight up Lottridge to Barton. Maybe if I had any money on me, grab something at McDonald's or Timmies.

The corner house on Lottridge and Somerset has a willow tree with a canopy of leafy branches that hangs over the sidewalk. If you're tall you have to stoop when you pass by. I don't have any problem with it, but tonight I slowed cautiously; something was different.

Someone was under there, hunched over in the shadows next to the parked cars. I heard the rattle of plastic blue boxes and thought of Dana. He had made his living any way he could – hourly manual labour, sidewalk retail, scavenging garbage for scrap metal or blue boxes for returnables – until one night, in the basement of the derelict, old PoW, he'd been ripped apart by the Hounds of Tindalos, summoned by the Resurrection Church of the Ancient Gods to punish Dana for sneaking into their late-night ceremony – and for bringing me with him.

In the shadow of the willow tree, someone dropped a beer can onto the sidewalk. It banged like a cowbell and rolled toward me. Steely Dan Magnum. I scooped it up, and saw a hand extended out of the shadow into the light. The figure looked like a woman, tall and broad at the hips and shoulders.

"Here ya go, ma'am." As I handed it back, I saw that there was someone with her, a figure in a wheelchair. The yard wasn't fenced, and I went up onto the grass to go around the couple.

"Thankya, sir." Something familiar in her voice.

"Betrayed," said the man in the wheelchair. "Stolen from me."

Something in his voice creeped me out, but I didn't recognize this pair as any of the local street people I knew.

"Hey, you are welcome to that can," I said, "and have yerself a good night."

They weren't the baseball-capped couple who roamed the east end throwing reusable garbage, scrap metal and, if no one was looking, garden tools and lawn furniture into the baby trailers behind their bikes. The woman wasn't the European lady who came by on Wednesday mornings, so grateful to be handed a beer can or a wine bottle (I don't know where she came from, but I always wondered if this place was better). This man wasn't Dana, or any of the other street people who disappeared when it got dark, and reappeared at dawn, stumping wearily through empty parking lots or along the train tracks from wherever they'd spent the night.

"I had it all," the man said.

Something in his voice. I turned around and backed toward the street corner, keeping my eyes on the pair. Now I remembered – the woman was Clare, the personal aide (one might say henchperson) to Raphe Therpens, the head of the Resurrection Church of the Ancient Gods, the cult behind the midnight games. And the man in the wheelchair – it was the Proprietor, Therpens himself.

Was this an ambush?

The Proprietor rolled closer, painfully inching forward in his manual chair, squinting at me from the shadows of the willow.

"This poverty and pain we live in now" – slumped in his seat, he gestured with a gloved hand – "the Great Old Ones – they'd take care of that . . . with me as their minister . . . their prime minister . . ."

Tssking and swearing under her breath, Clare came trotting after the wheelchair. She looked at me apologetically. I twigged that neither of them recognized me.

"Prime minister of Canada?" I said.

"Prime minister of *everything*." He coughed, and the cough grew and shook him, and Clare leaned over to straighten him in his chair. I fidgeted, wanting to get out of there before either of them recognized me from last fall, when for several days we were pitted against each other, pretty much in a kill-or-be-killed situation.

"You hafta excuse him," Clare said. "He was in a real bad accident."

That's for sure. I'd seen him get blown right off the edge of Ivor Wynne Stadium, and it was a long way to the ground. I had been certain that he was dead or at best, strapped to the ceiling in some hospital ICU. But here he was, still rattling around these tired old streets like the Energizer Bunny in an empty bathtub.

I waved a hasty good night and started to turn up Lottridge.

"I'll be back," Therpens said. "The stars are turning in my favour. Even as we speak."

"That's great," I said. "Have a good —"

"Even as we speak," Therpens said, "the Great Old Ones are mustering their powers" — I tried to turn and keep walking, reminding myself he was sick and in pain, telling myself that what he said couldn't be true — "to rise again. But don't listen to me, you idiot."

Now Clare was shushing him, but his voice grew steadily louder. "It's not just the devils or the exanimators. Much more — the likes of you won't stop them."

I whirled around. "Actually," I said, "we did stop . . ." Nate, shut up, I told myself.

"The Church can't do it on its own. But the cavalry's coming. The Four Horsemen of the Resurrection. You just have to look."

The Proprietor squirmed in his chair. I cringed, ready for him to miraculously regain the use of his legs and throw himself at me, drag me to his followers to berate and torture and kill. But I knew that whether or not he still possessed that power, I had to practise not being afraid.

"Even as we speak . . ." His head drooped, then he took a deep breath, rallied the remains of his energy. ". . . the stars –"

"You mean, even as *you* speak," I said. "You're full of crap as usual." Nate, shut up.

". . . the stars are turning in our favour, and the seas will part. Look to the west –"

"No, they're not," I barked at him. Nate, shut up. "The stars *aren't* turning in your favour. The waters *won't* part. You guys are dead in the water, and you're going to stay that way." Nate, shut up.

Clare bent down, squinting to recognize me. "The Silva kid."

"I got the scars to prove it too."

Dana dead in an abandoned school basement, the horrors in the stadium, the dritch, the Hounds, the buzz in my head as Yog-Sothoth, the Great Old One second only to Cthulhu himself, seeped like a bloodstain out of the night sky, calling to those assembled to go down on their knees, to obey. I didn't need to shake up these memories. There was something in the air – something that Therpens's rant had summoned. I could feel my scars itching and throbbing. Now a light went on in the

Proprietor's brain. He leaned forward and squinted at me.

"You're just another pawn, you – a pawn of the old ways of thinking."

"Old ways, old man," I mocked. The Proprietor, I figured, was at least forty. "Yer still a flunky for some tentacled alien slimebag that doesn't give a damn for you or anyone or anything else on this planet."

"It's already happening. The Great Old Ones will triumph. Cthulhu will rise again, from his ancient city at the heart of the world. And so will I. I will rise again."

"Gotta go," I said to Clare. "It's been a slice."

I turned and kept walking, determined not to run, as behind me, despite Clare's efforts, the man who had been the Proprietor began to shout.

"Go ahead, you moron – strut and boast, and think that this planet is yours to own. The stars are turning and turning and turning in our favour. Something in the west is rising – something is coming out of the west. It will be here before you know it. Everything we lost will be gained again when our saviour comes from the west, when our salvation comes from the west. You can defy us now, go ahead, but look to the west!"

His voice echoed off the wall of the new PoW. Last fall, not thirty metres from where we stood, the Hounds of Tindalos had found my friend Dana and decapitated him. Killed him at the bidding of this man, the Proprietor. But I was putting all that behind me, I had to. I kept walking.

"LOOK TO THE WEST!" he shouted. "SOMETHING IS COMING."

PART 1
A BRIEF HISTORY OF AIRSHIPS

In some places they was
little stones strewed about
– like charms –
with somethin' on 'em like what
ye call a swastika naowadays.
Prob'ly them was the Old Ones' signs.

– H. P. Lovecraft, *The Shadow Over Innsmouth*

CHAPTER 1
THE HAUNTED CHURCH

"Nate Silva, you are full of it. Never been good at nothin'. Ya go to school up on the Mountain with all those faggots. Not man enough to stay down here with the real people, down here where it's like . . . real."

"Ya know, Cody," I said. "It doesn't make much difference what you think."

Actually, whenever he was around, it was worthwhile to pay attention to what Cody was thinking. He had always been a loose cannon, liable not only to collide with you when you were least expecting it, but also to shoot off his mouth, and his boots and his fists too, at the least provocation.

When I was five he had tackled me off a teeter-totter so that my head smashed on the asphalt; when I was eight he had beat me up for missing a fly ball in a baseball game; when I was eleven he had sucker-punched me in the hall and when I punched him back, he'd hit me so hard my head rang and blood spurted from my nose and ruined my shirt. Cody was the same size as me, but I couldn't match his need to hurt.

When I had the chance to go to high school up the Mountain at Westmount, the prospect of furthering my education in a Cody-free environment was a point in its favour. But we still shared a neighbourhood and sure enough, stopping at the Big Bee to provision myself (one chocolate nut bar) for my latest experiment in interplanetary relations, I had run into him.

"And what is *that*?" Cody rattled on. "You gonna pull some kinda martial arts crap if I get in your face?"

I sighed. This was early in the new year, just a few weeks after I'd run into Clare and the Proprietor. I still chuckled sometimes over Raphe Therpens's raving. "Look to the west!" What a loser.

No way. No way I was looking to the west! I had enough to deal with right here. As I pocketed my chocolate bar, I was thinking of cancelling this expedition and heading home. The scars still itched and burned. I got tired way more easily than I used to. Early this morning though, before sun-up, I'd sprung awake with a plan. Now I was carrying a length of bamboo from our garden, a shaft almost two metres long, thick at the bottom and tapering at the top to the width of a finger.

"You wanna know what this is for, Cody, I'll show you. But here's the thing: it's dangerous."

I don't know if this was the right thing to say. I just knew that once Cody came at you, you could only run away, stand your ground and risk getting beat up, or do something to impress him – and Cody was hard to impress. I thought to myself, This project might just win his respect, or get him killed, maybe me too. Either way, Cody would be off my back once and for all.

"I don't want to get into anything that might freak you out," I said.

Cody swore. We went out to the parking lot of the Big Bee and, between his reminders of what a loser I was, I told him my plan.

"You gotta be kidding me." But he didn't back down.

We headed east along Barton, and I tried to get a word in edgewise while Cody told me I was full of it.

12

"I got homies who were in the Church – I know it's all lies what yer saying – monsters and aliens and stuff."

"Monsters," I said, "are the least of our problems. The big problem is . . . was . . . these creatures called the Great Old Ones."

"Not what I hear. The Old Ones were on our side. We'd be better off with them, if you hadn't screwed everything up."

I wondered sometimes if the worst thing about the Great Old One Yog-Sothoth wasn't that it was a kaiju-sized tentacled alien, but its terrible power to inspire loyalty, to make people obey. I had seen this and felt it. Close up, it was like an electrical shock buzzing through your nervous system, a voice inside: "Worship me – and your troubles will all be over. Worship me – and anyone who stands in your way, we'll get them. Every one of them." A buzz that was hard to resist.

At the railway tracks we paused for the traffic. As I scanned the situation, Cody found a break and went for it, making a cab squeal its brakes. He turned and gave me the finger from across Barton. "Chicken."

I sighed and wondered if there was some way, any way, this would end well. I looked both ways and caught the next break in the flow. "Almost there," I told him.

This old track was a strip of the wild, slashed through the middle of this built up and broken down old city. Early January, the winter snows still holding off, and the leaves were off the dense bush that bordered the tracks, turning it into a gauntlet of lifeless grey branches, brittle winter vines and naked thorns.

Three months ago, I'd been to the old chain factory that had housed the Resurrection Church. Now as we approached, I thought the place looked more busted up than ever. Of course, the chain-link gate over the spur line to the factory's old loading dock was rusting in the weeds; I'd been there the night the black freight car had smashed it down, in its failed attempt to rescue the dying being called the Interlocutor.

"What the hell we doin' *here*?"

"Going in."

The front doors of the Church were also busted off; bits of them were scattered to each side of the steps, as if the entrance had been rammed open from the inside. I thought of the dritch that my friends and I had barely escaped from in that desperate hour before the last midnight game. A couple of plywood sheets had been nailed over the door; now they hung like tattered flags, the work of either vandals, or the dritch.

I was betting that the dritch was still around. I knew there was a tunnel in the basement that could lead anywhere: up into the city, or out into the lake. Dritches are good at digging, and they can grow as long as a school bus.

Inside was the usual mess that piles up wherever people have been and gone: flattened water bottles, scrunched beer cans, coffee cups, Timbits boxes. There was no sign of the electric scooter that I'd seen the last time I was there. Like the Interlocutor herself, it had been kicked, bashed and beaten into a near-death condition. But there had still been a spark of life. When I'd pushed the panic button the Interlocutor had described to me, I'd heard a voice in her native language: "Ensse . . . n'hraggi akh menganah . . . srrrubi . . . ?" That was all I could make out. I followed her instructions, and soon a black freight car had blasted down the track to the rescue – too late to save the Interlocutor, as it happened.

In a corner was a tattered sleeping bag, as if someone had figured this would be a good place to camp out. But the bag was slashed and tattered, and dark smears led from it across the pitted hardwood toward the basement door.

"This place is gross," Cody said. "Let's *go*."

"We just got here."

I saw something at the edge of the stage where the Proprietor had made his rousing speech, where I had cleverly slipped him the parchment that (if it hadn't been a fake! – I still got mad thinking about it) would have led the Hounds of Tindalos to him, instead of to my father. A bit of turquoise fabric peeked out of the rubble on the floor. I slipped it into my pocket, then pulled out a flashlight.

"N'hraggi akh menganah," I said to myself.

"What's that mean?"

"I dunno, but let's check out the basement."

OVER THE course of a long night and day, I'd gotten pretty familiar with this basement, but I'd spent that whole time mostly in pitch darkness, so this was my first good look. There was the wall where the Interlocutor had leaned, slowly dying from her beating at the hands of the mob, the glow of her fishy flesh growing steadily fainter. There were still a few scattered bones . . . and a hole in the floor, wider than I was tall, like the mouth of a deep well. I shone my light down it, but the mouth of this abyss was plugged with dirt and debris. Around its lip the soil was moist, as if freshly dug.

"What kind of craphole is this? What're all these bones here?" Cody kicked at something in the dirt.

"Human bones. Some of them." I found a section of rib cage and pinned it with my foot to the dirt floor. I began rattling the ribs with my bamboo staff.

"The hell you doin'?"

"If something comes up through that hole," I said, "if you see anything move or even hear anything coming, take off. Up the stairs, fast. Get out of here."

"What makes you so bad, Silva, that you can stay and I can't?"

"I *think* I'll be okay. It's an experiment." I raised my voice over the rattling of the bamboo. "But I'm not so sure about you. You see, to get the Great Old Ones through to this world, the Church has these ceremonies where they open up something called a continuum threshold. So far, Yog-Sothoth hasn't been able to get through – as far as I can tell, he's just too big, and the threshold is too weak – but other things get through. Little things called dritches, that grow to be huge. And the last time, the night I got hurt, something else came through, a whole flock of them – they had wings."

"Yeah, sure." For the first time, Cody was listening as if I was credible. "The Devils. Those things are real."

"I saw them that night – coming at me out of the threshold. Just shapes in the dark, bat-winged, along with –"

"They're here for real. They mostly go for animals – cats, birds, squirrels, little dogs. Sometimes they attack people."

This was interesting to me – the media called them Stipley Devils. They treated it like a hoax, "mass hysteria," like the supposedly crazy things people said about the midnight games themselves. Even newscasters on Y108 and CHCH made smart-ass cracks about the Stipley Devils. To me, beneath the sarcasm, they sounded just a little bit nervous.

16

"What was that?"

Speaking of nervous, Cody's general nastiness was cracking a little. Under our feet, we'd felt a shudder, as if something big had awakened, rolled over sleepily and was coming our way. I kept rattling the bones.

"Like I said," I repeated to Cody, "as soon as you see or hear *anything*, take off."

Last night, I woke up with the memory of the stadium. The turf opening up, and the dritches emerging en masse. Enormous centipedes with long bony feelers, they had milled through the frightened crowd, not in a feeding frenzy (lucky for the crowd) but to make a rush for the continuum threshold before it closed again. I remembered that whenever one dritch came close to another, over the general hubbub I could hear a buzzing sound. Finally, I figured out what that sound was.

"Screw you, ya dork." Cody pushed me and I felt the staff pulled from my hand.

"Don't . . ." I raised my arm and felt the fabric of my hoodie rip as Cody flailed at me. My baseball cap flew off my head and I dropped my flashlight. "What the hell you doing?"

"You've always been *lame*, Silva. What are you bringin' me here for, ya perv?" He whacked me with the staff again, but I'd made a dive for the flashlight, so he hit my back and not my head. Now I crouched on the dirt floor of the basement, littered with bones and debris. I felt that floor throb under my knees.

"Stop. Listen." As I pushed myself up, I held out my hand to ward off another blow, and the staff really stung. I guess Cody was right in seeing it as a weapon – slender as it was, it could really hurt. "Gimme it back."

Cody turned and headed for the stairs. He took the staff with him.

"Give it back," I yelled and, unconsciously echoing what the Proprietor had yelled at me the week before, "Something's coming!"

Cody reached the wooden steps.

Beside me in the dirt, the earth heaved and parted like rapids around rocks and I lost my footing. Like a tree trunk erupting roots-first out of a flood, a dritch reared up out of the hole in the floor. I heard Cody swear, and I groped around for something, anything that would help me. The dritch's bony feelers rattled the air, centimetres from my face. I rolled away, and it lunged toward the stairs where Cody stood petrified, staring. The staff dropped from his fingers.

"RUN," I shouted, but I was too late. The dritch had seized Cody and pulled him into the air. Suddenly my fingers felt something long and narrow. I picked it up. It was an old garden hoe. I turned it backwards and rushed at the dritch, striking its rear feelers with the hoe's long handle. I rattled them just as I'd rattled the bones with the bamboo staff.

Cody screamed, and I smelled something in the air that stung my nostrils, something acrid and burning. I kept at the dritch, and then, without thinking, using its long feelers like tree branches, I pulled myself up onto its back. My only chance – the only chance for Cody and me – was if my dream last night turned out to be true.

CHAPTER 2
GARDENING WITH EXTREME PREJUDICE

The first time I'd met a dritch, it had pushed up out of our backyard bamboo patch and attacked Rocky, the neighbour's black Lab. I'd used the hoe as a weapon, but it was useless against the tough chitin of the dritch's exoskeleton.

Now I realized that what had saved me was that the hoe had struck repeatedly against the dritch's feelers; that was why it had suddenly stopped attacking. It had spared me (and Rocky) and retreated into its hole not because I was hurting it or scaring it (my blows against its stony hide had been painless), but because I was rattling its feelers. To a dritch that meant that I wanted us to be buddies.

That was then, this was now. I was clinging to the back of a dritch three times bigger than that backyard one. The creature flexed and my head banged into the low ceiling. I felt it coil around to try to get at me and as it did so, it dropped Cody to the floor. This was it: do or die.

I jumped to the floor, dropped the hoe, seized the staff, turned and continued rattling the bony feelers. I could use one hand because the staff was lighter. In fact, the staff was a lot like a dritch's feeler. At my feet, Cody sobbed and pulled himself across the dirt floor.

All this was happening in almost complete darkness, all of us – me, Cody, the dritch – just moving shadows against the glow of bright LED light from my dropped pocket flash. Now I rattled and buzzed the bamboo staff against the dritch's feelers. The creature drew itself erect, jamming its head against the low ceiling, and looked down at me.

"We met before," I said to it. "Me and you, or something like you. We're not enemies."

Actually, I wasn't worried that the dritch would think I was an enemy. I was worried it would think I was food. I looked at Cody, dragging himself toward the stairs. A ripple went through the dritch's body; instead of a nose and nostrils, it breathed through spiracles along its belly, like earthly arthropods do. I wondered if it was sniffing me now.

I paused and then did a drum roll with the staff between the two nearest feelers. I could feel the dritch's stare. How did a dritch think? *Buzzes my feelers, is friend. No buzzes, is food.*

I yelled at Cody to keep moving. He'd reached the bottom of the stairs. Keeping one eye on the dritch I ran to him, grabbed his shoulder. Something wet stung my hand, like alcohol in a wound, but I winced and pulled on his hoodie. He got to his feet and we stumbled up the stairs and through the door into the dim light of the old factory.

Cody pulled away from my touch like I was the walking dead. The front of his hoodie was in tatters. My hand really smarted; and I looked around for something to wipe it on.

"You're . . . This is like . . . *voodoo* or something."

On the floor, beneath a stain on the ceiling, a puddle of rain-water. At least, I hoped it was rainwater. I went and wiggled my hand in it. The sting cooled a little.

"Take off your hoodie," I said. "It's got acid on it, or something."

Cody still stared. "It *bit* me. But it didn't touch you."

"I don't think it bit you, Cody. If it bit you, you'd be dead. But it sure messed up your clothes, and maybe *drooled* . . ."

"Get away from me." Cody turned and ran. "Don't ever come near me. You're, jeez, you're cursed or something . . ." He reached the front door and I heard his footsteps on the pavement outside, reaching the tracks and fading in the distance. "Voodoo pisshead." He'd got his strength back pretty fast.

I turned toward the basement door, my flashlight and my staff in hand, now totally unafraid, though for all I knew the dritch might change its mind and decide that food was more important than whatever bond we'd formed by rattling feelers. But when I went back into the basement, it was gone.

Half an hour later I walked in the front door of my house. I could smell dinner, and heard cooking sounds from the kitchen. Unsteadily, Dad got to his feet and greeted me, and so did Uncle Don. Melanie and the kids just stared.

"What's that you got there?" Dad asked.

I held it up. "Our old hoe. I got it back."

CHAPTER 3
THE SCARS

Visits to the Shirazis' usually meant snacks and video games, but tonight Sam and his dad were out somewhere. When I got to the meeting, I saw Evie's old convertible parked on the street, and Meghan's Toyota. Except for me, the meeting was all women. They immediately tried to get me to take my shirt off.

"No way."

"Nate, we're not after your body," Meghan said. "You're not the hottie you think you are."

"Jeez, Meghan. All I mean is . . ."

Sensing that Meghan was taking the wrong approach, Evie stepped in. "Scars are knowledge," she said. She was very old, in her fifties or sixties at least. "We've all got them."

"But . . ."

"I had my own run-in with the Hounds," Evie said, "but I never got face to face with them like you did. I suppose Howard told you all about it."

To be honest, I was wondering whether it would be a plus or a minus if Mehri, who was in the kitchen talking on her phone, saw me with my shirt off. Would she think that Sam's buddy Nate was looking good? Doubt it. I was still skinny, and since I'd spent a lot of the past couple of months in bed, not in great shape. And the scars – red against my pale skin, like the severed roots of some gross tree that had been ripped from my body, yuck.

22

I decided that, overall, it would be a minus, and I should continue on like I always had, hoping that Mehri liked me for my personality.

"Nate?"

"I don't remember him saying much."

"The scars on the inside," Evie continued, "they go just as deep, and burn just as hot."

This wasn't turning out to be much of a fun party.

"I'll tell you, I got around in my day," Evie said. "A hot young east end girl partying with the gold cufflink crowd. Believe it or not, those guys . . . some of them were trying to get the Resurrection Church going even back then."

"So this was back in –" My mind was racing through the decades before I was born. When would Evie have been, don't know . . . twenty, twenty-five? I knew that older people could be sensitive about their age. "– the 1970s?"

"Pay attention, Nathan Silva. It was the forties."

That got my attention, all right. In the first place, I hadn't been 100 percent sure that Evie even knew my name. All I knew about her was that at some point the Church, or the Great Old Ones Yog-Sothoth or Cthulhu, or the Hounds of Tindalos, had reached out and touched her. And the Church's touch leaves a scar.

"Nineteen forty-six."

I blinked. It was now December 2012, so Evie had been, say, twenty-five years old in 1946. Hmm. If she'd been born in 1921 . . . I blinked hard. "Jeez, Evie, you get around pretty good for a ninety-year-old."

"And you've got the attention span of a June bug – tonight, anyway. What the heck's on your mind?" Evie glanced at the kitchen door. "For your sake, I'll take that crack as a compliment, young man, though actually I get around pretty *well*. Use your adverbs. You've got important work to do and you can't afford to talk, or think, like some illiterate hoser with his hat on backwards."

"Yes, ma'am."

"My scars are more on the inside. What those people did to me. There was a man called Weston – one of those rich people who make you think, That's how I'd like to be, like him. Then you find out that there's nothing there – that all he wants to do is get richer –"

"I wouldn't mind being a *bit* richer . . ."

"– and that something human's got burned out of his soul, and something awful has taken its place. And this *something* . . . it doesn't want anything or anyone to get in its way. Weston, that's who set the Hounds on me and my family."

Evie paused. The room had gone quiet.

"John, he tried to lead them away . . . he'd been told that if he went out in the woods, where there were no right angles, the Hounds couldn't get to him. But they found him, all right. They tore him apart."

I'd heard this story before – everyone in Hamilton had in some form or other – but if what Evie said was true . . .

"It's the angles that lead the Hounds to our world – the perfect right angles that don't exist here, not anywhere in nature. Only when they've been measured and built and fitted . . . So when those men . . . those *monsters* . . . targeted my baby, I did what I thought was the only thing I could. I lined a case with concrete . . . pressed and smoothed all the sharp angles out of it. And when the time came I put him inside. But nobody told me how long it would take that concrete to set. It loosened and let go and flowed around my little boy . . ."

The room had gone silent. I'd seen these women rally around Evie before, when she was having a bad night – but no one approached her or said anything. It was like she'd retreated into her past and was still back there, suffering, needy, but out of reach.

"The wet concrete engulfed him." She looked up at me. "Like the *vulsetchi*. Drowned and smothered and took his life as surely as the Hounds." She took a deep breath, trying to restore the protective gap of years. "And here I'd thought I'd save him . . ."

"Evie," Meghan said. "You know you can't go over this again."

Evie shook her head, as if she was surfacing from underwater. "You're right, hon." She looked around. "Sorry, you all." She cleared her throat. "But maybe this will remind us why we're here. Nate."

"Yeah. Sure."

"The scars?"

"Phew. Okay." I took off my hoodie, and shrugged out of my T-shirt.

Evie had thin grey hair, brushed back in a ponytail. As she brushed her fingers over me, I felt the amazing softness and dryness of her skin, like some luxury gift wrap designed to hold together old people.

"As I was saying," she continued, "scars are knowledge."

"Whatever, Evie. They haven't made me any smarter."

Evie shook her head. "Scars are like the sulci and gyri, the grooves and folds that knowledge carves into the smooth flesh of the brain – the inner brain, that is; the mass of grey tissue inside our skulls. The body itself is our outer brain. Every scar is a special knowledge – and not all scars can be seen."

Goosebumps were rising along my bare arms. When at night the scars would start to tingle and burn, and wake me up, this was because they were still healing, Doctor Martin had told me. "After all, Nate, they're deep, and they heal at different rates of speed, the burned and the unburned flesh." He'd shaken his head. "I've never figured out what kind of a weapon they used on you."

I'd told Dr. Martin about the Resurrection Church, and the midnight games, and the Hounds. He'd explained that these were hallucinations brought on by my brain's attempts to make sense out of fear, shock and blood loss, on a night when fanatic cult members had set off improvised explosive devices during a mass meeting in Ivor Wynne Stadium.

I'd gone home and thought about it, and at the next appointment I told him he was correct, and didn't bring up the subject again.

"I'll tell you, Evie, they still itch, and sometimes they hurt," I said. "But they're just scars. I don't know what I've learned from them."

"Of course you do, hon. You've learned that you can come through the flames, and survive."

As far as I was concerned, I'd just got lucky, but why argue with Evie? For all I knew, she was right. She was a weird old bird and there was no telling what she might know. For example, she'd compared the concrete that killed her son to "the vulsetchi." What the heck's a vulsetchi? I thanked her for the valuable insights and put my shirt back on, grateful my command performance was over.

I went into the kitchen. Mehri was just off the phone and Meghan was making tea. Mehri was wearing black leggings, and a black hoodie over a red Delta Red Raiders T-shirt, and very white shoes. As usual she looked like a million bucks, maybe two million.

"So, Mehri," I said. "Maybe you'd like to, uh, check out my scars. Evie seems to think they're quite something."

Mehri looked at me from across the table.

"No kidding." I reached over and took her hand. "It's cosmic."

Mehri snatched her hand back. "Don't." She pushed herself back from the table and took the teapot. "It's a good thing my father wasn't here. For that, he would have you killed."

I snorted sarcastically, but I was thinking, Hmm, I've never seen that expression on her face. Mehri has dark, expressive eyes. I thought I saw a glint of humour there, though I wasn't quite –

"Slowly and painfully." She kept looking at me with those awesome eyes. "Sam would help him."

She took the teapot and tray, and looking back at me before she headed into the living room, added, "You're their friend, Nate. They love you. So it would be nothing personal. It's just a Persian thing."

"Heh heh," I laughed feebly. "Yeah, well, uh . . ."

I watched her go and thought of a time when she'd come to our house with Sam.

"That girlfriend of yours," Dad had said afterwards, "she looks like a goddamn movie star."

"Come off it, Dad. She's not my girlfriend." I'd tried to disguise the pang of agony I felt when I said that. "She's Sam's sister."

"Nate, a word of advice," Meghan said. "You should never take a girl's hand and try to put it anywhere."

"I was just . . ."

"Anywhere on your body or anywhere else. She is perfectly capable of putting her hand where she wants to put it."

"You're a big help." I could tell that Meghan was being supportive, but sometimes I hate that.

27

"You know that she was joking. About Sam and his dad."

"Yeah yeah yeah." I took a sip of tea. "Jeez . . ."

"Actually, Nate, Mehri really likes you."

Meghan in "supportive" mode was making me feel worse by the second. I changed the subject. "Can you tell me why I'm here tonight? I thought this was going to be some kind of anti-Resurrection Church / Great Old Ones what-to-do-next strategy-type meeting."

Actually, I would much rather have talked about how Mehri really liked me, my feelings for her, what to do about that and so on. But taking on the Resurrection Church and the Great Old Ones was easier to talk about. I guess Meghan felt the same way. Love is better than war, but war is simpler. (I don't know if that's a saying, or if I just made it up.)

"It is, kind of," she said. "What happened back in October was so incredible. In a few days, you and I both had our eyes opened to something enormous – you'd have to say impossible – that was taking place right in front of us – right where we live."

"In my opinion," I said, leading up to telling Meghan about the Cody fiasco, "there are still a few dritches around. Underground, and maybe out in the lake."

"Exactly. We've got to research this stuff, and find out what we can. And how about the Church? Sure, that guy they call the Proprietor is out of commission – but I bet someone's stepping up to replace him, right this minute, if they haven't already."

"That reminds me," I said. "I got you a present."

I brought it out, neatly washed, folded and tied with a ribbon, and gave it to Meghan. She untied the ribbon, and for a moment her face lit up.

"It's my scarf!"

"You said it was your favourite."

"Where did you get it?"

I told her. Among the wreckage on my visit with Cody to the ruined factory. Months before, when the Church had kidnapped us by scooping us into a van, Meghan – in one swift, graceful move, as if she did this kind of stuff every day – had whipped her scarf around the driver's neck and tied him to the headrest. That had screwed up his driving considerably. We had escaped in the ensuing chaos, but Meghan had made it known she had sacrificed her favourite scarf for us. Now, she examined it for stains, sniffed it gingerly.

"Don't worry," I said. "I washed it."

"Hmph. Machine washed?"

"Oh yeah, for sure. In hot water, too. I wanted to do a real good job. It feels a bit stiff now, but I'm sure it will, you know, loosen up."

"Well, thanks." Meghan folded the scarf into her purse. "That was so thoughtful."

Despite her words, I felt a chill. Somehow, putting the scarf in the washing machine – what else would you do with it? – seemed to be an issue of some kind, but I didn't know why.

"Anyway," I continued. "I totally agree. There's lots to be discovered. For example, where is that airship, *Sorcerer*? If we could find it . . ."

"Give it up, Nate. Nobody else saw that thing."

"How could you miss it? It was as big as the stadium."

It came and went so fast that nobody I talked to seemed to have seen it. Maybe instead of arguing I could ask Clare, or the Proprietor, if I ever saw them again. Or maybe I could ask the man who called himself H. P. Lovecraft – and I would if he hadn't, on that fatal night, chosen that exact moment to turn tail and flee the stadium, never to be heard from again.

There was no point in bugging Meghan about this; I would pursue it on my own. I was sure her new group would find lots of other stuff to investigate.

"So you'll be like the Lovecraft Underground," I said, "only local?"

"Exactly," Meghan replied. "Right here in Hamilton, so quicker to respond in an emergency, and more hands-on."

Outside of Howard, who had introduced himself as a sort of proxy who had only taken on the name for this mission, the workings of the Lovecraft Underground – LUG – were mysterious. Meghan liked to call it "The League of Unmarried Gentlemen," as if LUG was just a bunch of geeks who got together to play Cthulhu-themed video games, but I suspected there was more to them than that.

"Are you going to call yourselves 'Lovecraft Underground – Hamilton Branch'?"

"No way," she said. "Those guys are useless. We're the Furies."

"Pretty badass." I had a vague sense that Furies were something out of ancient myths. I would look them up. "Do you want me to join?"

Meghan frowned. "So far it's just women. Me, Mehri, Hamideh, maybe Mrs. Shirazi, though we haven't asked her yet, one or two people from our English for New Canadians group. Evie, of course."

"Evie will vote me in," I said. "She says that my scars are –"

"We'll talk about it," Meghan said firmly. "I'm not sure about having men in the group. They like to take over the discourse."

"Even me?"

"Frankly, Nate . . . I mean, you're a great guy, but like so many guys, you are just, when it comes to women, kind of dumb."

CHAPTER 4
A BRIEF HISTORY OF AIRSHIPS

Back in October, on my third night in the hospital, I woke up with a clear memory of the ID I'd seen on the airship's side. I found a pen, grabbed the nearest Get Well card, wrote it down and then forgot all about it.

Once I got home, stronger and less dozy from pain meds, I started to do some searching online. I looked up "airship," "dirigible," "zeppelin," all in various combinations with "Sorcerer" . . . and got nothing. The words were too common: there was too much information out there. Then I remembered the card.

I shuffled through the stack that I'd brought home in a shopping bag: there was one from Meghan, one from Uncle Don's family (at this point, still living in Woodstock), one from the Shirazis, but the ID was written on the one from school. There it was, scribbled as if some shaky old guy had written it, standing out among all the questionable quips, puns and good wishes from people at school who never talked to me in person:

R102 G-FAAX.

At first, a search for "R102 G-FAAX" got me nowhere. There are just so many numbers and letters online, in every imaginable configuration. Then I thought: if *Sorcerer*'s ID was part of a series . . . I searched "R101 G-FAAW" and kapow, pages and pages came up, about a series of British airships that had been started before the Second World War – the R100 and

32

the R101. The next thing I knew, I found a site called Flight 33: Unsolved Mysteries of the Sky, and a page with exactly the header I was looking for: R102 a.k.a. Sorcerer.

I started to read. Airships, it turned out, were a big thing up until the 1930s. Unfortunately, they seemed to crash a lot, and after the *Hindenburg* disaster in 1937, the technology was discarded as being too unstable. Up until then, however, people thought they were a great way to get around. In England, for example, they had the R series – a series that came to an end in an unusual way. According to Flight 33:

> The first two of the R series ended in disaster. R100 was an airworthy vehicle, but pressured by the ambitious Secretary of State for Air, Lord Christopher Thomson, into making a maiden voyage it was not ready for, R101 G-FAAW crashed and burned in the north of France in 1930.
>
> After the R101 crash – a tragedy far deadlier than the famous *Hindenburg* six years later – the British airship program was terminated. Even the R100 – which flew perfectly well – was deflated, disassembled and sold as scrap.
>
> There were those, however, who saw the program's abandonment as premature. In the midst of the general disenchantment with lighter-than-air travel, a catalyzing figure appeared: Marthe Bibesco, French-Romanian heiress and friend of Lord Thomson. In 1931, she journeyed to London to meet with William Mackenzie, who had succeeded Thomson as Secretary of State for Air; Commander Dennis Burney of Vickers-Armstrongs, which had manufactured the R100; and Prime Minister Ramsay MacDonald. Bibesco brought to the meeting a brilliant young German engineer, Maxmillian Nordfeld.
>
> Nordfeld had developed a new and far more reliable airship design, powered by a revolutionary electric battery of his own invention. The airship was smaller than the earlier models in the

R series – 500 feet from stem to stern, versus the R101's 700 feet. It gained its buoyancy from helium, an inert gas, rather than from hydrogen, a gas that is anything but inert – in fact, it was the flammability of hydrogen that had caused so many worthwhile airship enterprises to literally go up in smoke.

These innovations, however, represented only the beginnings of Nordfeld's ingenuity. Having designed his craft to be lifted by helium and powered by electricity, he had devised a way to distill helium from the atmosphere itself, where it exists in very small proportions. His batteries could be recharged from a variety of sources, including an inertial charging system that harnessed the energy of the R102's ascent and descent.

With her money and influence, Bibesco was able to help Nordfeld's design into production. The prototype, the R102 G-FAAX, was completed in 1937. On its test flight from Howden, Yorkshire, to Cardington, Bedfordshire, a return trip of almost 450 kilometres, the R102 functioned perfectly.

Soon afterwards, Nordfeld suddenly insisted on launching a more ambitious trip, to Friedrichshafen in southern Germany. Although the reasons Nordfeld gave were vague, his destination was not surprising: Friedrichshafen was the manufacturing site of the Graf Zeppelins, so it had mooring and maintenance facilities that made it the logical destination if one were flying an airship to Germany. That in itself, Nordfeld's partners argued, was not enough reason to undertake the flight. Nevertheless one cold January night Nordfeld – with a skeleton crew of his most trusted pilots, technicians and deckhands – started up the R102, cast off the mooring lines and set a course for Germany.

As it happened, however, Nordfeld had lied. He wasn't going to Friedrichshafen, southwest of Munich, but to a destination just north of the city. The Nazis had been in power since 1933, and Adolph Hitler was initiating the first stages of his Final Solution, imprisoning immigrants, Jews, gay people, non-white German citizens, Communists, Socialists and the mentally handicapped, and artists, writers and journalists who were critical of the Third Reich. It was a time when creative thinkers such as Nordfeld – liberal in his opinions, and for that matter, half-Jewish – were fleeing Germany, not flying into it with millions of dollars' worth of new, easily weaponized technology. Why, historians ask themselves, did Nordfeld want so badly to return to Germany, and why did he make his destination the Nazis' already-notorious internment camp at Dachau?

Evidently he landed the R102 outside of the Dachau camp, treated its commandant and senior officers to a tour of the airship and then, in the dead of night, orchestrated a massive escape attempt that liberated as many as 100 prisoners, although casualties were high. The R102 took to the air but, its gas compartments shredded by machine-gun bullets, seemed to have trouble gaining altitude. Finally, it vanished into the night, heading south toward the Alps.

At this point, I almost gave up, thinking I'd got the wrong airship. None of this seemed to have anything to do with what I'd seen. Then I glimpsed the name further down the page: *Sorcerer*.

Apocryphal Accounts
Since that night in 1933, the R102 has never been seen or heard from again – not officially. Over the years, however, there has emerged an impressive cryptohistory of alleged sightings and encounters:
Providence, Rhode Island, USA, 1937.
Rimouski, Quebec, Canada, 1958.
Amchitka, Alaska, USA, 1971.
Juarez, Mexico, 1993.
Hamilton, Ontario, Canada, 2002.
In the more recent of these sightings, witnesses report that a new name has appeared on the side of the vessel, plainly legible as SORCERER. This was thought to be a different vessel until a Juarez photographer caught it in a photograph at the

1993 event (which took place, as have so many R102 sightings, during a violent thunderstorm). In this photograph, the original 1937 ID and the name SORCERER can both be seen clearly marked on the vessel's side.

This was all new and exciting. I reread it, and downloaded the information. Once I had my own copy, I went to the list of sightings and scrolled down to the Hamilton entry. I was about to correct it. After all, I had seen *Sorcerer* just last October – October 2012, not 2002.

Then I paused before changing the 0 to a 1. What if it *wasn't* a typo? What if *Sorcerer* had appeared in Hamilton before? If it shadowed Resurrection Church attempts to conjure a continuum threshold . . . or was aiding, or trying to block the ceremonies . . . or was itself somehow summoned by the excited crowd, then maybe it *had* been seen in 2002 – the year that, at the age of six, I had lost my mother when, for reasons I didn't quite get, she became a victim of the violence that follows the Resurrection Church like a school of piranha. While I was lying in bed asleep, taking for granted that I'd see her first thing in the morning because I always did, something terrible had reached out of the sky and taken my mother out of this life – did all that involve *Sorcerer*?

CHAPTER 5
JANUARY 1937:
DACHAU, GERMANY

Dear God, strike me dumb / So I won't to Dachau come.

The guard had taken a toilet break, so Tobias Edenshaw strolled over to talk to his new friend. Checking that no one was looking – everyone here was a prisoner, but that didn't mean you could trust each other; you never knew what someone might do to gain favour with the guards – he tugged at the knots that bound the Interlocutor. Finally one came undone; he quickly retied it, but more loosely. There was no point in freeing the creature – if he did that, likely both of them would be taken out and shot – but he couldn't stand to see it suffering. The thing's mask had come loose during its capture, and now behind its wilting human face he glimpsed its real face, a wobbling mass of grey, pebbled flesh. It turned to him and although he couldn't always make sense out of its jumbled syntax, this time he understood what it was saying.

"*Danke schön.*"

"*Bitte,*" Tobias said. "They'll let me out of here soon, and I'll figure out some way to free you, too. Tell them you should be in a laboratory, being tested and interviewed and studied, not in a jail."

The thing shuddered. "These in charge – these Nazis – their laboratories are more bad than their jails."

"Still, I have lots of influential friends," Tobias said. "Fritz Lang, Karl Hartl, Leni Riefenstahl: You've heard of them? Maybe you've seen me in the movies?"

He stopped. This creature showed no sign of recognizing any of these famous names. Why would a space monster come all the way from another planet, and then not go to the movies? He changed the subject.

"Good news: My best friend Max. I saw him today. From a distance; they were giving him the grand tour. He's the *Kapitän* of that airship, the R102." He gestured out the window where the huge English dirigible hovered, lost in the darkness above its network of mooring lines. We could see it earlier, Tobias thought. What happened? Why would they turn out all the lights?

Then he heard Max's voice, calling his name.

Tobias looked around. Still no guards. He went to the window. There, in the darkness, was his friend's face.

"Max . . . how?" He put his fingers against the glass, then tried to get the window open, but it was stuck. He raised his voice, to be heard through the glass. "*Wunderbar.* Great to see you. Did you bring anything to eat?"

"Shut up and listen." Max put his face up against the bars so Tobias could hear him through the glass. He was still talking when Tobias heard the rattle of metal and the groan of splitting wood. Everyone else in the barracks looked up. Next to the window, the door to the prison yard was locked, but it sounded as if it was being seriously compromised.

The door swung open, admitting the freezing night air and a whirl of snow, and Max appeared. "Now," he urged. "*Jetzt.*"

Tobias started barking orders in the loudest stage whisper he dared muster. "Go now." He pointed toward the rope ladders that dangled out of the dark sky. "Right now. Climb for your life."

Most of the prisoners hadn't been in the camp long, but knew enough to seize the moment. They swarmed out of the barracks into the snow-covered yard and threw themselves onto the nearest ladders. Others, confused, ran toward the fences. Tobias ignored them. There was a good chance that none of them would make it anyway. Any second now, the alarm would be raised and all hell would break loose. He pointed prisoners at the ladders as best he could.

"Climb! Faster than you've ever climbed anything in your life."

Not far above, the R102's electric engines were shifting and reversing, spinning and adjusting to keep it in position. Up on the bridge, Max's crew was doing a hell of a job. But with a fresh gust of wind, the R102 began to drift toward the guard tower on the edge of the compound. To catch hold of the rope ladders, prisoners had to chase them as they skittered across the yard. There was a burst of machine-gun fire, and Tobias ducked back inside the barracks and threw himself on the floor.

"Are you Tobias?" In flashes of machine-gun fire from outside, Tobias could see a large male shape holding a crowbar. "I'm Eadric. Max says he'll kill me if I don't get you on board."

"Do you have a knife?"

Eadric pulled out a large clasp knife, extended the blade. "What are you doing?"

Tobias grabbed the knife and ran to the back of the room. Eadric cursed and followed him. Tobias started cutting the bonds from his new friend. Around them the camp was dissolving into chaos: running, shouts, screams, gunfire. Tobias saw that the guard had returned, brandishing his rifle. Eadric knocked him to the floor with his crowbar and took his weapon.

Tobias looked away and helped his strange friend – my god, the guy was sure heavy – out the door. They got out into the yard and suddenly Max was at his side.

"Tobias, we've got to go now. Leave this *kerl*." He looked at the huge prisoner, and flinched at the grotesque, half-masked face that looked back.

"No." Tobias cast away the last of the rope bonds. The prisoner raised itself to its full height, stretched. "Go," it said in a raspy, burbling chuckle. "I am following."

Running for a ladder himself, Tobias saw a spray of blood on the churned snow. A body fell out of the darkness, hit the ground and lay still.

"Dammit, Tobias. Come on. We've saved all we can save." Max pointed Tobias at the ladder, and grabbed onto another.

As Tobias climbed, he looked back. Something strange was happening with the prisoner he had just risked himself to save, but in this light it was hard to tell. Shrugging off the heavy coat it wore, it reached down – what kind of arms did it have? – ripped the wooden step off the side of the barracks and, with uncanny strength, threw it up and out of the prison yard, directly at the guard tower. Wood clattered on metal. The gunfire stopped, and the bulky prisoner shuffled and grasped the last rung of Tobias's ladder as it left the ground. From the tower came rifle fire; either their machine gun had run out of the bullets, or the wooden steps thrown by the prisoner had really messed things up.

Now the R102 was gaining altitude, the lengths of rope ladder slithering across the dusty yard, desperate prisoners grabbing at them as they lifted into the air. Nine metres up, one woman lost her grip and fell; another held on for dear life and climbed, and when she missed a rung, Max's accomplice dropped his crowbar to put his arm around her, the last one to leave the ground.

Bullets whistled through the dark. Carried irresistibly aloft, Tobias felt himself clear the camp fence, struggling rung by rung up the ladder, twisting and throbbing in flight, as below the great prisoner gained on him. Tobias felt a hand on his shoulder, and someone wrapped a harness around him to lift him into a long room lined with parachutes, lit by electric light. He held onto the frame of the loading door and looked for the prisoner to emerge out of the darkness. He felt Max put his arm around him. They hugged, then Tobias watched as the prisoner reached up and gripped the floor of LOAD/EVAC with two long, glistening arms, hauling its weight easily into light and safety.

"Tentacles," Max said to Tobias. "This *kerl* has tentacles."

"I can't pronounce its proper name," Tobias whispered in his ear. "It calls itself an Interlocutor."

CHAPTER 6
A NIGHT IN THE NORTH END

In January I'd gone back to school. During gym class, I would exercise gingerly over at the side of the gym: for example, trying to do just one chin-up while everyone else ran and yelled and pounded balls back and forth. During the winter's first snowfall, I headed out and ran around the football field. Every now and then, Mr. De Barros stuck his head out the door and checked that (a) I was actually running and not goofing off, and (b) I had not collapsed and died. Last time he pushed open the door just as I was coming in. He could see that I'd worked up a sweat.

"Good on ya, Silva. Take it easy, eh?"

"Nothin' to it." Actually, I was so wrecked I could have barfed. I couldn't catch my breath, and the scars on my chest and shoulder burned like I'd been whipped.

This was after Cody's and my encounter with the dritch. After *that* I'd gone home, skipped supper and slept for thirteen hours.

DESPITE THE long months of winter, by March I was feeling more or less myself. In fact, one evening I set out to do a quick scouting expedition in the North End.

The only thing was, sometimes in the spring around here, when the days are getting longer and the bite of the breeze isn't quite so sharp, you can start to think that winter is over and that you can relax and put your boots away. But you shouldn't relax; you should be on your guard more than ever. As I headed out on this chilly evening, for example, it started to snow. And snow. And snow.

I reasoned to myself that the bad weather gave me an advantage, even as I leaned into the north wind, brushed snow out of my eyes and headed for the howling expanse, all snowdrifts and shadows, of the North End. If *Sorcerer* was there, I bet that its hideout was guarded, but this weather would compromise any surveillance. Guards or no guards, anyone in their right mind would be huddling inside, thumbing their smartphone or reading a classic of Canadian literature. Visibility was so bad that even if anyone saw me, they likely wouldn't recognize me, or be able to identify me afterwards.

I was wearing a T-shirt and hoodie, the hood tied tight around my baseball cap, and over that, a parka my aunt Melanie had given me for Christmas. With cotton long johns under my jeans, and two pairs of socks inside my gumboots, I felt like I was dressed to climb Everest.

Still, I walked with my hands in my pockets; my dollar-store gloves weren't quite keeping out the cold. What if I fell or, I dunno, got stuck somewhere outside – I'd freeze to death unless I phoned for help. The falling snow would obscure me, and my tracks, but at the same time, it covered any other tracks that I might want to see – tracks that could tell me if I was alone in the deserted North End, or if someone or something was out there, shadowing my moves, following these train tracks to nowhere in the dead of night.

SORCERER. I was gambling that it was still here somewhere, in this wilderness of crumbling chimneys and rusty NO TRESPASSING signs. You would need a huge space to hide something that big, and the North End had more empty factories than Chernobyl.

Tonight it was an arctic desert, but when the snow was gone, you'd see that the neighbourhood was gradually going wild. Weeds sprouting along the railroad tracks, or in corners of rusting chain-link fences, were morphing into trees ten metres high with birds' nests and squirrels. At this rate, someday it would be all forest, a sea of leaves pierced here and there with a crumbling brick smokestack, corrugated metal roof or rusty air duct making a home for local wildlife.

For grade five, I'd done a diorama of the Mayan cities in Central America that, like the North End, now stood still and deserted, no one knew why. My dad told me that free trade was what did in the North End. When import tariffs were eliminated, we stopped making our own clothes, tools, appliances and steel, and started buying them cheap from other countries. But since we weren't making and selling stuff, we had less and less money ourselves. I wondered if that's what had happened to the Mayans.

But if it wasn't steel that the Mayans made, what was it? I only had vague memories: clay pots, sacrificial knives, funny hats. When the market for those things dried up, what did the Mayans do? Moved away, I guess, to open bed and breakfasts, or give surfing lessons to tourists, or run cocaine cartels, or work in the car factories. Only their buildings remained: empty of life, full of echoes and secrets, wind and time pulling memories out of their cracks and seams.

Besides my arctic clothing, I was travelling light with just a few essentials: flashlight, pocket knife and the bamboo staff that had almost brought about my (and Cody's) downfall. The North End was even bleaker and emptier than I'd imagined. At first the snow made things more ghostly and mysterious, but soon it became just a big fat drag, making me cold and weighing me down a little more with every step. No matter, I told myself, this was just reconnaissance. I would follow this little-used railway line from our neighbourhood near the closed-up stadium, across Barton, passing the derelict Resurrection Church headquarters with the dritch in the cellar, and out past the weed-covered side-tracks, and see if I found something, anything, that might lead me to *Sorcerer*'s hiding place. Nothing along the way encouraged me. The tracks were full of shadows, my hood was full of snow and the signs on every side were meant to discourage.

No Trespassing

Trespassers Will Be Prosecuted

Private Property

Danger

Keep Out

In front of me, the track made a white tunnel through the dark fences and undergrowth on every side, and at the end of that tunnel I saw movement. Something dark shifted and changed shape. At night in a snowstorm, in the middle of a semi-derelict industrial area where no one lived, someone or something was coming down the track. I gripped my bamboo staff more tightly, though I didn't think a dritch was on the way. A sensible dritch would be underground on a night like this, or snoozing somewhere in the depths of the lake.

I had just passed a junction where the tracks went off to the side. I thought of taking it to avoid detection, but when I started to retrace my steps, I heard voices. People were coming down the tracks, but who were they? I looked around for a place to hide, waist-high snow gushers erupting with every step.

Someone cried out: they had seen me. Lights flared in my eyes, and someone shouted.

Then, as I headed back toward the glow of the city, that glow intensified, blazing above the white dots of flashlights that were pointed at my back. Like the shock wave from a nuclear blast, a whirlwind of light swept down the tracks at me. It was coming so fast that it was all I could do to struggle to the side as the firestorm approached. I lost my balance, and plunged into a patch of thorns, layered with snow. A train rumbled past, its powerful headlight diffused not only by the falling snow, but by a mini-blizzard generated by powerful air jets that blasted the tracks before it.

But there was so much snow on the tracks that, as it neared the approaching crowd, the train was forced to slow and I saw it was no everyday train. This was the black freight, one sooty engine and one windowless boxcar, that I had seen on the night of the final midnight game. The Interlocutor had instructed me to call it, as she lay dying from the beating she'd taken in the church, her great bruised tentacles coiling and flexing painfully as they drooped from the ruptures in her thin human-like fake skin. The freight had arrived, but not in time; and I'd fled as the door flung open and someone roared at me angrily, mistaking me for the Interlocutor's murderer.

As the freight continued to slow, the hiss of the pneumatic blasters went up in pitch as it laboured to clear the tracks ahead. I pulled myself out of the frozen thorns, and as the train crept past, I saw an access ladder on the back. Clearly, I wasn't heading home just yet.

I thrust my bamboo staff under one arm, threw myself through the cloud of blown snow and, casting aside years of teacherly warnings about the dangers of hopping trains, grasped the steel rungs of the black freight.

I climbed to the top. The freight slowed even more and I heard shouts as it inched its way through the crowd of people I'd just avoided – from the noise they made, there were eight or ten of them. Shouting, swearing and then for some reason, a cheer, and then the train picked up speed, leaving the mystery hikers far behind. On my right, I saw the great green bulk of an old steel factory. Up here the sting of the wind was even more bitter. Hooking one arm through a top rung, I retied my hood more tightly and fiddled with the fastenings on the parka, which I'd hardly ever worn before.

Something grabbed my leg. I almost lost my grip, then I kicked backwards, broke free and pulled myself up onto the roof of the freight as it gained speed.

I scrambled away from the edge and turned in a crouch, trying hard to keep my balance. From the end of the car, a hooded figure pulled itself onto the roof and rose to its feet, towering over me.

I felt like yelling, *Eh bud, what's your problem?*, but in fact, I didn't know if this person had a problem with me or not. They'd scared me to death by grabbing my leg, but maybe they were just trying to get up the ladder. For the longest moment they stood there, looking down at me, then their hood blew back and I saw that this was no stranger at all: it was Cody. He recognized me in the same moment.

Something dropped out of the storm and fastened itself onto Cody's shoulders. He shouted and fell to his knees. The thing clinging to him looked up at me: for a full second I caught a glimpse of angry black eyes and the rippling of brittle, multi-jointed legs; the mark of the insect, weirdly compounded with the mammalian-like fur that covered its limbs, and pink-veined, leathery wings. The wings flapped, and Cody was pulled off balance.

"No, help, no!"

He stretched his hand toward me, I rose to my feet and reached toward him, and then the wings flapped, he reared back, fought for balance on the edge of the train car and was gone.

The freight was slowing, and I teetered to the side as it changed direction at a junction and angled down yet another sidetrack, through a corridor of fences and bushes shrouded in white. Up ahead, I could see the dim border of yet another chain-link fence, and beyond it a vast galvanized metal wall, yet another temple to some long-dead industry.

Then, with a screech of rusty metal, a gate opened, and the black freight lumbered through.

CHAPTER 7
A VERY ODD BUILDING

As the freight slowed to a crawl, I swung myself off the roof and onto the ladder. In the factory wall, a door was sliding upward and the freight was heading inside.

What was in there? Given the ongoing storm, the crowd on the tracks, the creature from the sky and my precarious position on the train, this had to be a better option. The moving freight train was failing to provide me with a nurturing and supportive environment. The door was already sliding shut. I backed down the ladder and as soon as the boxcar cleared the threshold, jumped to one side as the door closed.

The thing is, the closed door left this loading dock, or whatever it was, drained of light. Mid-jump, I glimpsed a pile of cardboard boxes, but the lights went out and I landed on them with a crash. Picking myself up, I blinked and waved my arms around in the pitch darkness.

A line of windows glowed faintly over the entry, but their grey sheen was too dim to show anything inside. The nuclear superlight at the front of the black freight's engine had turned off, and the throb of its engine was dying down. At the far end of the room, a door opened and against the lighted doorway I saw hooded figures in heavy coats and toques enter and heard them clatter down rickety stairs.

In my leap from the boxcar I'd found out something useful:

most of the boxes I'd just crashed into were empty. The racket I'd made was masked by the sound of the freight's engine. I grabbed a big box and flipped it over my head. As I crouched inside, the noise of the freight's engine died away, and silence spread through the dark space. If I wanted to stay concealed, I'd have to move very quietly or not at all.

"You hear that? Something moved."

"Just before we let the freight into the compound, I saw one of the Church people climb up onto it . . . but one of those devils got him."

"What do you mean 'got him'?"

"Attacked him. Knocked him off the freight."

"Knocked him off? Where'd it go?"

"Dunno – knocked him off, flew away."

"You sure? I heard something in here. Just now."

"I've been telling Tobias – there's too many holes in this old place. We're supposed to reinforce the nacelle, but I don't even wanna go near it. There's Stipley Devils nesting under there."

"D'you think there's one here now?"

I heard the clatter of doors opening on the black freight, both on the engine and the boxcar it towed, and weary voices exchanged greetings.

"Get outta there, guys," one of the men called from the stairs. "We think there's a *thral* in here."

"Jeez!"

"Come inside. We don't wanna turn on the lights 'cause of those creeps from the church. We'll get some decent flashlights, a couple carbines from LOAD/EVAC . . ."

Together with the crew from the freight, they clattered up the steps. The door closed. I was alone in my cardboard box. I

50

pulled up a corner. It was still as dark out there as it was in the box. My phone rang.

"Nate, what the hell," my dad said. "Where are you?"

"I'm up in the North End," I whispered. "Looking for clues about, uh, the Resurrection Church." I'd never told Dad about *Sorcerer*.

"On a night like this?"

"I'm fine. I've got that parka Aunt Melanie gave me."

"It's a school night."

"Uh. Yeah. But look, Dad, I'll check in later. I'll be home. Take care."

"Why are you whisp–"

I hung up and muted the phone, grateful Dad hadn't called a minute earlier. For the moment, I crouched in the box and weighed what I knew so far.

Whoever these people were, they were clearly opposed to the Resurrection Church – and friends of the folks who ran the black freight, so they must also be on the side of the aliens called Interlocutors. I hoped this meant they were the good guys, though I might have gotten off on the wrong foot by secretly crashing their stronghold and being mistaken for a Stipley Devil.

I wiggled out of the box. Fumbling my way back to the boxcar, I tripped on something – my bamboo staff. I picked it up, found the boxcar, then felt my way along it to the engine – which, though I expected it to be steaming hot, was barely warm to the touch, and didn't stink of diesel the way trains usually do.

I heard voices, and ran around the base of the landing so I wouldn't be seen. The door opened and a crowd of people poured through. A woman's voice said, "I'll hit the lights. Fan out. Find it and kill it and let's unload this train."

51

The lights went on, and I pressed myself against the wall. At least a dozen people, some in heavy coats and parkas, some shivering in plain beige coveralls, poured down the stairs into a space that, as I blinked against the light, I could see was like an enormous barn, with a corrugated steel roof and cobwebbed beams. A coated figure carrying an axe came my way.

"In the corner!" I pointed. "I heard something there."

Most of the crowd were pretty much featureless under hoods and parkas, but when this person turned around, I saw a dark-skinned woman, her face framed by thick black hair. She frowned at my bamboo staff.

"You couldn't get a better weapon?"

"All I could find." I rushed ahead of her, pushed between some steel oil drums and started poking at boxes with my staff. She flanked me, looking this way and that, holding her axe ready. I breathed a sigh of relief.

After a minute or two of this, there was still no Stipley Devil a.k.a. thral, and someone shouted orders to unpack the freight.

With a crash, a rock flew through one of the windows and we all dodged a burst of shattered glass.

"Lights out!"

Work continued in relative darkness. Mingling with the crowd, I picked up a couple of cartons and was told to take them to the kitchen.

WHAT KIND of a warehouse was this? Even given that it had probably been empty for years, and that everything looks kind of sinister seen only by the light of moving flashlights, I found the place weirdly designed. Up the steps, through a door in the rusty galvanized wall, and down some stairs, into a space with crusty weeds sticking wanly through the dirty concrete floor. What a dump, I thought; do these people live here, or what? And then up stairs again, suddenly into a quite different and more livable space, heated and lit: painted metal walls criss-crossed with pipes and conduits, up more stairs into some kind of lounge area with tables and chairs, like a nightclub in an old movie. Across the room, a line of large windows opened into blackness. Under a black quilted cover, a big shape like a pool table or shuffleboard.

I stopped and looked around. This was a mistake in terms of blending in – everyone else kept moving. Suddenly I was all by myself, standing in a sort of empty nightclub, holding two cartons of COFFEE – 12 x 750 g, not knowing which way to go. This place was ringed with entrances. One of them must lead to the kitchen.

Then another freight carrier reappeared, shrugging off his hood to reveal a tall white guy with untidy hair and a greying beard.

"Kitchen?"

He pointed ahead of me and to the right. I nodded thanks, and went down a corridor where a heavy rope ran through steel rings along each wall. To help inebriated customers get to the john? If this place was some kind of restaurant or tavern, or Depression-era resort, what was it doing up here in the middle of the North End? Who were its customers?

I felt a hand on my shoulder, then I was spun around to face a crowd. The boxes were pulled out of my hands, and a group of large walking parkas, led by the man I'd just talked to, frogmarched me into the lounge.

I was pushed into a chair.

"Hey, guys . . . I was just walking home when it started snowing," I lied feebly, "and got lost."

"This is a secret government facility," said the bearded man. He had a growly voice and some kind of Euro accent and acted like he was in charge. "You're under arrest." He turned to the others. "Get him out of here."

"I was just walking past, minding my own business, when it started to snow, and then some *thing* swooped out of nowhere . . ."

"Boy, just shut up." The leader stuck his hand in front of my face. "You are this far," he said, holding his gloved thumb and forefinger together, "from us calling the police. You'd end up in juvenile court in a second. And from there . . ." He reached for my collar. I tried to pull away, but he held on tight.

"But tonight, maybe we'll give you a break. Maybe." He gestured to one of the others. "Take him to the main gate and boot his ass out into the storm."

"You can't do that," I said. "I'm invited here."

He ignored me. "Take him to the gate. Where the hell's your stick?"

"Sorry, Eadric," another man said. "I put it down for a sec outside, and . . ."

"Carry the stick," Eadric said. "At all times when you're outside at night. You don't want your throat ripped out by a thral."

I raised my voice. "Howard asked me here. He won't like it if you throw me out."

Now everyone stopped and looked at me. "Who?" said Eadric.

"Howard emailed me," I said, "and asked me to come down."

"Howard?" He looked at his companions. "Does he mean . . ."

"Lovecraft, of course."

Eadric shook his head disgustedly. "That fruitcake. No one's seen him in months." He looked down at me. "You better not be lying to me, kid. You're sure that Lovecraft told you to come here?"

"Yes, sir," I said. "My man H. P. Lovecraft. Back in the fall, we got to be buds. If it wasn't for us, you'd all be mindless slaves of the Great Old Ones. Can I see him?"

Eadric sighed. "That's it. Boot him out." People started zipping up their parkas. "Wait a minute." He pointed a finger. "You. Stay right where you are." He left the room.

At least it was warm in here. Fluorescent lights hummed and flickered in funky old round ceiling fixtures. A line of people filed past, unloading and stowing boxes and bottles and canisters, too busy to give me a second glance. From the way they were treating me, this place was some kind of prison, but there was a polished linoleum floor with rugs, decorated in stark designs with sharp corners and dark colours, high fashion but from another time. The big windows reminded me of the Toronto Island ferry I'd been on once when I was a kid, but they were set oddly, slanting outwards from the bottom.

Next to the door that Eadric had gone through hung a red fire extinguisher, and beside it a sign with one word – FIRE – and an axe in a glass-fronted case. I wondered if he had gone to fetch Howard, or if these people, who seemed to know him, were as stumped as I was by his disappearance. During that last ceremony, back in October, Yog-Sothoth had appeared, been blasted with fire by *Sorcerer* and cried out something like "Father, save me!" before the continuum threshold had collapsed, and Lovecraft had taken off.

EADRIC WAS back. "Now that you're here," he said, "how about this: let's get some work out of you."

"How about not?" I stood up. "How about, I take my chances outside, and come back tomorrow?" Everyone else had gone off somewhere: If this outfit hadn't wanted me to come here in the first place, they wouldn't try to stop me from leaving, would they?

"My friend, it's a simple job that all of us have had their turn at. You only have to dispose of some, uh, materials."

"Why don't you just do it yourself?"

"It's . . . it's too, uh . . . too personal. Sentimental reasons."

"What kind of materials?"

"It's really just sort of a ritual. You have to shove a bundle into a hole, but you have to do it fast. Because it's a reverse air pressure situation. When the door opens, it could release, uh, dust . . ."

"Dust?"

"Exactly. Dust which will, uh, clog our ventilation system."

"Why don't you just open the windows?" I gestured around at the rows of glass on either side of this peculiar room.

"We can't do that."

"Sure you can. Just blow all the dirt —"

"They don't open." He sat there looking at me. That, apparently, was that.

"I'll tell you what," Eadric said. "I'll pay you a hundred bucks."

I heard a popping sound outside, and suddenly I was thrown off my feet as the whole building lurched to one side. Someone rushed by, keeping their balance by grabbing one of the thick ropes that served as a handrail.

"They're trying to break through the gate. At least one of them has a gun."

I reached for the rope and pulled myself to my feet, but

suddenly I seemed to have trouble standing. The floor was tilting thirty degrees and counting. If this kept up, the handrail would be on the ceiling. The building shuddered, and the floor began to right itself. I looked over at Eadric.

"Is this an earthquake?"

I didn't let go of the rope. I looked back into the lounge with its weird downward-facing windows where, even as the floor tilted and swayed in the opposite direction than it had before, all the furniture stayed put – because all the furniture was bolted to the floor.

"This is *Sorcerer*," I said. "We're on board *Sorcerer*."

"Where did you think you were?"

"*Sorcerer* exists," I said. "It really exists. And now it's taking off. I found it."

"You found it all right," Eadric said, feet firmly on the floor and both hands on the rope, as if he'd done this a thousand times. "If you're like most people, you'll be sorry you did."

CHAPTER 8
FEBRUARY 1937: SWITZERLAND

"I'm *no* friend to the Nazis! But I can't put you up forever."

Walking with long, graceful strides, dressed all in black, the young woman couldn't stop moving as she led Tobias and Max through the dining room of her Swiss estate.

"It's true, we have buckets of money but only buckets, not truckloads. In fact, the Nazis are playing havoc with Hugo's assets. If they had their way they'd put him out of business."

"You've been wonderful," said Max. "You've saved lives. But we're under a lot of pressure here."

"Yes, you're really roughing it," snorted Brigitte Helm. "Three to a featherbed in a Swiss mansion with croissants for breakfast."

"I've been meaning to talk to you about that," said Tobias. "Can we reinstate cocktail hour? Everyone really misses it."

"So funny."

"We got fifty-two people out of Dachau alive," said Max. "Without you, they would have had no place to go. Now some of them are on their way home –"

"Stop buttering me up. For their sake, I hope their 'home' doesn't have bathrooms full of foreigners, an airship tied up in its back garden and a monster in the garage." Brigitte headed down a corridor, through the kitchen (the kitchen, Tobias reflected, was twice as big as the house he'd grown up in) and out into the back garden.

"– and some of them are being trained as crew," Max continued. "God knows, we've got no one else."

"Well you'd better hurry up and get them trained and take to the air and get out of here. The British Embassy phoned me the other day. They want their airship back. The way the envoy talked, you'd think I'd taken it."

She talked as she walked and without the slightest gesture or command, they knew they had to follow. Brigitte was that sort of person.

"And this story about a sick person quarantined in the garage is not going to stand up. Hugo asks, if they're sick, why don't they go to the hospital? He wants his garage back."

"He'll get it back soon," said Max. "For now, we need the workshop."

"And for someone who's supposed to be sick," Brigitte added, "that thing eats like a horse. A horse that only eats seafood and apples, and looks like one of Satan's minions."

They'd reached the side door of the garage. Max knocked, paused for a second and they went in. Wrinkling her nose, Brigitte gingerly lifted the hem of her black dress, though she didn't have to. Despite the smell of hot solder, gasoline and rubber, oysters and rotten apples, the floor was clean and the windows were open. In one corner, a metal floor fan kept the air circulating. At a workbench, sloppily shrouded in a checkered cape Tobias had made from one of Brigitte's old blankets, the Interlocutor laboured over a large console constructed from welded metal and electronic parts. As they watched, it flicked a switch, and lights began to pulse dimly within the device's glass front.

"We look for more power," it said in German. "*Stromspannung.*"

"We can run a cable from the R102," Max said. He turned to Brigitte. "Amazing things are going on here. Amazing."

"From your batteries of wonder cells," Brigitte commented, "all charged up with our hard-earned electricity."

The Interlocutor squirmed. "The vessel cannot stay. Everything must be done to . . . make a crossing. There is less duration available before an event that will happen soon, and must be taken under control. This creation . . ."

"What's it talking about?" Brigitte huffed.

Night fell in the room as a shadow filled the garage windows, eclipsing the thin winter sunlight.

"We're supposed to be moored and secured," Max said. "Tobias, can you find out what's going on? I want to figure out what our friend is trying to tell us."

"I'm coming too," Brigitte said. "I need fresh air."

They left the garage and took the flagstone path to the back garden. Tobias heard Brigitte gasp as she saw, though not for the first time, how filthy the thin layer of muddy snow was, how beat up and trampled the property looked, from the passage of equipment, supplies, human feet and whatever those things were on the Interlocutor's bottom end. The garden took up several acres but the R102 – secured by a web of mooring lines, constantly monitored and trimmed so that its buoyancy would keep it just touching the ground, neither landing with its full weight or bobbing into the air – was big enough to cast its shadow over all of it, plus a healthy slice of the Swiss forest it backed onto.

The R102 was still moored, but its stern had swung around in the wind, brushing last year's apples, now brown and withered, from the top branches of the estate's orchard, and casting its shadow over the house and garage. As they approached, Max's assistant, Eadric, ran to greet them.

"No damage done," he said. "Honest. We had to unshackle one of the cables to thread some wiring, and before we could reattach it, a wind came up . . ."

"Wiring?" Brigitte looked dubiously at the equipment that occupied her garden's gazebo. Another of the Interlocutor's devices was mounted on a table there, blinking and humming, connected to cables that led, in turn, to the intricate tattoo of almost-invisible copper wires that now covered the huge airship. They felt the sun on them again as, through winches, ropes and sheer muscle power, the vessel was brought back to its resting place. "You people are wired enough as it is. Me and my husband, my family, my staff, we're nothing but tubes in your massive radio set."

"Brigitte — we'll be out of here soon." Max appeared behind them, blinking uncertainly in the sunlight and looking a bit stunned. "I promise. Tobias, the stakes have gone up a notch. This new device the Interlocutor is making — it's absolutely astonishing. I've come up with a name for it." He grinned with pride. "The *Raumspalter*."

"A space-cleaver?" Tobias scratched his head. "That doesn't make any sense."

"We can't test it until it's on board. The technology, the Interlocutor says, is all ours. It will give it to us. *Give* it. In return, it wants us to carry out a mission."

"A mission? Against the Nazis?"

"A mission to save a man's life. A man who, for some reason or other, is important to the Interlocutor and its people. We have to ready the R102 and plot a course to the USA — to a town called

Providence. I think it's on an island somewhere off the coast."

"The USA? You want to fly the R102 to the USA? Max, that's crazy. You need to file flight plans. No one's going to accept a flight plan for a stolen dirigible. This will be a completely illegal, pirate operation. The Yanks will turn us over to the British. If they don't shoot us down first."

"They can't shoot us down – or catch us – if they don't know we're there," Max said smugly.

"How do you hide an airship the size of a city block?"

Max went over to the gazebo and checked the cables leading from the device on the table. He looked at Tobias.

"Like this." Max flicked a switch.

From the garden came cries of alarm. An African French teacher on top of a ladder, tarring fabric over a bullet hole in the gondola's underside, had carefully clipped a safety strap in place and tied himself to the ladder. Suddenly, he found himself strapped to nothing, on a ladder that was hanging in nothing, leaning on nothing. But he didn't fall. He could feel the gondola, centimetres in front of his face, but it had become transparent. Far above him, an Italian labour organizer from a German clothing factory was patching the gasbag, roped to an access port on top of the airship. Now she found herself straddling nothing, roped to nothing as far as she could see. Yet, the R102 was still there.

"Technology so advanced," Max said proudly, "that it's like magic. A cloak of invisibility."

"So American fighter planes won't shoot us down – they'll simply ram into us by accident."

"The Interlocutor has also helped me get my Magne-tron-Erkennungssystem up and running. We'll use radio waves to detect and avoid approaching aircraft."

Tobias sighed. Max clearly had made up his mind. "An island off the US coast. Please tell me it's not the Pacific coast. Already we have to cross France, the Atlantic Ocean and then . . ."

Max grinned and put his arm around him. "Don't worry, my friend, this Providence is on the Atlantic coast. I've got charts: Rhode Island. There's a man there who's dying . . . I don't quite understand his problem, but there's something inside him that must be removed before . . . the Interlocutor says before . . ."

"Before it kills him?"

"The word it used was 'hatches.' It has to be surgically removed before it hatches."

"And who is this man?"

Max shrugged. "The Interlocutor moves in mysterious ways. He's not a scientist or philosopher or statesman, but some crummy pulp writer no one's ever heard of, although he has a wonderful last name: Lovecraft. If we can nab him, and then fire up the *Raumspalter* . . . then, the Interlocutor says . . ."

"Monsters from space . . ." Brigitte hissed. "Flying radio-wave detectors . . . cloaking devices . . . a *Raumspalter*, whatever the hell a *Raumspalter* is." She hurried back toward the house. "When I got out of the movie business the first thing I said was, *NO MORE SCIENCE FICTION*. And now look at me."

PART 2
SORCERER

I conceived the idea that the great brownstone
house was a malignly sentient thing – a dead,
vampire creature which sucked something out
of those within it and implanted in them the
seeds of some horrible and immaterial psychic growth.

– H.P. Lovecraft to Bernard Austin Dwyer,
1927

CHAPTER 9
THE THING IN THE HOLD

"Not only have I found *Sorcerer*, I'm on board *Sorcerer*." I ran to a window. Below us was only a swirl of snow, a few moving lights, then the glow of the city through the storm.

"Now that we're in the air," I said, "how do I get off?"

"A matter of minutes," Eadric assured me. "We're gaining altitude; soon we'll be over the escarpment. We'll, uh, cruise by the airport and find an empty field somewhere. You can walk toward the lights, take a bus home." I looked out at the snow whirling past the huge windows and hoped the buses would be running.

Sorcerer was the ghost that had haunted my dreams for months. Where had it been for all these years . . . decades, if what I'd read on Flight 33 was true? Why had it, instead of Yog-Sothoth, slipped through the continuum threshold during the last of the midnight games? Where had it come from? Did it appear from another part of the world? Or had it indeed slipped through all the way from the terminus the Interlocutor had called "the northern volcanic desert of R'lyhnygoth," the planet of the Great Old Ones?

A lot of questions were in my mind but foremost among them was: I had just been offered a hundred bucks to carry out what was, allegedly, a minor housekeeping task. Was it doable? Was it as simple as Eadric said it was? If I did it, would I actually get paid?

"Do you still want me to do this so-called task?"

"What?" Eadric asked.

Now I wanted out of here more than ever. "If this is some sex thing, you can take your quick hundred bucks and shove –"

"No, no, no. Strictly on the up and up. There will be other people there, believe me."

"I don't know," I said slowly. "This all sounds to me, kind of . . ."

"Two hundred dollars."

"Cash?" He nodded.

"Let's do it."

"There's something here we have to get out of the way first." He gestured with his arm: around us in the lounge, some strange ritual or meeting was unfolding. Some sort of table or dais had been set up, and people – crew members, I guess – were congregating.

"And then I can go home," I said.

"Of course."

A simple stretcher – just a sheet of canvas between two long wooden handles conveying what was obviously a human body, wrapped in cotton like a mummy – was brought in and laid across the dais.

Fidgety and impatient, Eadric clapped his hands and called everyone to order. "Can we get started?"

"Where's Tobias?" someone asked.

"Rescheduling, organizing damage control, calling ahead to Georgia and helping secure the supplies from the freight," Eadric snapped. "He told us to go ahead. He's got a long flight to plan."

Long flight? I was antsy to do this alleged task, get my money and get dropped off. Eadric started the ceremony.

What could I do? I wasn't about to stomp around and throw a tantrum during some guy's funeral. I stood at the back of the sparse crowd and listened. In a moment, someone came and stood next to me: a dark-haired white woman in her forties a few inches shorter than me.

"You're new here," she said. I nodded. "Did you know Gyorgy?" I shook my head and told her my name.

"Agnes." Wait a minute, I thought. I know an Agnes.

"We are here to honour our brother and comrade Gyorgy Prohaska, whose journey aboard the R102 has come to an end. Like so many of us here, Gyorgy has been raised from the dead once before. As the citizen of a proud nation, he survived internment at the hands of the state . . ."

I know *this* Agnes.

"He means the death camp of a madman," Agnes whispered. "Hitler."

Jeez, I thought, Gyorgy must have been pretty old. Agnes did her best to bring me up to speed as Eadric continued, and although I listened with one ear, my mind was racing. Where had I met her?

". . . to become a citizen of the vast universe. Even as the R102, a voyager between the earth and sky, between countries and continents, became *Sorcerer*, a voyager between worlds, each of us has survived death, to become something, someone, a new being quite different than the person we set out to be. Our friend Gyorgy was such a person. From a Hungarian . . ."

"Actually, Gyorgy was Roma," Agnes whispered.

". . . tinker and traveller, to an aeronautics and lift mechanic without parallel. From . . ."

"So, Italian?" I whispered back.

"Nonono," she hissed. "Not Roman, Roma. The people once called 'gypsies.'"

". . . a simple man who had travelled the back roads and byways of eastern Europe, to a voyager among the clouds, and then the stars . . ."

I looked around as I listened. This funeral had a loose dress code: my winter coat, hoodie and gumboots were all I had, but the rest of the mourners were just as informal, dressed in frayed and faded overalls, blue jeans, cracked and stained work boots, and winter coats. Then I remembered. That night at the stadium, my father in danger, the crowd gathering for the ceremony, Agnes had tried to help us. I'd only met her for a few minutes, and it had all fallen apart into chaos, but she was a friend of Howard's.

"Unto him we wish the deep peace of the running waters and the free open air; unto him we wish the strength of the quiet earth and the hum of the stars. *Amicus mea, daemones illi non dominabitur tui.* Unto you, Gyorgy Prohaska, we wish the glory of the universe, world without end, amen."

When I turned, Agnes was looking at me. "*Dios mío,*" she said. "I just put it together. You're Nate."

"Uh, yeah?"

The ceremony had ended. Eadric was consulting with someone at the stretcher. He caught my eye, raised his hand.

"Don't go away," Agnes whispered.

"I've got to —"

"I'll be right back."

Agnes disappeared in a flurry as the crowd got ready to move on. I found myself holding onto the rear right handle of the stretcher, a muscular Filipina woman to my right and, at the front, two tall Black guys who talked non-stop to each other in French. Eadric led us down a passageway. We took a sharp left and were now, I figured, pretty much at the stern of the ship, or at least the stern of the long enclosure (I found out later it was called the gondola) that housed all of the airship's working parts besides the gas cells within the enormous upper hull.

To the left was a door marked LOAD/EVAC, but we went to the right, through a door marked PRESSURE, where to one side was a wall of gauges, switches, fuses and circuit breakers. The rest of the room was taken up with huge shiny tanks of gas, ceiling-high and extending back to the very end of the airship's gondola.

Gradually, the rest of the mourners filed in after us, until the room was crowded not only with people but with lengths of wire and conduit, scattered tools and piles of cardboard boxes that had just come off the freight car. Dominating the space was some kind of glass-walled enclosure that looked much newer than the rest of the fittings around me. A fluorescent tube glared from its ceiling, shining down on a trap door set in the floor and sealed with a great wheel like a door in a submarine. It looked like it was made of heavy steel, barred and padlocked.

I had attracted a lot of curious glances at Gyorgy's service. This was a place where outsiders were noticed immediately. Someone in the group called out to Eadric, *"Wer ist das?"*

"This is Nate," Eadric said. "He's agreed to do the honours. For a very modest fee."

"Just to be clear," I said, "two hundred –"

"Take off all that –" Eadric gestured at my coat and boots, and in a few moments I had stripped down to my jeans and

T-shirt. I don't know if I could have gone any farther, with all these people watching, but fortunately we stopped there. I even kept my socks on. "– and put on this." A couple of his helpers were dragging over a huge rubber suit. Its steel helmet looked like it had been clumsily augmented with rubber patches, leaving only a tiny glass faceplate to look through.

"You want me to get into *that*?"

Eadric and a couple of helpers guided my legs into the suit and sealed it up around me. One of them fiddled with a valve on the outside, and stale air, stinking of rust and WD-40, flooded the helmet. I staggered in place for a few moments, getting my balance, then took a few careful steps. Already the suit was getting uncomfortably hot.

"Can I get my two hundred bucks now?"

Eadric gestured to a switch on the suit's breastplate and, as he donned a black plastic headset, I turned it on and could hear his voice inside the helmet.

Eadric dismissed the other carriers, took the front of the stretcher himself and led me to the windowed booth that dominated the centre floor. A sign over the door read OFFLIFE ACCESS / AUTHORIZED PERSONS ONLY. Inside, a great wheel secured the metal hatch in the floor. Eadric undid the lock, slid a bolt and looked back at me.

"Here's what we'll do." Through the suit's headset, he sounded the way I felt: like Neil Armstrong speaking from the moon, although at least astronauts had low gravity on their side, whereas my arms and legs seemed to have been tied with dumbbells.

"I'll set down my end on the rim of the hatch, and leave the room," Eadric said. "We'll open the hatch remotely. As soon as it's open far enough, slide the bundle" – by this he meant Gyorgy

– "into the hatch. There will be negative air pressure – that will help to pull the bundle into the hatch, but you must slide it in all the way as fast as you can, before the pressure equalizes."

Ever since I had come out of the blizzard and onto *Sorcerer*, I had felt a strange sensation in my bones. Like when you have a ringing in your ears, only this was a ringing that resonated through my whole body. It reminded me of the psychic buzz I had felt during one of the Church's ceremonies, when a continuum threshold was being fired up and Yog-Sothoth was drawing very near. Something about *Sorcerer* generated that same kind of uneasy, sickly excitement.

Now, as I approached the hatch, the feeling grew, like I had a gutful of nerves and a head full of bees.

"You got that, young man?"

The buzzing in my head wasn't bees, it was a voice. I could only think of one thing to say.

"Someone's in there."

Eadric blinked and recoiled as if I'd spat blood.

"Do as you're told," he replied, "and they'll stay in there."

Eadric left the room before I could ask what he meant, leaving me balancing Gyorgy's corpse uneasily on one end of the stretcher. I heard the clatter of the metal door latch as it turned and locked in place, and then there was Eadric, pointing urgently through the glass at the floor in front of me.

Sure enough, the wheel was turning and the hatch was opening. Hearing the rush of air into the hatch, I pushed up my end of the stretcher. The handles bumped against the metal rim. Through the opening, I could see a torrent of mist flowing downwards in the darkness, being sucked into the hold by Eadric's "negative air pressure." The mist billowed up, then like a waterfall flowed back into a darkness lit intermittently by flashes of blue light. Those flashes of light revealed a brown, seething mass of ropy muscles, nerves and muck that looked and smelled like a blocked sewer. Let me outta here. I tilted the stretcher.

Suddenly, I felt a tingling in my right shoulder, and veins of subtle lightning flowed down my chest and shoulder blade. A damp coil like living rope flung itself out of the hatch and lassoed the stretcher's end. I heard a pounding on the window, and looked up to see anxious faces, and Eadric gesturing me to raise my arms higher, to tilt the stretcher up, to dump Gyorgy as quickly and unceremoniously as I could. The tingling was stronger; my shoulder stung like lactic acid was bubbling and burning my muscles.

I shook the stretcher to dislodge Gyorgy's corpse, and the dark tendril reached up farther. I could hear the rush of air growing quieter, and the pounding on the window grow louder, and then with a smooshing sound, the tendril flowed up the stretcher like mercury and touched my gloved hand. The veins of fire burned like a snakebite, the tendril flinched as if it too felt the pain, and somewhere, somebody was screaming.

Stop this! Stop this! I beg you!

I was locked in a dark place where they had stripped me naked and thrown me, and *things* were eating me alive. Things that lived on pain. They made sure every feeling I had turned it into pain.

Why won't you free me?

They sucked me in like a whirlwind of ground glass, so that every part of my body, starting with my eyes and my mouth and the softest and most sensitive organs and openings, burned and burned, day and night. Burned like fire and acid, until there was nothing human left inside me except sickness and suffering and self-pity. *Stop this!* I cried. *Stop this! I beg you!*

I turned toward the horrified faces outside the window. Eadric and another man were fumbling with some piece of equipment with tanks and tubes and a blackened brass nozzle. As the black tendril swelled and circled me like a hungry python, I fought my way forward and pounded on the glass. From the other side, I faintly heard Eadric shouting, "Light it! Light it!"

There was a spark, and then a tongue of flame shot from the nozzle the two men held gingerly before them. I squeezed my eyes shut against the glare, although no heat penetrated the glass wall or the layered materials of the suit. The tendrils that held me flinched, and pain shot through every part of me, from my toes to my eyeballs.

The tendrils withdrew, sliding back along the floor and embracing the corpse. Gyorgy was pulled off the stretcher and into the darkness below. I backed away, pulling the stretcher with me, and the trap door thumped back into place, leaving no trace behind. The wheel spun, sealing the hatch.

There was shouting outside the compartment. "What the hell are you doing?" A woman's voice.

The door burst open and the room was flooded with some sort of chemical mist. I raised my arms to shield my helmet as it fogged over. Agnes and another woman, wearing masks with heavy filters hanging off each cheek, rushed into the room and started spraying me directly from tanks hanging off their shoulders. Blinded and confused, I let them lead me out of there, down a hallway and into a shower room. With gloved hands they started undoing the suit fittings.

"We can't undo the helmet. Nod. Shrug your shoulders," Agnes ordered. I did what I could and they lifted the helmet off and set it on the floor. I reached from inside and started unzipping the suit's collar, and with their help, I shrugged off the upper half of the heavy contraption.

"Oh my god," the other woman said. Blinking and snorting, I registered only that she was blonde and younger than Agnes.

As soon as I was able to step out onto the tiled floor, the blonde woman took my arm and, wearing thick rubber gloves, inspected my hands and arms where the dark tendrils had touched me.

"I don't see any sign of incursion. But look. It's him." Her voice broke. Eadric and the other man appeared behind her.

"I don't get it. We saw what we saw," he said. "Jiang, do you see any sign of contamination?"

"*Nein.*" Jiang continued speaking in German, and Eadric answered him.

"You were going to burn me," I said. "You started up a flame-thrower."

"That was for the vulsetchi."

"Eadric, get out of here." Agnes sounded ready to bite his head off.

"Take a shower," Eadric said to me, "and count your blessings."

"Get out *now.*"

"So big. But it's him. Nate, you don't recognize me?" I looked at this woman, dirty blonde hair over her face, mask hanging off her neck, and blinked.

Agnes stepped between us. "He's lucky he's alive, but he's covered with disinfectant and who knows what else. Give us five minutes, dear."

She took me to a tiled room with a line of six shower nozzles. She turned one on. I was only too happy to start peeling off the few clothes I'd been wearing inside the protective suit.

"Quick. You can't waste water. It shuts off in ninety seconds."

Agnes left me and I started counting down – ninety thousand, eighty-nine thousand, eighty-eight thousand – and checking my aching body for wounds I could feel but couldn't see. What kind of a ritual had I just been through? I could still hear that voice in my head. *Stop this! Stop this! I beg you!* I lathered up fast and stood under the nozzle until the water stopped. I could hear an echo off the hard walls around me, like a ghost in a castle.

Why won't you free me?

Drying off, I found myself alone and my clothes gone. In their place was a checkered dressing gown, an old set of flannel-ette pyjamas and a pair of felt slippers. Suddenly the voice from the vulsetchi's hold shut off. I was back with my own thoughts, and I realized who the blonde woman was. She and Agnes appeared when I was almost dressed.

"Oh god," she said. "Oh god. Nate."

I stared back at her. "Mom?"

My mother put her arms around me. She smelled like sweat, harsh detergent soap, hot metal and boiled vegetables: in fact, she mostly smelled like everyone and everything else on *Sorcerer*.

"You're alive," I said.

"You're so big," she said. "Look at you. Why are you trying to kill yourself?"

"Nobody told me it was dangerous. I slid a guy's body – well, his name was Gyorgy – into a hatch. Something came out, and . . . anyway, how are you alive?"

"I missed your whole childhood."

"Why are you and Agnes dressed like Ghostbusters?"

"I was supposed to inter Gyorgy," Agnes said angrily. "Unlike you, I know the dangers. I can prepare. Are you sure you're all right?"

"I'm fine!"

"When I realized who you were, I had to let Nell know. There was no time to lose. We can explain."

"Go ahead and explain but . . . is there anything to eat on this airship?"

CHAPTER 10
THE ABSENT PARENT

After unloading the black freight, and being shot at by the Resurrection Church, and after the (from my point of view, scary and harrowing) funeral ceremony for their oldest crew member, *Sorcerer*'s inhabitants were ready to party. As we entered the lounge, a crew member was folding and stowing the black quilted blanket, uncovering the object I'd thought was a pool table, and that turned out to be a grand piano. We sat down as the young Black woman I'd met in the loading dock, wearing jeans and a hoodie (on board *Sorcerer*, this was really dressing up) propped the lid in place (rather than black like normal pianos, this was some kind of brushed metal) and tried out a few initial chords.

"It's like the café in *Casablanca*." I'd watched the film with Dad. "But in the movie, people were more dressed up."

"Speaking of movies," my mother said. "How's the store doing?"

"Touchdown Video? It's 2013 now, Mom. What planet have you been on all this time?"

"Since you ask, R'lyhnygoth."

"Anyway, Dad closed it down, like four years ago. He works at Sears now."

I remembered my mother as a reassuring presence, huge and all-powerful. In fact, more as a presence than as a person. And here sitting across the table from me was this woman with dark circles around her eyes, wearing the crew members' standard beige coverall and a familiar ribbed, charcoal-grey sweater.

"Agnes calls you 'Nell.' Your name's Eleanor. Eleanor Fraser."

"People call me Nell, Elle, Nellie, Lennie."

We had a book of clippings at home, newspaper stories my mother had written.

"I always just called you Mummy."

"Not the last time we talked, you didn't."

"Jeez." When I'd gotten out of the hospital someone had phoned claiming to be my mother and I'd threatened them with death and torture if they ever called again. But something in that voice kept nagging at me. "That *was* you."

"We touched down in Hamilton, then Tobias took us to some other hangar way up north. I managed to slip out, then I hiked ten or fifteen kilometres to get to a gas station. It had a phone booth, thank god – why are those so hard to find now? – but they caught up to me. I just had time for you to yell and call me names before I was swarmed." She pointed across the room, where Eadric sat with a circle of crew members. "*Him*, in fact, and his cronies."

Agnes shrugged. "Eadric is afraid of the sporifidae, and he has every reason to be."

"He's a paranoid creep."

"Being paranoid about the sporifidae is a good idea."

"I thought you were some creep from the Resurrection Church, pranking me," I said to my mother.

"I missed your entire childhood," she said. "You're not my cute little boy anymore." She reached out to touch my face, and instinctively I shrank back as if from a stranger.

"I thought you were dead. Everyone does."

My mother drew back, embarrassed. I don't know why, but I

felt like she wanted our reunion to have more hugs and tears, and I felt a kind of sullen satisfaction that I wasn't giving them to her.

She sighed in frustration. "And since when," she continued, "did 'pranking' become a verb?"

It's been ten years, I thought. You couldn't get back any sooner? Finally, when the silence was getting uncomfortable, I came right out and said it.

"There was a ceremony," my mother explained. "I do – did – freelance journalism, and I was trying to get a story on the Resurrection Church. My editor thought they were harmless crackpots, but I was sure there was something more, that they were dangerous. What I wasn't ready for was that they actually *were* in touch with real extraterrestrial life forms that are very nasty, and want to colonize Earth. I snuck into a couple of meetings, and I have to give myself credit; along with a bunch of other media people, we raised some ruckus against the Church, but . . . there was kind of a riot. Next thing I knew there was fire, bullets, people screaming and getting hurt. And suddenly there was *Sorcerer*. The guys on *Sorcerer* convinced me to come on board to escape. That was the biggest mistake of my life. As soon as I was on board, they took *Sorcerer* through the continuum threshold to R'lyhnygoth."

"You've been to R'lyhnygoth?"

"*Sorcerer* can make that jump – it's a unique entity, that's for sure."

"You've spent these past ten years on another planet?"

She sighed. "For me, it was ninety days."

She leaned forward and showed me her digital wristwatch. The luminous letters at the bottom read June 14 • 2003. "And what's the date today?"

"It's March," I said. "Twenty thirteen. Your watch is busted."

"I boarded *Sorcerer* on October 10, 2002. You were six years old. I told your dad I'd be back before midnight. Then I went through the mob at the ceremonies, escaped onto this tub – if you can call that 'escaping' – and crossed the continuum threshold. I spent three months surviving on R'lyhnygoth – I've made enough notes to write a book, if I can ever get back to civilization."

"You should come home with me . . ." It sounded weird to say this. "You know, to live with us."

"Then we found out that Yog-Sothoth was preparing an assault on Earth," my mother continued, "that he would try to cross over, and that would give us a chance to breach the threshold again. That's when we came through at the stadium. As far as I was concerned – and I'd been looking at my watch every five minutes for three months – the date was January 8, 2003. But time runs differently on R'lyhnygoth."

"What do you mean? Time is time."

Agnes said, "The hub-rim differential."

"For me," my mother continued, "it's been bad enough being away from you and your dad for three months. For you, and everyone on Earth, it's been ten years. Look at you."

"So why did you even get on *Sorcerer* to begin with?" I asked. "It was terrible for us. Why didn't you just come home?"

"I was being chased," she said. "There was nothing around me but gunshots and violence. Someone yelled there was an IED. Then suddenly there was something *there*. Someone came out of the darkness: Eadric and the others. They told me to get on. They said there was no time."

"You could have escaped. You could have just run, and not

screwed off to another planet for ten years. Why get onto *Sorcerer* instead?"

"You want to know why?" A definite edge was creeping into my mother's voice. "Because they told me *you* were on board. They told me that if I wanted to see you again, I *had* to come. I boarded *Sorcerer* because I thought you were there."

Trying to make me feel crappy? Mission accomplished.

"Is that why you've done the same thing to me?" I asked. "Eadric said I'd get dropped off, and look . . ." I gestured at the row of windows. Outside was blackness, with the occasional whisk of the waning snow swirling past. "Where are we going? Where am I getting taken to?"

"It's not me. I'm not in control. I want to get off *Sorcerer* more than you do."

"Why don't we just eat," Agnes said, "and be quiet for a minute."

The food was like cafeteria food from ancient times: dried-out deep-fried chicken, mushy steamed vegetables, rice. Conversation remained minimal. After our years-long separation, my mother and I were not getting off on the right foot. I was worried that my ride on *Sorcerer* might not be the eye-opening chance of a lifetime that I should gratefully accept, but instead a downward slide into a world of crackpot science and bad food that would keep me out of school just as I was trying to catch up. I had lots to worry about without getting caught up with *Sorcerer*. For one thing, I was still traipsing around in someone else's old pyjamas.

When we had eaten, my mother took me down some corridors to a laundry room where I hauled my clothes out of a dryer, toasty and clean without a trace of melted snow and ice, or of the vulsetchi, or any of the stinky gunk that came with the vulsetchi.

My mother wanted to talk . . . and talk . . . and talk . . . but when I told her I was tired, she took me to a cabin, sparsely furnished with a few bunk beds and a desk, and pointed me to a top bunk. Only one of the other bunks was occupied. She put her finger to her lips, and insisted on giving me a good night hug.

Once she was gone, I looked at my phone. It wasn't that late, and I had unfinished business.

APPARENTLY, WITH the disposal of Gyorgy's corpse, I had passed some kind of test, or security check, and was now an honorary crew member, allowed to wander around *Sorcerer* at will. Exploring the airship's corridors, occasionally passing a crew member who would nod or say hello. My cellphone showed zero bars. I wondered if we had gone through some kind of continuum threshold, like the one that had opened up over the stadium that night, and had now left the planet, but then I remembered that I was surrounded on every side by metal walls and floor. To get a signal, I had to get to a window.

The lounge was silent and dark. Once again the piano was an anonymous covered shape. I went past it to lean against a window. This was Earth all right, at the tail end of a cold winter. I looked down at a white landscape criss-crossed by ribbons of glowing streets, infested by the moving lights of cars like tiny fireflies. I figured we were several hundred metres up. In a pool of light beneath me, a tiny black car pulled into a snow-covered yard, a door opened and a tiny black flea-sized dog bounced out into the snow, followed by a tiny black flea-sized person, then *Sorcerer* passed over and they were gone.

At least I could get a signal here. This was my chance to phone 911 and report that I'd been kidnapped by the crew of an antique dirigible. No, I didn't get its plate number.

Instead, I phoned home.

Dad's phone rang . . . and rang . . . and rang. I pictured him, still not feeling 100 percent after the events of last fall, still not 100 percent on board with having Uncle Don and his family invite themselves to move in, still not 100 percent sure how this cell phone thingy worked, giving up, dismissing me as a junk call, letting it ring . . . Finally he answered.

"Dad, I just want you to know, I've gone off on a kind of a drive, with, uh, friends, so I might not get back home tonight."

"You told me you'd be home."

"Yeah, well, I ran into some friends and we're, you know, gaming and stuff."

"You're gaming in a car? Where the hell are you?"

I sighed.

"It's a school night."

"Dad, I'm in good hands." I wished I believed that myself. "You might say I'm, uhh, having kind of an adventure."

"This sounds totally bogus. If you're not safe, tell me. Tell me where you are."

"See ya tomorrow."

"Dammit, Nate . . ."

I hung up, put the phone on mute and wandered the corridors until I found the cabin my mother had found for me. There was someone in the far corner, and across from the bed I'd claimed with my coat and boots, there was a new tenant.

I climbed into my bunk and lay there listening. Around me, all that was solid and inflexible – the steel bed frame, the light fixture, the tiny porthole – hummed along with the huge engines that were taking us, according to my mental calculations, south by southeast. Water moaned and chuckled through the painted radiators. The winds outside rose and fell and all around me, from here in *Sorcerer*'s belly, I heard great sounds of hissing and sighing. The segmented gasbag above me pushed back against atmospheric pressure, shrinking and expanding against the outside air and as it worked to keep us in the sky, the airship sighed and shuddered like a huge beast with a broken heart.

From time to time, crew members would pass by my room, sometimes solo, sometimes two or more talking or arguing, usually not in English or my high-school *sur le pont d'Avignon* French. I tried to remember what I'd read of the history of the R102. Manufactured in England, it had made an unexpected trip to Germany in the early days of the Third Reich . . . innovative new batteries . . . concentration camps, jailbreaks, gunfire . . . and then I slept.

I dreamt that I was swimming in some huge windowless tank or sewer, in murky waters through which, intermittently, flashes of blue lightning showed an underwater jungle of numberless tendrils. The tendrils clung to me, to my skin and fingers, and I knew, in the dream, that this was only a lull in my normal state. As I swam I could feel a current of pain push against the soles of my feet as it overtook me, washed over my legs and then enveloped my whole body, and the current was a sheer, all-embracing burning.

CHAPTER 11
THE HUB-RIM DIFFERENTIAL

I woke up to the porthole admitting a dim grey light. "Hey," somebody said, "you okay?"

"Uh, yeah." I looked to see who was talking. The bed across from me was empty, but from the corner, a young Black woman was eyeing me warily.

"You were yelling."

I shrugged. "No way . . . maybe it was a dream."

"You were yelling, 'Get me outta here, you bastard torturers.' In German."

"Not very likely, since I don't speak German."

"Come and have breakfast," she said.

We introduced ourselves. Margrit seemed to know to everyone we met, and when we got to the well-lit lounge, I realized she was the woman I'd run into in the loading dock, and that she was also last night's pianist. A line of folding metal tables were set up along one wall. I joined the lineup and had oatmeal with brown sugar and milk with that chalky, made-from-powdered taste. From a nutritional point of view, I would have liked to add some fruit (actually what I really wanted was bacon and eggs with toast and jam), but found only raisins, which I dutifully spread on top. Margrit invited me to sit down, and from across the table she peered at me over the tops of old-fashioned gold-rimmed glasses.

"Who are you, anyway? Where'd you come from?"

"I snuck in on the black freight," I said. "Looking for *Sorcerer*. The next thing I knew . . ."

Margrit kept up the questions, not all of which I could answer. Who was my favourite musician? What did I want to be when I grew up? Who won the latest World Series? I asked her questions back.

"Hell, I'm just an unemployed piano tuner from New Jersey. Who was hoping to study in Germany and become a concert pianist, but ended up playing the piano in bars. The wrong bars, it turned out, with the wrong people, in the wrong place, at the wrong time."

"How old are you?" Margrit looked to be in her early thirties.

"Hmm." She looked thoughtful. Just why this was a hard question, I didn't know. "What year is it?" she asked. I told her. "I guess that makes me ninety-seven years old."

"That's ridiculous." I looked around the room. "The hub-rim differential thing. I think Agnes mentioned it last night, but nobody explained it."

"It's simple. The universe –" she gestured at her oatmeal "– a great big mass of galaxies, nebulae, black holes, stars and so forth – is constantly expanding outward from its origins, whatever that might be."

"The big bang theory."

"I guess," Margrit said. "And as it expands, it also rotates. It spins, and on a scale too vast for us to imagine – too vast for me, anyway – it spins not just through space, but through *time*.

"We think of time as this big static thing that we, living things, move through. We move, change, get older; time itself doesn't. But time isn't static. It's also moving. There are some who say the universe is alive; I don't know about that, but I know this: everything in the universe moves, everything is in motion. Including time.

"So when the universe expands and spins, it's like a gigantic bicycle wheel. R'lyhnygoth is near the centre of the wheel, the hub, and Earth is out near the rim. Can you picture that?"

"Sure," I said. "You're saying that each planet, in fact its entire solar system, is moving on the wheel not only through space, but through time?"

"But like a wheel, the closer you are to the outer rim, the faster you move. For the planet R'lyhnygoth and Earth, the ratio is something like forty to one. Once you're through the threshold, for every hour you spend on R'lyhnygoth, forty hours elapse on planet Earth. In 1937, we got into this without knowing. I wouldn't be here today if Max hadn't got me, along with a bunch of us, out of Dachau. We stayed at this country estate in Switzerland, then took the R102's first extended voyage – across the Atlantic to pick up Howard. Then we had to make a super-extended voyage – through a continuum threshold to R'lyhnygoth, so the surgeons there could save Howard. They also saved the thing growing inside him, which if you ask me wasn't the best idea in the world, but that's the *hihyaghi* for you.

"So on that first visit, we accomplished an enormous amount in six months. We survived great dangers, and we learned some astonishing things. But we got displaced in time."

"Wow," I said. "That must mess you up."

"What's worse is," Margrit said, "after a while, you get used to it. If I add up my time on *Sorcerer*, I'm probably thirty or so. But just look at this crowd. Look beyond their clothes – they issue us all these same dowdy coveralls: makes it hard to look snazzy. Look at all these people. You name it, we got it, from Ethiopian Muslims to Bavarian Jehovah's Witnesses."

I glanced around. There were people who looked like they, or their parents, might have come from Japan, India, El Salvador, Norway, Kenya, wherever. It wasn't much different from my school cafeteria, except that they were all adults. I couldn't figure out what Margrit was getting at.

"So . . . the crew was chosen according to maximum, uh . . . political correctness?"

Margrit laughed. "Political correctness – that's a new term, isn't it?"

I shrugged. "Not for me."

"It's something I could have used a lot more of, in my life and career, but anyway if we're talking about *Sorcerer*, I guess you could say political correctness in reverse. Romany, foreign workers, Jewish writers, Black musicians, touring artists, actors and acrobats, gay and trans workers, everyone just trying to find a place for themselves, as we all do – the crew of the R102 is what you get if you stage a jailbreak at a Nazi concentration camp in 1937."

She shrugged, looked at her watch. Around us, people were getting up, stacking dishes, heading out to start their workday.

"You were playing the piano last night," I said. "That sounded good."

Margrit raised her hands in acknowledgement. "Who'd think you could get that tone? An aluminum grand piano. Every piano bar and speakeasy should have one."

"My dad gets together with his buddies," I said. "They play the blues and uh, so forth."

"The blues and so forth. That's practically the definition of Western music." She waved. "Gotta go – I never know who

Tobias has let pilot this thing, or where we'll end up next."

Nineteen thirty-seven. The year that the R102, a.k.a. *Sorcerer*, had taken its inaugural flight. I looked around at the funky old design, the faded rugs and curtains. Everything looked in awfully good shape for an airship that had been in service for seventy-six years. So . . . if it had spent a certain amount of time at the far end of this hub-rim differential, then the time elapsed . . . I shook my head. These ideas were hard to get around.

I saw, through the clear centre of the frost-covered window, and through gaps in the clouds outside, that we were heading out over water, leaving behind the snow-covered checkerboard of southwestern Ontario's fields and suburbs. The lounge shuddered in a blast of wind, though I couldn't feel so much as a draft through the double-glazed windows.

"Tobias. I've been hearing his name all night. I should meet this Tobias."

"You should. Right this way."

We left the lounge and headed up the main corridor toward the front of the ship, until we came to a door that, like all the doors on *Sorcerer*, was painted institutional grey with dark green trim. Margrit turned the lever handle, and we stepped over the threshold. The door swung shut behind us.

At the front of the bridge were two pilots' chairs hung with belts and headphones. Beyond the floor-to-ceiling windshield, enormous wipers squeaked and shuddered back and forth, beating back the oncoming assault of wet snow. In one chair was Eadric, who was leaning forward, earnestly lecturing the other chair's occupant: a tall, slender man with long black hair and a pockmarked complexion, who was lying back, thumbing his cellphone and very much trying to ignore Eadric.

I looked around. Behind the pilots' chairs was some kind of light table with pencils, compasses and charts, and around the cabin were different control stations with desks and dials and huge shiny microphones and tangles of black wire. Like a lot of the R102's interior, it had the same "museum" vibe I got from touring the antique destroyer that's tied up in Hamilton Harbour. As soon as we were in the door, Margrit left me to join a tall white woman with broad shoulders and frizzy hair who was already stooped over the light table, pencilling lines with a compass and yardstick.

Over to the right of the windshield, however, was a console that looked definitely out of place. Chest-high, of shiny brushed metal in contrast with the chipped, painted-over look of the rest of the airship. At first I thought it was one of those old jukeboxes that light up in front, then I wondered if it was some kind of aquarium. Behind its front glass panel, a mass of lights dimmed and brightened, shrank into nothing, then burst into fireworks, slithered and slid into writhing multicoloured shapes, as if the machine was a nest of luminescent undersea life. On top of the console was some kind of dial, and a panel of lights and switches. A red light shone there; as I watched it began blinking and went out. Beside it, a green light came on.

With the front of the gondola almost all windows, the bridge had the best view on board.

Suddenly the tall man sat up and raised his voice. "Look, I'm trying to plot a course here. We've interred Gyorgy already? Why does nobody tell me anything around here? Where the hell are the navigators?"

"Tobias, I'm right here." The woman at the light table held

up her hand, and gestured at Margrit and me. "And look, here's Margrit."

Eadric fumbled for an explanation. "Everything happened at once . . . unloading . . . gunshots . . . surprise takeoff . . . vulsetchi . . . Agnes . . ."

So, really, I thought, who's in charge here? Did clothes provide a clue? Margrit and the other navigator could not have looked less alike as people, but they wore the identical brown pocketed coveralls that seemed to be the *Sorcerer* uniform – clothes that also looked as if they might date back to when the R102 was first launched. Despite the airship's age, everything on board, including the crew, looked to be in awfully good shape, although if you asked me, they all could use some new clothes.

Tobias, on the other hand, seemed to wear what he wanted. Tall and skinny, he had on a soft, comfortable-looking hoodie, teal green lined with salmon pink, over a white T-shirt printed with some kind of stylized black raven–type bird.

"Thrals nesting under the re-entry nacelle," he said to Eadric. "So what?"

"Put on some gear and go up into the cell three access, right under the nacelle. You can hear them."

"I don't much care, as long as they don't gnaw on the rubber. But it's awfully cold out there. Thrals don't like the cold. Bet you any money, by now they're dead or flown away."

"I'm telling you, they *do* gnaw on the rubber. If they're still up there –"

"Eadric, I've got bigger worries than a few vermin who can't even get inside the ship. It's the vulsetchi I worry about. I worry about using that *thing* as our power source. What if we spring a leak and the vulsetchi gets out of the hold and into the ship – or even worse, gets *out* of the ship? Then what do we do?"

Eadric said, "Make sure it doesn't get out. The experiment with the boy was encouraging. For some reason, it didn't take him. Meanwhile, Gyorgy's . . ." Eadric paused, looking for the right word.

"Corpse," Tobias offered.

". . . remains . . . will power the R102 for months. Flesh into energy, and we need lots of energy. *Sorcerer* needs power. The sporifidae are a blessing."

"Flesh into energy. But in your opinion, we get more energy from the flesh of creatures with highly developed nervous systems."

"It's not an opinion, it's research. We did tests."

"Okay, human beings make the best possible fuel. So if Gyorgy hadn't died, what would we be doing – robbing graves to keep the lights on?"

Eadric shrugged. "Think of how many people there are in the world now. A human being is nothing – a human body, easy to come by."

"Sometimes I think we should burn up this tub and everything in it, starting with the vulsetchi, sporifidae, whatever you want to call them."

"They could be the power source this world needs. Organic matter to electricity. The flesh is the fuel; the nervous system, conduits that literally transform matter to energy . . ."

"Aside from the moral issues, Eadric – you've heard of those, right? – there's the problem of control. One leak . . ."

". . . flesh into electricity with incredible efficiency."

". . . and the next time, the Valley of Bones will be Shanghai or Paris or Valparaíso, and the vulsetchi will *keep* spreading." Tobias sighed. "And what about Kaindl? He's getting into my dreams too, and it's no wonder, I don't blame him, after what's been done to him. What were we thinking? Damn. I wish Max was here." He turned and saw me standing there.

"Experiment?" I said. "I was an experiment?"

Margrit and the other navigator looked up from their charts.

"So I was an experiment, and now I've been kidnapped. And ripped off," I said. "I'm supposed to be in school today, not going to Georgia. What am I going to do in Georgia? How do I get home from Georgia?"

"You see, I told you," Eadric said to Tobias. "He's okay. No one on board has symptoms. And we know vulsetchi infection spreads very fast. Your quarantine has worked."

"Except that the crew are pissed off, depressed, fed up and on the verge of mutiny."

Eadric pointed at me. "And this boy . . . the sporifidae couldn't touch him at all. He's completely immune."

Immune? After sliding Gyorgy's corpse into a hold full of these sporifidae/vulsetchi things, I felt like I'd been tasered. My body was raw and sore, as if I'd gone over Niagara Falls onto the rocks. And there was that voice, and the feeling that came with it: unending, desperate pain and utter hopelessness. Last night had been a restless sleep.

"Eadric, we need a plan," Tobias said. "We've been skipping over decades like a rock over the water: 1937, 1958, 1974, 1993, 2002 and now whatever this year is. We need a break. Our people need the chance to have lives."

"With the resources we have at our command, with this ship," Eadric said, "we've got more important things to do than –"

"Nell, for example. Keeping her on board was a mistake."

"The first chance she got," Eadric huffed, "she jumped ship and –"

"I don't blame her. She has a family. She didn't need to be hunted down and captured by your Nazi thugs."

Eadric shot to his feet. "Nazi thugs. You're the one who treats *Sorcerer* like a flying leper colony."

"If the vulsetchi get out – you know how serious that would be. *Sorcerer* is supposed to be helping to save life on Earth, not play Russian roulette with it."

"If it wasn't for Max and me, Nazi thugs would have made an ashtray out of you."

"If it wasn't for Max, you'd be a Munich street vendor. Selling ashtrays."

"I don't have to take this from you." Eadric pushed past me, headed for the door to the corridor. He looked back as he reached the door. "I'm not about to take crap from some Indian picture painter."

"An Indian picture painter . . ." Tobias leaned back in his chair and put his feet up on the dashboard. ". . . who's piloting a frickin' spaceship."

"I've got half a mind to go back to Germany," Eadric said.

"You wouldn't like it now. It's a liberal democracy."

CHAPTER 12
THE DEMONS WILL HAVE NO DOMINION

Eadric slipped out, swearing under his breath. Maybe, I thought, these people have been cooped up together for too long.

Tobias looked at me. "Nazi thug," he sighed. "Jewish thug. Haida thug. Romany thug. What's the difference?"

"Sometimes I sense a kind of tense atmosphere here on *Sorcerer*."

"'I've got half a mind to go back to Germany,'" Tobias mimicked. "When we land, I've got more than half a mind to head back to the Haida Gwaii. For good."

"It sounds like you and Eadric are on the same side, but have, uh, different priorities?"

Tobias laughed.

"Speaking of which . . ." I introduced myself and explained the deal that Eadric had offered me, to perform what seemed like a minor custodial task, in exchange for two hundred dollars.

Tobias nodded. "Really? Eadric took it on himself to do *that?* No."

I explained yes, he sure had. "But what was *that?*" I asked. "The darkness in the hold – it was like it was alive. And it flowed up through the hatch . . ." For a moment I lost my voice. "Intense pain," I said, "and someone in there was speaking to me. *Stop this!*

Stop this! I beg you! It's not so much that I 'heard' it," I said, "more as if it came from inside me, inside my head. As if . . ."

"That's what the voice said?" Tobias finally looked at me, as if whatever ghost he was watching had drawn near, come through the wall of the bridge and drifted down onto me like a cloud of smoke. *"Hör auf damit. Hör auf damit. Ich bitte dich?"*

"What? No." I was confused. "That's not it."

"That's what you just said."

"I said . . . that is, I said that what the voice was saying was 'Stop this! I beg you!' I don't know why you're translating it into, I dunno, German or whatever that is."

"I'm not translating it. You may not know this, what's your name again? . . . Right, Nate. Nate, do you not realize that when you repeat what the voice said, you're speaking in German?"

"But I don't speak . . ."

"Does the name Gustav Kaindl mean anything to you?"

The excitement of being on board *Sorcerer* was wearing off. "How about my money?"

"Ahh. *That.*" Tobias went to a cabinet, brought out a key and rummaged around in a drawer. He locked it and handed me a bundle of bills.

"There you go, young man. A bargain at twice the price. Money, that's no problem. The thing in the hold, however . . ."

"What I don't understand is what kind of a *thing* it is."

I flexed the bills. The one on top was a twenty – the older kind, before they were made of plastic. I thought it might be rude to count. Anyway, it felt like there was enough.

"Awful as the vulsetchi may be, there's something at their core that's even more awful. And Eadric – he gets along with

98

hihyaghi really well but who doesn't? – has a skeleton in his clos-
et, literally! But wait a second. What's going on here?"

Tobias pulled his feet off the dashboard and strode over to
the console. "Why is this light green?" The navigators looked up
with their first flicker of interest.

"We're not going back there, are we?" the white-haired woman asked, a quiver in her voice.

"That's the thing, Gretchen. We shouldn't be able to. The
light's been red for months."

As I approached the console, the scars on my chest and
shoulder started to itch and burn. In a moment, I was standing
beside Tobias. This was my first good look at this weird piece
of equipment.

"There have been power surges too," said Gretchen. "Ever
since last night."

"That happens whenever the vulsetchi are newly, you know,
fed."

"If you say so." She went back to her work.

"Yikes." Something had jumped inside my shoulder, like
a loose cable being pulled tight. I reached over and gingerly
scratched my shoulder. The scars were coming alive. Now it
was like a squirt of boiling water on my shoulder blade. Tobias
glanced at me and thumped the metal top of the console. It
sounded as solid as the rear end of a Hummer.

As he clapped his hand on the console, Tobias squinted at
the lights, looking for some change. "This can't be happening,"
he said.

"I noticed this earlier," I offered. "When I first came in and
looked around, the light was red. Then it blinked and went out,
and the green light came on."

"You don't say? You should have told us."

I shrugged. "I don't even know what this is. Does it play MP3s?"

"This could change everything."

I followed Tobias back to the pilots' chairs, where he took his seat, checked dials, looked at our course ahead. *Sorcerer* was crossing some big body of water. There must be some big lake south of the border that I didn't know about. Wherever we were, things didn't look much warmer there than back in Hamilton.

"It's a long way to Germany from Georgia," I said. "Eadric will have a long way to go home. In fact so will I, if you guys ever let me off . . ."

Tobias chuckled. "Georgia. Of course. You think we're going to Georgia." He looked out at the slate-grey expanse of water below us, and the approaching ranks of tree-covered hills. "You don't have to worry about Eadric, my friend. He'll cool off by the time we land. He has to. By the way, we're not going to the *state* of Georgia, we're going to the *Strait* of Georgia. Hangar Georgia is what we on the R102 call our berth on Nelson Island in the Salish Sea – just off the British Columbia coast."

That made sense: I'd wondered why, if we'd been going south all night, we were still passing over frozen lakes and snowy forests. Yet I had the impression that the Strait of Georgia, a.k.a. Salish Sea, was at least as far from Hamilton as the state of Georgia, maybe even farther.

"How am I supposed to get home? It's like I've been kidnapped."

Tobias waved dismissively. He checked his instruments, glanced at the panorama outside the curving windshield and turned back to me.

"We, in fact, saved you from a dangerous situation. A very nasty group of people was closing in on us last night." He shrugged. "I guess we can't keep out of sight forever."

I told him a little bit about my experiences – 100 percent unhappy and dangerous – with the Resurrection Church of the Ancient Gods. Starting with the night that Dana and I snuck into the stadium to see what all the racket was about.

"You did?" Tobias raised his eyebrows. "Uh-huh."

I told him what had happened to Dana – torn to pieces by the Hounds of Tindalos – and about meeting the man who claimed to be a sort of proxy of H. P. Lovecraft.

"You know Howard?" Tobias was positively animated, nodding and twitching his feet. "And you've come up against both the Hounds, and the vulsetchi, yet here you stand unscathed. We're going to have to start calling you Teflon."

"No, you don't have to. Really." I chose my next words carefully. "So are you guys, like, space pirates, or interplanetary terrorists, or something? I mean, you're against the Great Old Ones and the Resurrection Church, right?"

"We certainly are, my friend. I'm proud to say we've been a thorn in the side of the Great Old Ones since 1937! Long story short: on their own home planet – I won't burden you with its name –" Tobias leaned forward to adjust a dial on the panel in front of him.

"R'lyhnygoth?"

He looked up in surprise. "Well well well! On R'lyhnygoth, there's a race that for generations has been pitted against the Great Old Ones and their dreams of conquest. They are smaller creatures than the old gods – no bigger than a human – and years ago they found ways – iffy, undependable and dangerous as they might be – that some of them could bridge the continuum threshold to Earth. These creatures are called the hihyaghi; on Earth they call themselves . . . damn, what is the word? Inner . . . I wish Max was here . . . Inter . . ."

"Interlocutors," I offered. "An Interlocutor did her best to help us back in the fall, but the Church caught her and killed her. If it wasn't for that Interlocutor – I never found out her name – I wouldn't be here now."

"Oh." Tobias kept his eyes on the course ahead but said, as if talking to himself, "Teflon, you're full of surprises."

"You'll be surprised what happens if you keep calling me Teflon."

Tobias laughed. "Look," he said, "I don't know when Eadric will be back." He gestured toward the empty pilot's seat. "I have a feeling we have a lot to talk about. Why don't you sit down?"

"I've got a question," I said. "That ceremony yesterday, the funeral. Or whatever it was. There was a line – in Latin I think?" I tried to remember. "Daemones, uh, dominus, dominoes . . ."

"*That*." Tobias frowned. "That's the ceremony we do aboard Sorcerer whenever one of us passes. *Amicus mea, daemones illi non dominabitur tui.*"

"Yeah, that's it. What's that mean?"

Tobias paused. It occurred to me that he wasn't having as much fun as it seemed.

"It means," he said, "that you've made it to the end, and that you can rest after all these years of hanging onto yourself, and helping others to discover, and reminding them, who they truly are. It means that because of you dozens, or hundreds, or millions of people haven't been sucked dry by the Great Old Ones, and it means that their servants, the Resurrection Church, will never get revenge, because when they come get you, you'll have moved on. It means that because of you, the Cthulhu Leviathan has not yet come to pass, and it's a promise that we'll work and struggle so that it never will. Literally, in English it means, 'Over you, my friend, the demons will have no more dominion.'"

CHAPTER 13
THE RE-ENTRY PRESSURE WAVE EFFECT

That night, back in October, of the last ceremony of the Resurrection Church, the wind rose, the clouds billowed and I'd never seen such lightning strikes in the sooty old neighbourhood around the stadium.

The thing is, all that really happened: I wasn't putting it in just for effect. We already had the chanting of the crowd, the appearance of the Hounds, the summoning of Yog-Sothoth, the intervention of *Sorcerer* – I didn't need to dream up a thunderstorm too. Besides, cliché already?

Tobias explained to me, however, that there's a hard science, real-world explanation for all this.

"We can't figure out all the real-world effects that the nervous systems of certain creatures from R'lyhnygoth seem to be able to achieve. Not to mention the arcane mathematics that link ancient runes, contemporary handwriting and the Hounds of Tindalos. But we do know that it's possible to open up a continuum threshold, a kind of wormhole that, with the aid of extraterrestrial technology, can be used to get from one point in the galaxy to another almost instantaneously. But the fact is, the sudden appearance of an object of a million cubic metres or so – *Sorcerer*, or a creature as huge as Yog-Sothoth – entering the atmosphere basically out of nowhere creates an enormous pressure wave. Successful threshold crossings – and no one does them better than *Sorcerer* – incorporate some sort of spoiler mechanism that diffuses the pressure wave. If you've ever had a good look at *Sorcerer* from the outside –"

"Not really."

"– you will have seen a metallic sheath that shields the nose of the gasbag and extends down the front of the gondola. That's the re-entry nacelle; it helps to diffuse the pressure buildup. This release of energy, although more gradual, still causes sudden changes in air pressure and temperature, so what do you get?"

"Uhh . . . storms?"

"Exactly. High pressure zones, temperature changes, cloud formations, static electricity, thunder, lightning . . . everything you need for a good apocalypse."

"So what happens if something big tries to come through without a re-entry thingy?"

Tobias made a face. "You've heard of the 1930 Curuçá River event in Brazil? That was the Great Old One Algol-Otenga attempting . . . Doesn't ring a bell?" I shrugged. "How about the Tunguska explosion over Siberia in 1908?"

"Sure. That's famous. A large meteor or comet frag–"

"Nice try . . . by which I mean to say, suit yourself. But . . . the cause of that massive blast was none other than an attempt by the repellent Yba'sokug, the first of the Great Old Ones to devise a continuum threshold that would actually get something as large as him to Earth. Of course, the poor bugger hadn't taken into account the re-entry pressure wave effect."

"Okay," I said. "So in October when I first caught sight of

Sorcerer, there was a burst of flame. Yog-Sothoth cried out . . . I heard him . . . and faded away."

"All thanks to Max. We were desperate to get home. The *Raumspalter* was acting up; when we found out that Yog-Sothoth had managed to open a threshold, we decided to try to piggyback on his efforts, slip in beside him and ride the threshold back to Earth. Max rigged an experimental rocket booster to give the R102 faster acceleration, but once Yog-Sothoth opened a threshold, Max turned it on him. He burned his butt so we could slip through," he explained. "Yog-Sothoth is as big as *Sorcerer* and a lot meaner. But we whupped his ass! All that was because of Max."

"When do I get to meet Max?"

He sighed. "Good question. Max did all this from the ground, and when we went through the threshold, he got left behind. We've got to go back."

"Max. This isn't by any chance the Max who designed this" – I gestured around me – "and got it built? Nordfeld?"

"Teflon – I'm sorry, Nate – you are a font of surprises. I met Max in Germany when I was working there as an artist. We became very close, but Max was obsessed with his work as much as any of the artists I knew. He went to England, where he was working on some big airship deal. He wanted me to come with him, but I was a workaholic too. I had a good gig in the movies – playing Indians in German westerns! – and because that gave me a name, I was selling paintings like crazy. I was sitting pretty.

"Then" – Tobias shrugged – "just like so many people who thought the Nazis would make an exception in their case, because they were so special . . . one night I'm sleeping peacefully, the door bursts open and I get dragged kicking and screaming into a lorry, and thrown into a freight car like livestock." He shuddered. "If two days on a freight car wasn't enough to kill us, we all ended up in fricking Dachau. Writers, artists, tourists, foreign workers, anyone who wasn't able to get out in time, or who hadn't had the brains when they had the chance."

"Like you."

"Exactly. But Max heard about what happened. Lucky for me. This was way before the internet, way before TV. There was the radio, but all the news coming out of Germany was strictly government-controlled. Max was in Yorkshire working on the R102, and heard about the Nazi crackdown on the BBC. Then he phoned to see if I was okay. Of course I didn't have a phone; he had to phone someone who might know somebody who might have heard something that they couldn't talk about over the phone. One way or another, Max found out where I was. Then he phoned as many of his connections in the German government as he could. Nothing was working – it's not like nobody wanted to help, but they were afraid. So he hijacked his own airship – made himself some powerful enemies in the British government, I hear – flew it to Germany and stopped by Dachau, on the pretext of showing off this new technology to the brass there. He charmed everyone – Max is good at that – and they gave him the tour. But all along he was casing the joint."

"I've read about this," I said. "It's on the internet. Max organized a massive escape attempt?"

"Eadric, too. He's kind of a prick, but I've got to give him credit. He was Max's second-in-command, and those boys got things done. They saved dozens of people who would have died. Including a prisoner who wasn't exactly a person."

That prisoner was an Interlocutor – one of that tentacled race

Tobias called the hihyaghi. Of the few species from R'lyhnygoth
I'd run into so far, the hihyaghi were the best-natured, and the
smartest.

"Once we reached Switzerland and found a temporary haven,
this hihyaghi – or Interlocutor, as you'd call it – convinced Max
that he had to build a machine that would help it return to its
home planet. But there were conditions to meet. Max – always
up for an adventure – was glad to help. Using the hihyaghi's
plans and design, we helped it finish that machine over there, the
Raumspalter" – he nodded toward the console he'd been fussing
over – "and carried out the mission. This, in fact, is where your
buddy Lovecraft gets involved. We crossed over to R'lyhnygoth,
and we managed to survive there for six months. And then we
returned to Earth."

"This is fantastic," I said. "Hard to believe."

"You're telling me. The thing is, we left Earth in 1937, and
after spending six months on R'lyhnygoth, we returned to Earth
– only to find that the year was now 1957."

"The hub-rim differential."

"You bet. And if you ask me, it's time to stop. No more
continuum thresholds, no more contact with R'lyhnygoth and
the things that live there."

"Sounds good to me." I was about to tell him that something
was brewing in Hamilton, that the Resurrection Church was
regaining its strength, that now was a great time to sever ties and
never let anyone or anything cross between planets again, when
he added:

"Except for one more trip. We've got to go to R'lyhnygoth
one more time. We've got to save Max."

CHAPTER 14
"THE WHALER THAT SAVED THE WORLD"

That night, my mother came to my cabin. It was just after supper, so Margrit was still in the lounge, immersing herself in playing the aluminum grand piano. The door was open, and over the piano's distant voice, I heard a knock on the door jamb.

"There's some excitement on the west coast," my mother said as she entered. "Mount Baker has just erupted."

Mount Baker, she told me, was an inactive volcano in Washington State, just over the border from British Columbia, snow-capped and visible for miles in every direction. "Don't tell me that it's destroyed Hangar Georgia," I moaned, "and now we have to go to the North Pole, or Egypt, before we can land."

"It's true that west coast air traffic is down," she said. "The air is full of ash, and that's hard on engines, especially jet engines. The people on the bridge say that with our electrics, and the propellers, it's not quite so bad, and with less traffic the chances of avoiding surveillance are better than ever. We'll stay on schedule. Here." She handed me a book.

"Yuck. What's this?"

It was a stained and dog-eared paperback that looked as if rats had chewed the edges.

"Read it."

I looked at the cover, a cartoonish artwork of a sasquatch peering from between tall evergreens in a dark wood, and in the background a lake or inlet with some Loch Ness–type serpent showing its head. *RainVisions: Stories, Tall Tales and Apocrypha from British Columbia's Mystic Coast.*

"What's an apocrypha?"

"A story that gets told so much, people start to treat it as true, whether it is or not."

I looked at the table of contents: "The Serpent of Sullivan Bay," "Redonda's Unearthly Visitors," "A Malibu Bush Ape Meets a Real Rangitang." My mother pointed to a title down the page: "The Whaler that Saved the World: The Last Voyage of the *Mary Maquinna.*"

"Read that one . . ." she said.

"What a cornball title."

". . . and when you're done, go visit the person who wrote it." There was an address written in pen on the inside front cover. S. Fraser, c/o General Delivery, Egmont, BC.

"Look" – I had a hard time calling her Mom – "I hafta get home. There's this thing called 'school' . . ."

"This is more important."

I looked at the name of the story's author – Sidney Fraser – and then at the book's title page. Third Eye Editions, Vancouver 1974. The book had come out almost forty years ago.

"This thing's older than Dad's VHS tapes. Sidney Fraser. Is this a guy Sidney or a girl Sidney?"

"He's your grandfather."

"I know both my grandfathers. Neither of them's called –"

"Sid's my biological father. He and my mum split up when I was like, five. I know what you mean: as far as I'm concerned,

Doug is my dad and always has been. But Sid's my biological father. Though I hardly know him myself. One of the reasons he and my mum split up was his obsession. He used to talk about this thing in the ocean – something he'd run into when he was just a kid – he and his crew had sent it to the bottom, but he was afraid it would come back. After they broke up he apparently went off and set himself up as a kind of sentry against this thing, and others like it. He talked about the Great Old Ones, but everyone thought he was just another west coast, uh, mystic, carving out his own reality. For a long time, I tended to agree with them, but just look at us now." She pointed at the book. "He claimed every word is true.

"Nate, I wish you didn't know a lot of what you seem to know. I wish you'd never found out. But with knowledge, there's no going back. And you're not my little boy anymore. Your whole boyhood, all the joy I might have had raising you to a young man, all that's dumped in the gutter, thanks to *Sorcerer* and the Resurrection Church. And I guess now you're part of all this, so you've got to see him, yes, because he's your grandfather, but mostly because – if we're going to push back the Great Old Ones from this world, and keep them away for good, and if you're going to be part of the struggle, without getting killed, or hurt more than you've been hurt already – I think you *need* to see him. He needs to see you, too."

"Do you think he'll like me?"

"Of course he will. If you're lucky."

"Will he be waiting for us when we land?"

"When we land. That's another story. I have to think of some way to get you to him. Let me think about this. Meanwhile, read what he wrote."

She was gone and I started leafing through the book, which was full of sensational stuff: ghosts, sea serpents, sasquatches, UFOs. I read a couple of them, but finally figured I'd better get to work. "The Whaler that Saved the World: The Last Voyage of the *Mary Maquinna*." Despite the title, I'd give it a chance.

Actually, to give ol' granddad credit, his story seemed to begin where the conversation I'd just had left off:

When you're young, and something unbelievable happens, you worry about people thinking that you're crazy. Later in life, that doesn't matter: you worry about the truth, because you've seen how easily the truth gets misplaced or stolen. Giving evidence is important; evidence that beyond the forces threatening this fragile and beautiful planet – as if its biggest threat, mankind itself, wasn't bad enough – there are greater forces, huge and intelligent and malign, that as I write scheme and contrive and lay their plans to cross the vast distance between their world and ours.

They have crossed it before.

Life as we know it could be over even now, or horribly changed beyond all recognition, if not for a battle fought in a rocky BC inlet in the summer of 1946: a battle between a hideous creature from another world, spliced into the body of a pioneering astronaut, newly emerged onto planet Earth and ready to grow and consume anything in its path, and a ragtag band of sailors on board the good ship *Mary Maquinna*.

Some might call the *Maquinna* the last of its kind, but I call her the whaler that saved the world. For a quarter century she's lain there on the ocean bottom, silted and rusting in the cold and dark, in the place where it all ends – the abyss where any chance to become better, any redemption for pain suffered or inflicted, any chance for love, hope or evolution, gets sucked into the blackness; that void in the ocean that the maps have one name for, but the sailors who have crossed it have another. Those who have lingered on the nearby shores or moored in the shallows, who have dreamt of awful things slithering up from those black depths, or awakened to hear their decks creaking from an invisible weight, or glimpsed an iridescent shape lurking in the dark beyond their dying campfire, those haunted souls, they call it the Medusa Deep.

C'mon, guy, chill! But it was an interesting story. The parts about whaling were pretty gross, but at the same time, it was kind of awesome that the person telling this story was some kind of relative. I wouldn't mind meeting him. This would be a guy who could remember stuff from World War Two: he'd been a kid, but he'd recall the time, and he could talk about what he'd seen and heard.

The summer of 1946 was not a great time for a teenage boy to get a summer job. The soldiers were back from the war, so there was a glut of able-bodied men. I was hoping to get a job delivering papers or selling hot dogs, but everywhere I went, older guys with cars and families were after the same jobs I was. Then one night my dad came home and it turns out one of his buddies knew a guy, and there was a whaling ship heading up the coast that needed a deckhand.

My folks argued about it. "You are going to send our boy up the coast in a boat full of hardened sailors and drunks and God knows what else?" my mother said. "He's smart. He's a bookworm. He's no whaler."

"It's good experience," my father replied. "It'll make a man ... what I mean is, it'll help him grow up to be a well-rounded individual."

"How is spending the summer on a floating slaughterhouse with a bunch of dumb clucks with harpoons going to make him well-rounded?"

"Thiessen's an experienced skipper – and they'll be back in time for school in September."

"Harpoons?" I interjected. "This is whaling, with real harpoons and stuff?"

"Plus," Dad added, "he'll make good money."

I skipped out of grade ten early so the *Mary Maquinna* could take me on in mid-June. I helped prepare the ship, and we left port on June 23. Nothing could dampen my enthusiasm that morning, even the biggest earthquake to strike the coast in years. At the mouth of Burrard Inlet, the ship shuddered as if we had struck a sandbar. Around us the sea growled like a Rottweiler, and looking back, we saw the Lions Gate Bridge sway like a clothesline in a windstorm.

To me, all that was like an omen that I was starting a life of adventure. Along with the Chinese cook An, a.k.a. Hank, I got all the dirtiest jobs, but as we headed for the open sea, I felt like a million bucks.

Six weeks later, we were tied up in a place called Egmont. It was ninety degrees in the shade without a breath of wind, and I was up to my knees in blood, guts and blubber. From toilet cleaning I had been promoted to flensing: that's what happens when the whale has been chased for hours, harpooned so it can't escape and stabbed a hundred times with lances until it finally dies and gets winched to the ship. You get a long-handled flensing knife, and you cut out sections of blubber from the corpse and pass them up to the deck to be rendered down into oil.

The one bright spot was, this whale wasn't that big, so I was able to work up on the deck, once the real pros had flensed it in the water. Flensing was a dangerous job, because as you cut strips of blubber, the carcass's buoyancy shifted, and the whole thing could roll under you like a birling log and dump you into the drink. Also, by that point, there had been blood in the water for hours, so you'd get sharks. It was a bit safer once you whittled away enough of the corpse that it could be winched up onto the deck, but then the August sun would go to work on it. The stink was awful, but it had no effect on the quality of the final product, so you just kept hacking away, cutting this magnificent animal into small enough hunks to go into the rendering pot and get melted into oil.

In June I'd thought of heading up the coast and never coming back – to hell with high school, to hell with the society it was supposed to be grooming me to enter. I'd spend the rest of my life on the high seas.

By August, however, hot and stinking of whale guts, I was counting the days till I could get home. The whale I was cutting up was a good thing – it meant that the skipper might have something to sell when we made it back to port; it meant we'd all get paid, and I would arrive back home and start school with money in my pocket.

At the end of the day I would fill a tub with sea water and take a bath on deck, and afterwards wash out my work clothes in the bathwater. Then I would get a bucket of fresh water and rinse myself off, and rinse my clothes in the same water. Then I would hang up my clothes to dry – preferably near the oil burner that ran the rendering pot or, if there was no room at the pot, I'd find a place below decks where I could dry them out. The engine room was usually the best bet. I'd walk around in a towel until my clothes were dry enough to put on again. But I still stank of rancid guts and whale oil.

We were just finishing up a right whale that Captain Thiessen assured us was the start of a winning streak. Having missed supper, I went in my towel to beg some food off An.

When I had come on board, An had been the one who showed me the ropes. At first, mostly cleaning. Cleaning clogged drains and toilets, cleaning grease out of the grill vent and stovetop, cleaning the kitchen floor, cleaning the corridor where an anonymous crewman had barfed up last night's supper, cleaning blood, guts and whale skin off the deck after a flensing. I worked hard and soon was calling An by his real name, An, even though Captain Thiessen insisted we call him Hank.

"Why would he do that?"

"Because he . . ." An paused, shook his head. "Everyone like me better if I have English name." He shrugged. "Maybe right."

From then on, I always called him An. It is a simple name, but the way he pronounced it was a challenge for me – different both from "Anne," the woman's name, and "an" as in "an apple." An helped me practise to get it right.

CHAPTER 15
THE THINGS
UNDER THE NACELLE

My mother and I had been circling each other warily amid *Sorcerer*'s long hallways and cramped cabins. I'd like to say that ours was a warm reunion full of love, tears and warmth, but it wasn't like that at all. Her curiosity about me and my dad and our lives bugged me – I felt like it was none of her business. I treated her like a stranger who was trying to get too personal too fast, because that's how I felt. Once when I was telling her something dumb, like problems with my math grade, instead of getting bored she threw her arms around me and started crying. I stood there patiently until she stopped, then mopped off my neck with some Kleenex.

To me, there was nothing left from when this woman, Eleanor, had been my mother and I'd been a little boy, basically with her for every waking hour. I'd had ten years to get used to not having a mother, and subjectively she'd only spent eight months away from her son. But as I was to find out, it was hard to ride a continuum threshold across the galaxy, spend time with completely alien places and peoples, and not come back a changed person.

At breakfast, she asked what I'd thought of my grandfather's story.

"It's okay. So far, I've only read the part about whaling."

"Keep at it," she said. "Just now, I need you to help me with something."

We were over what looked to me like an endless Arctic wasteland, but was actually the Prairies, the snow gridded by the straight lines of fields and fences and broken up by roads, ravines, rivers and towns. Ahead of us loomed a line of mountains like a wave of blue rock, snow-capped and frozen in place by the rising foothills. Kitchen staff cleaned away trays and dishware; otherwise the lounge was quiet. Everyone except my mother and me were on duty. But even my mother, it turned out, had a task.

A canvas bag hanging off one shoulder, my mother took me down a back corridor, and into the upper levels of the operations and living quarters. We left a hatch and entered a long walkway criss-crossed on every side by intricate intersections of aluminum girders, as if an army of giant spiders had been set loose with a giant Meccano set.

"When you read the whole thing – the whaling story – you'll see that for all you've been through with the Church, this isn't the first time that the Great Old Ones have come after us," my mother said. "Something happened in the summer of 1946, there on the coast . . . What's so funny?"

I told her what the Proprietor had said when I'd met him and Clare in the street. "Look to the west. Something is coming."

"At the time, I'd thought he was full of it. I mean, he's such a dork. Now here I am. West somewhere."

"Gaining altitude as we come over the Prairies. The thing about airships is, they don't go very fast. That's one reason they're the best vehicle for negotiating a continuum threshold. You don't always know what's going to be on the other side, or even what direction you'll be going when you emerge. So jet speed is not the best speed. Although airships have their own set of problems because of their huge displacement . . ."

We had reached one of the service intervals between two of the gas cells. Here the criss-crossing aluminum struts formed a rising wall of Xs going up and up and up, until they faded into the shadow of the rubberized gasbag far above our heads. The struts covered the walls of the individual gas cells, separating and supporting them. My mother explained that this was to ensure that the airship would never suffer a catastrophic loss of lift gas all at once. She pointed up into the dark. "That's where we're going. Here's your chance to really learn something about *Sorcerer.*"

With startling nimbleness she was up one of the ladders. Before I knew it, she was several metres over my head, looking down at me impatiently.

"Are you coming?"

I started up the ladder after her. It was not especially hard work climbing, but after a couple of minutes we were only half-way to the top.

"Where are we going?"

My mother was maybe more winded than she wanted to let on, and had to pause before she answered.

"If you're going to spend time on board *Sorcerer* you should get to know every inch of it. You got a head start at the vulsetchi cellar, though I'm so pissed off that Eadric made you do that."

"Well, I made two hundred bucks."

"I don't even want to talk about it. Listen!"

"Listen to what?"

"Shhh."

Sure enough, the sound was different here than it was down in the gondola. Above us was the rush of wind from *Sorcerer*'s passage through the prairie sky. *That* I expected, but what surprised me were the sounds from inside the gas cells themselves. Human-like sighs, distant banging and scrabbling; sounds that rang through the service interval like a string of tiny bells. As I listened, occasionally the fabric would flex and snap and stutter, like a squirrel scrambling on the roof of our house on Somerset Avenue.

"It's up here," my mother whispered, "that you start to feel it. That you start to feel *Sorcerer* is alive."

"Like a haunted house in a horror movie?"

"It's not ghosts that make those sounds. It's the life it lives. The gases that lift it up, the air it flies through that's always warming or cooling, the winds that come at it from every side, from up and down and from every point of the compass, the fabric that contains it, the metal that binds it, always expanding and contracting and flexing as it flies. And of course, the terrible powers that make it go."

"Speaking of terrible powers . . ." I was going to ask her if she knew who Gustav Kaindl was, the name Tobias had run past me, but she indicated we had a task that had to be carried out.

"The re-entry nacelle is a metallic sheath that shields the nose of *Sorcerer*'s gasbag and extends down the front of the gondola," she explained. "It disrupts the atmospheric tension, or whatever. It's something Max and the hiyaghi dreamed up."

"Tobias told me about that. I keep hearing about this Max. What do you think about Tobias's idea of –"

"Put this on." My mother handed me a mask attached to some kind of scuba tank and showed me how to put it on and get it going. She unsealed a numbered door and we pushed through a sort of big rubber valve onto the springy floor of a gas cell. She brought out a flashlight and leaned against me so her mask pressed against mine. Her voice sounded thin and far away, as if she were shouting from a distance.

"It's full of helium. Keep your mask on – a few lungfuls of helium and you'll pass out."

It was like we were at the bottom of a mine shaft. My mother shone the light up into the darkness and then flinched.

"Oh no!" She pointed. Away at the highest point, the darkness was stained with a blotch of washed-out grey.

"Eadric was right." The grey flickered out of existence, and then something fluttered through the darkness and landed at our feet.

The flashlight revealed what looked like a good-sized bat. It seemed sick or injured, its eyes closed, its wings fluttering weakly. I leaned over it. Too many legs to be a bat.

"Leave it!" My mother shouted, if only so that she could be heard through the mask and the thin intervening atmosphere.

The bat-creature revived, opened blank black shark eyes set in a bald, crocodilian head rimmed by spiny fur, and looked at us dubiously. Then it took to the air, only to come fluttering down a few seconds later. Amid all of *Sorcerer*'s other noises, I heard a thin scrabbling from high above us.

"Quick," my mother said. "We've got to get it back up there."

"I've never seen a Stipley Devil this close before. Much less a baby one."

"A Stipley what? It's called a thral. Now climb. Hurry. There's a layer of air on the floor, so it can breathe down there. But the rest of the atmosphere in here is helium."

A rope ladder was fixed to each wall of the gas cell. I grabbed the nearest ladder and began climbing. My mother began slowly; then, as the baby thral lost consciousness and went limp, she dropped it into a pocket of her coveralls and began overtaking me.

"We've got to hurry." She stopped just long enough to point upward. "The parents will be frantic. And if it's too long without air . . ."

Sure enough, the higher we got, the better I could see that the blotch on the ceiling was a hole, and right now, its tough fabric was being obsessively chewed and torn by angry creatures. I could see the glint of teeth, and black, scrabbling claws as they enlarged the hole.

We were almost at the top when my mother had to rest.

"If this thing dies," she gasped, "who knows what the parents will do."

We were almost at the hole, where a large ugly head was starting to poke through.

"Here." I reached into her pocket and grabbed the baby thral. It drooped motionless in my hand. I took several deep breaths and slipped the mask from my face. Cupping the mask in my hand, I tumbled the baby thral into it.

The thing twitched. A wing moved. Scenting its baby's proximity, the adult thral renewed its assault on the hole it was making in the tough material of the gasbag. Still holding my breath, I extended the mask, the baby on it now fluttering and opening its eyes. I pressed it to the opening, felt something jostle my hand, and then I pulled it back. The little creature had been snatched away. I pressed the mask gratefully back on my face, and took deep breaths. My mother pulled out a can of bear spray, leaned away as she sprayed a piece of duct tape and stuffed it into the hole. With another aerosol can, she filled the hole with plastic foam, and started handing me lengths of tape, one at a time. We made a rough patch over the hole in the thick rubberized fabric. "Talk about a band-aid solution," my mother said, "but it's all we've got."

CHAPTER 16
THE *OBERTH* A-7

Frankly, I wonder if there is any area, outside of a heartbeat or body temperature, where the word "normal" should be applied to any aspect of human beings. What, for example, was "normal" aboard *Sorcerer*, where people weren't sure if they were thirty or a hundred years old, and strange men bribed teenagers to deposit dead bodies into dark holds full of creeping fungus? My mother, I suppose, had given me at an early age my idea of what "normal" might be, but now she was quick to point out that her time aboard *Sorcerer* had wrenched her into a different reality and she could forget about ever being considered normal (either by herself, or by anyone else) ever again.

"Not that it – the term 'normal,' I mean – is anything more than a rough indicator of how people might be expected to think and behave under certain circumstances," she said. "Here on *Sorcerer*, for example, it's more normal to be liminal than to be actually normal." Liminal, she explained, means to be between states; either on a border between one place or another, or to be transforming.

"But if you're in a place, you're in a place," I pointed out. "If you're stuck on a border –"

"Not necessarily stuck," my mother replied. "The great thing about being on a border is that you've got two ways to go. Sometimes more than two."

"So it's like the border or being, like you say, liminal is actually normal."

"Nate, honey, that's what I just said."

Right, whatever, I thought. Once I could get off this thing, and get back to Hamilton, and catch up with school, and deal with the Resurrection Church, I would become Mr. Normal, and leave behind this dicey, un-normal world of antique flying machines, continuum thresholds and unpredictable, sometimes snarly alien species. If I could just get off *Sorcerer*.

When I picked up *RainVisions* again, I wondered if my grandfather might have found himself in the same situation. If leaving his everyday life in Vancouver to spend a summer on one of the last whaling ships wasn't enough of a departure from Sid's normal; if standing in blubber up to his knees, slicing up a marine mammal as big as a dinosaur wasn't enough of a break from normal; then what happened one August night in 1946, was definitely a one of a kind experience.

We put in to the dock at Goliath Bay, a big logging camp at the mouth of Jervis Inlet. This was a gala event. Not only could we go ashore at night, but there was someplace onshore we could go – what Captain Thiessen called "his house," which turned out to be a rented shack next to the camp cookhouse, where his wife, Iris, was head chef.

The *Mary Maquinna* anchored in the bay, and from the dock we hiked up the camp's muddy "main street" until it narrowed into a broad but overgrown path. Soon we were in the Thiessen home, crowded that night with six of us from the *Mary Maquinna*, the crew of the *Princess Becky*, a gillnetter that was also in for the night and Captain Thiessen's wife, Iris, and their five children.

Crowded as it was with people inside and mosquitoes outside, after a summer on the *Maquinna* this was paradise. We drank sweet tea and beer, and there was fresh bread, and blackberry scones, and smoked salmon. I took a pass on the whale meat that the captain had brought home and that Iris, who was of the Nootka, had accepted with great relish and stirred into a pot.

After dinner, I was sitting on the grass overlooking the inlet with Amy McKie, the sole deckhand on board the *Princess Becky*, which was owned and run by her parents. It was a still night under a clear starry sky. We were, regretfully, not sitting very close to each other.

"They told me whaling was on its last legs, but pee-yew," Amy said.

"At the end of the summer," I said, "I'll take lots of baths. I'll have money. Maybe I will go to one of the steam baths that are on Hastings Street."

Amy laughed, and when I asked what was so funny, she told me in shocking detail – in fact, I thought it all sounded highly unlikely – of what she'd heard went on in those steam baths. My folks had never told me about this. I looked for a chance to change the subject.

"Look" – I pointed – "a shooting star."

"There was one in the winter," she replied. "They say it landed in the next inlet, the place they call the Deep."

I had heard of the Deep, since we had passed it on the way up the coast. The so-called Medusa Deep, evidently a name that dated from the time of Captain Vancouver or maybe Cook. Marty, one of the deckhands, told me that it had a reputation as an evil place.

"Even among the Indians," he'd said, "and all in all, there aren't many places or things they call evil."

As I sat there with Amy suddenly a flash, like distant lightning, lit up the sky. I saw the outline of the islands along the coast to the northwest.

126

"Wow, that was something!" I said to Amy. "I wish one of those meteors would fall on the land. I'd like to collect one."

"You should be a scientist," she said, "not a whaler."

Just then, an unexpected sound echoed across the water. It was the ship's bell, rung in the case of any emergency – a bad accident, a fire, an uncharted reef. It was not something you rang as a joke: an old-fashioned school bell hung from a post, with a hammer dangling from a leather strap. If someone back on the *Mary Maquinna* had gotten drunk, they might take a few swings at it, but this time the bell kept on ringing til its reverberations bounced back to us off the rocky shores. Then I heard something really ominous: the voice booming out from the house was, to me, much scarier. From Captain Thiessen's voice, the sounding of the bell had definitely ruined a great evening.

"Where the hell's Sid?"

Amy jumped up to follow me as I ran up the slope toward the house. Captain Thiessen started shouting orders before I reached the porch.

"Get down to the ship," he said. "Find out what's going on. Tell them we're on the way. GO!"

It was my job to race against my captain and his crew. I turned and sprinted out of the yard, looking back to see Thiessen lumbering off the porch and heading after me. Soon I was at the shore, threading my way from float to float to the dock as loggers, some with families, some in nightgowns or underwear, opened the doors of their floathouses and scratched their heads. "Where's the fire?" somebody yelled.

I reached the dock, ran out to the end and waited until there was a break in the racket. I yelled over the water and heard one of the crewmen yell back. I turned and ran back into town, but didn't get very far, since the captain and the rest of our landing party were just making it to the shore.

"They say there's a plane crash," I gasped at them. "In the Deep."

"What about my ship?" barked Thiessen. "Is the ship okay?"

We clambered into one of the whaleboats and rowed back to the ship.

"It's that crazy Chinaman," Marty told us. "He saw that lightning and got skittish."

"What lightning?" said Captain Thiessen. "It's a clear night."

"We saw a flash," I said. "Coming over that ridge there." I pointed. "We figured it must be something coming down, like a meteor."

"Why didn't ya say so?" the captain said. "Where's Hank?"

They found An, who had been helping the mechanic finish off lubricating engine bearings. I told him I'd seen a shooting star, as well as a flash.

"Not shooting star," said An. "Not lightning. Airplane."

In a few minutes we had raised anchor and were heading northwest to cross the mouth of Jervis Inlet and round the point, and see if someone had crash-landed in the Deep.

I could feel my enthusiasm reviving for the life at sea. Here we were, on a rescue mission. A rescue mission! After months of slogging away at sea, we were setting off on an adventure – better yet, not in the middle of some godawful Pacific squall, but against the backdrop of bays and beaches on a calm and starry night.

"The rules of the sea," Thiessen said. "If a plane's down then it's in distress, and distress calls have to be answered."

"What kind of a plane was it?" I asked An.

"Not a plane, more like . . ." He searched for the words. "More like firecracker."

At that point, An had been in Canada less than a year. Considering he'd spent most of the time in Chinatown, his English wasn't that bad.

"It was burning, it was on fire?"

"No. Flies with fire. *Huǒjiàn.* Like firecracker, like . . ."

"You mean, like a rocket?" An nodded.

128

The new jet planes that had come out at the end of the war were pretty exciting. That's what I figured An meant. What one would be doing up here on the BC coast was beyond me, but I was worried that, being sleek, streamlined and made entirely of metal, any jet plane that crashed into the Deep would sink like a stone. If that was the case, our rescue mission would be too late.

I was spectacularly wrong.

The *Mary Maquinna* rounded the point through flocks of fleeing birds wheeling confusedly in the night breeze, roused from their slumbers by this mysterious thing from the sky. As the ship entered the mouth of the sound, before us a geyser of flame erupted from a circle of white water, illuminating an enormous pillar leaning like a steel Tower of Pisa that, as we watched, tilted farther into the cold waters of the sound. This was not a jet plane.

"It *is* a rocket ship," I heard myself say.

"Told you," An said.

"Stand off," shouted Captain Thiessen. "Sid, haul the skiff up to the side. You, you and you, into the skiff."

I waved to get his attention. "Can't I come?"

"You stay here, Sid. We'll need room to take on survivors."

We'd towed the skiff with us, and as the *Mary Maquinna* anchored, I hauled it around to where the rope ladder dangled from the ship's gunwale. An slapped me on the shoulder as he started down the ladder, and by the time Thiessen made it into the boat, both An and I had already taken up a set of oars, leaving the captain no time to argue. We pushed off from the hull and as I looked back, I thought how puny the *Maquinna* looked compared to the huge craft we were approaching.

The stern of this aircraft jutted from the water at least sixty feet; I don't know how much more was below the surface. Far over our heads we could see diagonal stabilizing fins, and between them the great propulsive rocket tube, still smoking and glowing in the dim starlight. We made for a hatchway that we could see, still a few feet above the surface. Under the captain's orders, as we rowed we kept a close watch around us for anyone in the water.

We approached the hull – and suddenly the monstrous ship shuddered and settled further into the waters of the sound.

"Get ready to row for your lives," the captain barked. "If she goes down fast, she'll take us with her."

We had almost reached the rocket when, without warning, the hatch banged open against the metal hull. Framed in the doorway, there appeared a bizarre creature the likes of which none of us had ever seen – a wrinkled body bedecked with tubes and dials, topped by an enormous glistening head from which a single shining eye stared out blankly.

"What the hell is that?"

As if to attack, the creature lunged forward, but falling short of the boat, splashed into the water where it bobbed, turned over and started to sink.

"Grab him!" the captain ordered. "It's a man, he's in a deep-sea diving suit."

He'd got a couple of details wrong, but not the urgency of the situation. I passed a boathook to An, who hooked onto a section of steel tubing on the struggling person's suit, and in a few moments we'd managed to pull them over the gunwale without swamping the boat. A shout from the rocket alerted us that there were more. Sure enough, what looked like a horde of Cyclopean monsters crowded the hatchway, awaiting rescue. We rowed the skiff over and helped three more suited humans down the ship's ladder into the skiff. Meanwhile, the first one took off their helmet, and turned out to be a woman of about forty with cropped brown hair, who called to us desperately.

"Hilf ihnen – aber nicht Magnus. Stoppen Sie Magnus!"

"Look," Captain Thiessen shouted. "There's another!"

We had just unhooked the skiff from the hatch cover and stood a few metres off, when a fifth person appeared in the hatch

– a pale man who was not wearing one of the elaborate diving suits, but was in fact completely naked. His body was completely hairless, and his skin had an unhealthy blue-grey tinge.

"What's the matter with this guy?" Thiessen fumed. "Did we interrupt his Sunday bath?" We took up our oars, but Thiessen told us to row not toward the wreck, but away from it. He gestured to the man in the hatch.

"Jump," he shouted. "Quick. Jump. Before it drags you down with it." But the man stood in the hatchway and glared. This evidently was the "Magnus" that the woman had shouted about.

"Hat jemand eine Waffe?" She held out her hands, imploring us. *"Töte ihn!"*

The great ship shuddered and started to heel over to one side. The man in the hatchway dove into the water, surfacing to swim toward us with powerful strokes. Thiessen shouted at us to row for our lives.

"Captain," I yelled, "we've gotta go back for him."

"We can't let him take us all down."

As we gained distance, the ship rolled in the water, and we saw, painted on its stern, its ID – *Oberth* A-7 – and then the ship's dorsal fin swung into view, revealing an enormous black swastika.

"We're takin' on a boatload of goddamn Nazis."

In a moment the hatchway was submerged, and then, the water still boiling around it, the ship began sinking very quickly. In a metre-high wave, we lost sight of Magnus as we fought to control the boat, and it was moments before we saw him surface and continue toward us.

"Row for your lives," Thiessen ordered. "He had his chance. We can't be anywhere close to that hot engine when it hits the water." A few moments later, he threw himself to the deck, shouting at us to do the same. As the rocket slid under, the surface exploded into steam. Pressed to the seat of the whaleboat, I could hear superheated debris whip through the air above me. Then the boat was heaved into the air by a wave that threatened to swamp us in hot sea water and a cloud of mist that stank of red-hot metal and burning oil.

Then it passed, and the ocean around us calmed. We rowed back to look for survivors. The rocket crew helped each other get their helmets off: two men and two women. They were all Germans; Inge and Arne spoke a bit of English, but Wolf and Lotte, not a word. As we searched, they argued among themselves: the issue under discussion, I later discovered, was what to be done with Magnus if he was found. Lotte maintained her hard line ("Töte ihn!" it turns out, means "Kill him!"), but others simply wanted to get away, and never return.

For the next hour we circled the crash site, at Thiessen's orders, giving it a wide berth, in case anything big from the wreck bobbed to the surface. As the wind and currents swept away the heated waters, the air cleared, and strangely enough, among the oil and clothing and bits of wood and paper, we soon found Magnus.

Lotte saw him first and cried out; Magnus's head had bobbed up between the skiff and the shore. The captain ordered us to the rescue.

"We need to get him out of the water, quick," he said, "before the cold gets to him." As we approached, Magnus fixed us with that angry glare – but instead of swimming our way, or waiting for us to get to him, he turned and with strong unhurried strokes, headed toward shore. With four men on the oars, we quickly gained, and when we were no more than a few yards away, Captain Thiessen called out to him.

As soon as he heard his name, Magnus dove under the water.

"What the hell's he up to?" We waited for Magnus to surface, and surface he did – a hundred feet away or so, no closer to the shore. When we started toward him, once again he dove, and dove again.

"How does he do this? Where's he get the energy?" Captain Thiessen wondered aloud. "If he keeps this up, he'll die of exposure!"

Magnus dove once more. We zigzagged over the surface of the sound, but after ten minutes, he did not reappear. We gave up and made our way back to the *Mary Maquinna*.

CHAPTER 17
THRALS

A Nazi space program launched in the last days of World War Two. A rocket ship sunk in the waters off western Canada. An astronaut, hated by his own crew, who takes to the water, refuses to be rescued and vanishes. This all made for a good read. My granddad's style was a bit old-fashioned, but when he told a story things moved right along. So far though – contrary to what my mother suggested – none of this shed any light on my own situation.

I wasn't going to be able to finish my grandfather's story anyway. I'd just got through the part about the *Oberth* A-7 when my mother came bustling down the passage from the direction of the bridge.

"Get your things. You've got to go. Now."

I didn't argue with her, just put on my coat and made sure I had all my stuff. I shoved *RainVisions* into one coat pocket, my phone into another.

"Are we landing?" I asked. "Where are we?"

"We've got to get you out of here."

"I don't get it."

"Eadric's getting fixated on this notion that you've got some kind of link to the vulsetchi – that now you're on board, they're acting differently. When we berth at Hangar Georgia, he wants to keep you on board and start up what he calls a 'rota of experimentation' on your relationship to the vulsetchi. He thinks you've got something special."

"Yuck. Meeting that thing, or substance, or whatever it is, that was scary. And I heard voices."

"He's almost got Tobias persuaded. But I don't want you going anywhere near that thing."

I nodded. "It gets into your head."

"You have no idea. I wish Max was here. Eadric listens to him, and Tobias is more focused when Max is around. They should never have let you anywhere near it. The vulsetchi is a sort of brainless, moving, predatory fungus – the kind of thing you'd only find on a place like R'lyhnygoth."

"Why does he think he needs me?" As I asked this question, I shuddered. "That whole thing was kind of horrible, but it was doable. I did it."

"Because you came through it so well," she said. "The vulsetchi doesn't usually pounce, but even so, almost everyone who does an interment develops terrible symptoms – cold sweats, shortness of breath, naked dread over the smallest tasks – if they're ever asked to do it again. Most of us suffer from it if we've been in touch with the vulsetchi."

"It was creepy, for sure."

"We call it . . . you've had experience of this, I know . . . neural suasion."

"Is that anything like per-suasion?"

"It's exactly like persuasion – only certain R'lyhni nervous systems can extend their signals – broadcast them, if you will – beyond the body's actual neurons; beyond the body itself."

"Neural Wi-Fi?"

"And like digital Wi-Fi, because of a variety of factors, some instruments pick it up better than others. And it's not the vulsetchi that broadcast it – it has about as many thoughts and feelings as a jar of yeast. But we don't have time. Let's get to the loading dock."

She looked both ways as we traversed the corridors and found LOAD/EVAC empty of any other crew members. We sat down on a pile of plastic pipe. My mother leaned forward, a familiar stance from lectures she delivered to me when I was little.

"The vulsetchi is a creeping, moving, thinking fungus that devours living, organic matter. Its attack is agonizing to any living being. It fixes onto its prey, dissolves flesh – *digests* it while the animal is still trying to escape – and liquefies and absorbs it the way a kidney absorbs blood. The vulsetchi evolved at the mouth of a volcanic vent on its home planet, but if it's brought into society, or any place where there's lots of animal life, the results could be catastrophic."

"What is it doing in *Sorcerer*'s hold?"

"The thing is, in the course of this digestion process, the vulsetchi generates tremendous amounts of electricity, and its waste product consists of pure H_2O. So as long as the colony is fed, it produces power and water – two things that *Sorcerer* and its crew need a lot of. But if there's ever a leak or a breach, and the vulsetchi get free . . ."

"Why does the vulsetchi affect me?" I shrugged out of my coat and hoodie, and pulled off my T-shirt. My mother saw my scars for the first time.

"What happened to you?" she gasped. "I should have been there."

"Why, when I get close to the vulsetchi, do these scars itch and throb? Why do I feel like there's some kind of link between me and something in the hold – something or someone that's in agony?"

My mother stared at me. "Gustav."

"That doesn't tell me anything."

"Nate, you've got to get off this ship right away. Besides, it sounds like your friends in Hamilton are in great danger. And I'm afraid that all this is connected to what's happening here on the coast." I put my clothes back on. She handed me a slip of paper.

"What's that?"

"Take it."

"No."

"What's your problem?"

I realized that my mother would knowingly do me no wrong. But I'd had bad experiences with accepting bits of paper from people.

She unfolded the torn fragment and showed me. "For god's sake, it's your grandfather's address. Go to him. Offer help."

"Help with what?"

My mother unhooked a bundle from the wall. "And maybe you'll get help in return. Here, put this on."

"What? You want me to *really* jump out of this thing? Don't you need training? Practice? Test jumps?"

"You're young and smart. Nate, trust me. This could be our only chance."

"Look at me." I spread my hands helplessly, showing my Walmart winter coat and gumboots, my Bluenotes hoodie. "Doesn't a real skydiver need, uh, gear?"

"You're not skydiving, it's just using a parachute. Jump, wait two seconds to clear the ship and then pull the rip cord." I felt the warmth of her hand as she opened mine, and wrapped my fingers around the rip cord's handle.

"Just a second here."

"It's got to be now. You won't be alone – we'll both jump. We're almost over the Caren Range – where it's not built up at all. We'll land in the hills. If we get separated, remember, head west, downhill, and you'll reach the highway. Go north along the highway, and you'll reach your grandfather. *Now*, before we're past the peninsula and over the water."

"But . . ." I had to stall for time. "There's more I need to –"

"So much work to be done. There's a great danger among us – a real menace, someone who will have to be stopped, even killed."

"What are you talking about?" I grabbed and tugged nervously at the straps, but I didn't really want to put this thing on. Why would anyone have to be killed? She reminded me of my grandfather's story: *Töte ihn!*

"There's a *thing* walking among us in human form – pretending to resist the Great Old Ones, but, I think, actually working on the sly to bring the evil to Earth from R'lyhnygoth. Someone's got to stop it." Parachute on her back, my mother checked all her straps, and looked ready to go.

"What are you talking about?"

"A malign host organism that will stop at nothing to hurt us and deceive us. A creature that's slimed its way out of the universe to bring humans to their knees. It has taken the form of a man without morals, a man without conscience, a man who is both less than human and more – as much alien as human."

"So – is this who Gustav is?"

"I'm talking about that monster in human form. The thing that calls itself H. P. Lovecraft."

138

Before I could react – Howard? Are you kidding me? – she slapped a red button on the wall with her fist and at one end of the room, the emergency access door began to open.

At the other end, the door to the corridor flew open. Suddenly Eadric and Tobias were in the room with us.

"What are you doing?" Eadric planted himself next to my mother, between me and the door.

"You can't do this!" Tobias said. "We need Nate. Since he's been on board, the *Raumspalter* . . ."

I remember the next few seconds in slow motion. I was frightened of jumping, and backed away from the door, even as it opened wider and wider. Then something came flying through the door and knocked my mother and me onto the floor. I heard my mother cry out, and Eadric cursing and struggling. Another dark shape came through the emergency door, and another.

The thrals, searching for a warmer place to nest than their windy niche between the re-entry nacelle and the top of *Sorcerer*'s gasbag, were swarming into LOAD/EVAC.

Scrambling to my feet, I saw that the largest animal had knocked my mother to the floor. She was pushing its head away from her neck, while it tried to wrap its clawed leathery wings around her shoulders. Jumping on top of the creature would only push it harder onto her body. I reached down, grabbed its short, bristly legs and threw myself backwards. At that moment, *Sorcerer* itself, struck by a side wind, lurched and, gripping hard to the thral's legs, I tumbled back, my shoulder bouncing off the threshold of the exit door, and then I was through and hurtling toward the ground far below.

PART 3
STARSCAPES YET UNTROD

From even the greatest of horrors
irony is seldom absent.

– H. P. Lovecraft, "The Shunned House"

CHAPTER 18
I LEAVE WITHOUT SAYING GOODBYE

The amazing thing, once I was falling, was how long it seemed to take.

Normally, if you grab the hind legs of a thral – especially one as big as the thral I'd pulled off of my mother – it will twist around and – if it doesn't rip your throat out with its powerful jaws – slash you with the sharp ends of its segmented legs, and puncture you and rake you with its clawed wings, until you are dead.

Unknown to me, as I'd been convalescing in the months after the midnight games, the scattering of thrals that had fluttered through the continuum threshold had started to colonize Hamilton. They nested in hard-to-reach places and only came out at night. Under certain conditions they would attack humans, but a thral isn't big enough to actually carry away a good-sized person, so for the most part they made do with starlings, pigeons, squirrels and unlucky pets. Soon, stories circulated, and those who found out about them – such as the group I'd met around *Sorcerer* that night in the North End – would patrol at night carrying long staffs that extended a metre or so over their heads. The idea was, these staffs would mess up a thral's sonar and foil an attack. If they continued to breed in Hamilton – even spread outside of the city – the thrals threatened to become as big a problem as the dritches, who knows, as big a problem as the Church itself.

In this case, while I hurtled out the emergency door, my reflexes made me grip onto the thral's hindquarters more tightly than I'd gripped anything before. Snarling and hissing, the thral writhed and twisted to get at me. A clawed wing raked the back of my hand. Meanwhile, we dropped like a stone, and in a second the thral realized that it was in imminent danger, and that as much as it wanted to get rid of me, as long as I was hanging onto its backside there was nothing to do but fly as hard as it could.

I have to give it credit, this alien creature was a hard worker: it put everything into pumping its mighty bat-like wings. Aside from the hideous, pants-peeing fear that came with the free fall, and a surge of rage toward my mother for getting me into this situation, I was worried about hitting the ground. Just how much was the thral slowing my descent?

Well, Nate, I answered myself, quite a bit, or you'd already be a bag of pink jelly and bone splinters leaking into the frozen ground. The thral went into a spiral, and through the mist, a curtain of cloud and drizzle, I saw a great orange glow frowning and flickering. That must be Mount Baker, I thought. The eruption. So that direction must be south.

Below us, the mist cleared and a snowy forest rose to meet us. I could hear the thral snarling and panting to save itself and (like it or not) me. The cold wind roared and foamed in my ears; and then – over my own moans of fear and grunts of effort as I struggled to keep my grip – I heard a cascade of binky bonky tinkly noises. This long fall was taking me back into a cell network, and in my coat's inside pocket, my phone was catching up on its messages.

Then the top of a fir tree hit my leg. The thral twisted toward a landing in the branches, but I kicked away, just as scared to be stuck in a tree with an angry thral as I was to hit the ground. The thral chittered in frustration. Suddenly I felt my face whipped and scratched, as if I was being flailed by a gauntlet of angry monks. I let go of the thral's legs, and I was dumped on my ass into a patch of bush.

CHAPTER 19
FROM THE REALM OF THE GODS

I could hear the thral horking and snarling and thrashing somewhere in the overgrowth, so I headed for the undergrowth, burrowing deeper into a thicket of evergreen seedlings, unfamiliar viny broad-leafed plants and ferns. Twigs and needles rained down on me. I pushed through a patch of light in the greenery, trying to put distance between the creature and me. Then I was on my feet, stumbling through cold, knee-high grass stippled with snow. I turned to see the thral erupt from a copse of fir trees and take to the air. I grabbed a rock and prepared to dive back into the trees as it circled, chittering and crabbing at me and the trees and the sky and the world in general, all the time gaining altitude until, to my relief, it disappeared into the low-hanging clouds. In what direction, I couldn't tell, but I assumed it was heading back to *Sorcerer* and the loving close-knit thral family it had nurtured under the shelter of the re-entry nacelle.

I was standing on a rocky slope overgrown with little Christmas tree–type firs and this leafy ground cover, interspersed with huge stumps. I realized that I had just done exactly what my mother had asked me to do, only in a way that guaranteed maximum fear and trauma. "Head west, downhill," she'd told me.

I had to laugh. Head west. It reminded me of the Proprietor raving at the end of my street – "Look to the west!" – and I'd thought, what a dork.

Now here I was. About as far west as you could get; next stop, Japan. I rubbed my forehead and my hand came away with streaks of blood. I had scratched my face, landing in the bush, but eyes, ears, hands, legs, et cetera, still seemed to function. Nate Silva, I thought, so badass.

I scanned the skies – in the distance, clouds and more clouds and the white peaks of the Coast Mountains. Jeez they were tall. I scanned until I saw far in the distance, the orange radiance of the Mount Baker eruption. If that was south, then west must be on my right. I hiked through a rocky and overgrown meadow toward a line of trees, past stumps and exposed rock faces, and saw a flicker of movement up ahead. Someone was waving at me. I walked into a dip in the ground and lost sight of them, skirted a pond with a razor-thin rim of ice, and regained high ground.

Sure enough, there against the dark green of the tree line was a grey pickup truck, and standing beside it were two people. I waved back, although my arms were cramped and my fingers stiff as a bunch of carrots from gripping the thral's legs during that long desperate descent. I wondered how long I had been falling. It had felt like an hour. I tried some sort of mental math: if *Sorcerer* had been a thousand metres up, and if the thral, while desperately trying and failing to gain any altitude, had fallen ten metres a second, then my descent took maybe a minute and a half.

But then, I thought, as I kept walking, ten metres a second would equal six hundred metres a minute, which means, if six hundred times sixty equals 3,600 – nope, 36,000 metres, I'd been falling at thirty-six kilometres an hour. That was about the speed, I guessed, of a car driving down the street in front of my house back home. But if one of those cars hit me, I'd be seriously crunched, whereas, except for my scratched face and hands, I seemed to be unharmed. So maybe, by the time we hit the ground, the thral had been descending more slowly, more like . . .

"Aymash!" I had reached calling-out range. The person waving was a woman with streaked grey hair under a multicoloured woollen toque, wearing layers of dark clothes and a big grin. The man, long black hair under his cowboy hat, looked at me impassively, leaning against the box of the rusty Ford pickup. I reached a ridge of dirt and rock that put me a bit above them, then I tumbled down a slope into a ditch, barely keeping my feet, and climbed up onto a dirt road overgrown with weeds.

"Hello there, ma'am."

"Aymash! Aymash!" She was wearing blue jeans, gumboots like me and a yellow rain jacket over a heavy sweater. She came forward looking as if she was going to hug me, thought better of it and extended her hand, first pulling off a rubber glove. "Aymash! Aymash!"

"For sure." I shook her hand.

"I'm, I'm . . ." *I'm lost for words,* I should have said, since I wasn't sure where to begin. "My name is Nate."

"Ahh." She thought for a moment, and turned to her bearded partner. "'Ma-namisnate': now that's a word I don't know. I should have brought my phrase book. Do you understand him, Ernie? This is so exciting. I think we should take him to . . ."

The man sighed, looked into the distance, and then at her. "Jeez, Phyllis, he said his name is Nate." He looked at me, raised his eyebrows. "Nate. Right?"

"That's me."

"See. He speaks English."

Phyllis looked at him skeptically.

Goddammit, I thought. Next thing, they'll be telling me I'm

148

speaking German. "My name is Nate Silva. I'm trying to get to . . ." I pulled out the slip of paper my mother had given me, read the address ". . . a place called Egmont."

They laughed. "This road won't get you to Egmont."

"Which way do I go?"

"We can give you a ride down the mountain. We can't take you to Egmont, but we can put you on the highway that goes to Egmont."

In the back of the truck were cardboard boxes lined with plastic and filled with greenery. "We've been picking fiddleheads," Phyllis explained. "First of the season." Before they invited me into their truck, I couldn't help but notice that Ernie pulled a rifle out of the box of the truck – all along it had been close at hand, though out of sight – unloaded it, slipped the cartridges into his pocket and locked the firearm into a case behind the truck seats.

He noticed me watching him.

"When we saw you and your buddy come flyin' out of the clouds, I didn't know what to think."

"It was a first for me, too."

They folded me into the crew cab, cluttered with rain gear, thermoses and gardening tools. I rested my feet on the gun cabinet. With Phyllis driving, the truck bounced onto this overgrown track they called a road, and Ernie turned to get a good look at me.

"I still don't know what to think. What's your story, son?"

I wished they hadn't actually seen me fall out of the sky clinging to an angry thral. Then I could have concocted a story about partying in the bush with some buddies. But it was too late for that. Ernie looked through the windshield as the truck rolled and shook into the trees. "Remember that windfall," he said to Phyllis. "Dontcha get gillpoked."

"Coming up," she said, and branches slashed the passenger side as Phyllis swerved to avoid a broken treetop that was jutting into the road.

"What we saw, in fact," Ernie continued, "was a great big bird, or pterodactyl thing, flap out of the clouds, and crash-land into the trees, and this whatever-it-was, it had you hanging off its rear end."

"I took pictures," Phyllis said.

"It's a long story. You won't believe parts of it. Maybe none of it."

"You can try me," Ernie said.

"Back in the fall . . ." I started, and began telling them – keeping it as short and simple as possible – about my run-ins with the Resurrection Church and the Great Old Ones, and their followers and detractors. When I got to the part about the continuum threshold, Ernie held up his hand.

"This is just stupid," he said.

"With a continuum threshold, certain things can get through easier than others. I think the Great Old Ones are too huge and heavy to get through the threshold easily, although of course they're the ones who want to get through the most. They try and try and try, and so far they've failed. But if a threshold is open long enough, other creatures manage to slip through, like the dritches I told you about, and these flying things, the Stipley Devils or thrals."

I took them right up to my unwilling excursion aboard *Sorcerer*, and my latest mishap in LOAD/EVAC.

"That reminds me. My mother. She must be freaking out."

"Can you phone her?"

I groped through my pockets. I seemed to have lost nothing during my long fall into the bush. My phone still had a charge.

"Dammit. My mum doesn't have a phone. Someone on *Sorcerer* must have one. But I don't have anyone's number." I felt an ache when I thought about what my mother must be thinking. I looked out the truck's window at the sky, as if *Sorcerer* might suddenly appear, and I could just wave. Lookie here. It's me. I'm okay.

Sometimes all conversation stopped, as the truck rocked and creaked and shook like a Wonderland adventure ride. Then we skidded up out of the trees, off this dirt trail, and onto a gravel road. This place, the west coast: it was like if the Hamilton escarpment went on forever, but with bigger trees. I had never been in a world like this before – a world that, in fact, seemed to be mostly trees. I braced myself against the back of the front seat as we headed steeply downhill. In a few minutes we pulled onto an actual paved road with traffic, but one that nevertheless also wound through a wall of trees like a path through a hedge maze.

"Do we get to a highway soon?"

"This *is* the highway."

Phyllis, talkative and even exuberant when we'd first met, had been quiet as she concentrated on the torturous drive down the mountain. Now that we were back in a world of paved roads, stop signs and overhead power lines, her excitement caught up with her. "We should take him to the band elders."

"Jesus, Phyllis . . . really? Let's just drop him off at the bus stop." Ernie turned in his seat. "You got money for the bus?"

"I'm good." Thanks to Tobias, in my wallet there was more cash than I'd ever seen in one place before.

Phyllis steered the truck onto a side road, and then up a rocky driveway into someone's front yard. There was an old SUV, a swing set, a black Lab who barked and ran up to us as we climbed out of the truck.

"He's clearly no ordinary young man. He came to us on the wings of a thunderbird.

"Daisy . . ." Phyllis addressed the dog, then spoke a few words in that same language with which she'd first addressed me. The dog ignored her, and came toward me with its head lowered, sniffing.

I leaned over and extended my hand slowly, fingers closed in a fist, as Dad had taught me to do with dogs.

"She thinks you're interesting." A stocky woman in a checkered shirt and blue jeans had appeared on the porch, the storm door hissing shut behind her.

Daisy approached, audibly sniffing, nostrils trembling. She headed toward my boots but when she reached my hand, backed off, growling.

"You've been handling something she doesn't like."

"That's for sure," I said.

This was Ernie's house, and he let me wash my hands at the kitchen sink, eyed by the woman, Mae, and Lena, a girl about my age who barely gave me a glance as she shuffled through papers at the kitchen table and consulted her phone. Ernie sat down and as I dried my hands, Daisy approached me again. I thought I'd scoured off most of the thral scent, but when I held out my hand she still shied away.

"Our guest today is no ordinary young man," Phyllis announced. "I believe he's a gift from the gods."

I moaned. "Didn't we clear that up?"

"Nope," Ernie said glumly.

"He understands the she shashishalhem word for welcome," Phyllis continued. "Aymash! Aymash! He answered me right away."

"You were waving. I figured you were saying hi," I said.

"He fell from the sky." Phyllis didn't want to give up any of my godhood. "In the belly of a thunderbird. Just like in the stories we tell right here on the coast."

"Actually, Phyllis." Ernie's voice boomed in the little kitchen. "They're the stories *we* tell."

"Okay, maybe he's just a person. As we can all see. But he's obviously someone special. Why else would he come down right in front of me and Ernie, in broad daylight – the exact two people who could understand and help him?"

"If he'd intended to get to me, or my people, it would make a lot more sense if he landed here in the yard."

"Dammit, Ernie." Phyllis's voice started to break. "When something cosmic happens . . . something spiritual . . . you shouldn't deny it. I say he's a gift from the gods."

"If the gods are giving out stuff, can we take him back and get me a set of all-season radials?"

"We should just thank Phyllis for explaining this to us," Mae said. "Thank you, Phyllis."

"What about all these fiddleheads?" Ernie said. "They won't keep forever."

"It's chilly out. They'll keep." Phyllis looked like she was formulating a new argument for Ernie, on behalf of my godliness.

"There goes my phone," I said. "Excuse me, I should get this."

Actually my phone hadn't stirred or made a sound, but I

exited quickly as if it had buzzed, pulling it hurriedly from my pocket as I went out the kitchen door. I had just remembered that, having survived an experience that I bet no one else ever had, I still had responsibilities. I phoned my Dad.

"Nate! Where in hell . . . ?"

I spent a couple of minutes assuring him that I was really okay. I tried to make a long story short.

"With the Resurrection Church thing, Dad, there are bad guys, and there are good guys, and I'm with the good guys. But it's taken me a long way away." Maybe thinking that since he was also recuperating from great mental and physical trauma, he shouldn't have to cope with unprovable facts no matter how potentially important, I had never told Dad about my sighting of *Sorcerer*. "I'm on the west coast."

"What? Vancouver?"

"Kind of. Why didn't you ever tell me about Sid Fraser?"

"Your mum's biological father? Never met him. I had a hard enough time getting along with Doug."

"I'm going to see him."

"What the hell for?"

"Mum's alive."

"WHAT?"

"It's a long story. She's trying to get home, but she's been taken . . . taken by the good guys, don't worry . . . to some kind of island."

I wanted to tell Dad the whole story – seeing *Sorcerer*, then finding *Sorcerer*, getting shanghaied onto *Sorcerer*, very unwillingly, and then the whole story behind *Sorcerer*. But Ernie and Phyllis were coming out of the house.

"Dad, I gotta go."

"Goddammit, Nate, come home."

"I will," I said. "As soon as I can." With all this money I had, I was sure it would be easy to get a plane ticket.

"What about school?" he said. "And for god's sake phone Meghan. She told me she heard from you once, thank goodness, but she's been calling me twice a day, bugging me for news."

I assured him that all was well, and finally managed to sign off.

"I sure can't thank you guys enough," I said to Phyllis and Ernie.

"Good luck getting to Egmont," Phyllis said. "Unfortunately, I'm going the other way."

I looked back down the driveway at the highway. "Is Egmont far to walk?"

As Ernie explained where the nearest bus stop was, Phyllis stood to one side and regarded me keenly. "You're sure you're not on a mission from the gods?"

"I seem to have a relative up in Egmont," I said, "who can help me with something. So I've got to go meet him. That's all I've got to do. As far as I know."

"We're happy to help. Here's my cell number. Ernie, give him yours."

"Phyllis. The ferry." Bickering about the relative freshness of their fiddleheads and the ups and downs of that particular market, eventually Phyllis was persuaded to back out of the driveway and head for a ferry that would get her to Vancouver. I waved as she pulled out of the driveway and headed down the highway.

Ernie headed inside. It seemed to me that he and his family had had enough of white people claiming to be awesomely connected to the mythic gods of the west coast First Nations. Then I had a thought. Didn't I have Agnes's cell number?

"Who knows," she'd said up on *Sorcerer*. "Someday, when we're back on the ground . . ." She answered after two rings.

"Agnes, it's me. Nate."

Silence on the other end of the line.

"Agnes? It's me, Nate. I was worried that you'd think I'm dead."

Still silence.

"When LOAD/EVAC filled up with those Stipley Devils, I mean thrals, one of them jumped my mother. So I grabbed it, and . . . Agnes?" I was worried that we'd lost the connection.

"Nate?"

"Next thing I knew, the thral and I had both been sucked out the door –"

"Is this . . . how is this possible?"

"– so what could I do? I was flying through space. I hung on."

"How could the fall not kill you? How could the thral not kill you?"

I gave her a short description of my descent, landing and rescue. "I'm a hundred percent alive. I want you to let my mother know."

"This place is in an uproar. Nell's been asking about you, but we lied. We kept telling her you were cleaning up, or that you'd gone to the bathroom. Nobody wanted to break the news –not until we got her patched up."

Agnes explained that although I'd dragged the thral off my mother almost immediately, it had scratched her arms, and clamped its jaws onto the base of her neck. "It grazed a jugular. You must have pulled it off just as it was opening its jaws to bite again. If it had closed them again, she'd be dead. A thral has a bite like a crocodile."

"'Patched up'?"

"Blood squirted out like a water pistol. Eadric nailed a thral with his carbine and tied a handkerchief around the wound. Then help showed up. We managed to chase those vermin away and Eadric got the door shut while crew members did first aid. The only word Nell said was your name. Eadric told her you'd gone."

"I'm not gone. Tell her I'm not gone."

"He meant, gone out for a second. While we were treating her, she kept asking for you, and Eadric – even Eadric's not a hundred percent heartless –"

("Thanks a lot, Agnes," I heard Eadric say in the background.)

"– changed his story and kept making excuses for you not being there."

"Agnes, can you tell her I'm alive and well? I'm on the way to see my grandfather."

"I'll go get her. Nate, everyone will be glad to hear it. *I'm* glad to hear it. Your death was depressing news for everybody."

"Sorry."

Silence. I said Agnes's name, and repeated it, and still there was nothing. I hung up and looked out at the trees across the road. Beyond them was the ocean, and somewhere *Sorcerer* had just descended behind a mountain, or maybe just passed out of cell range.

Then the storm door opened and Lena appeared.

"If you're heading up to Egmont, we can give you a ride."

Egmont, as it happened, wasn't walking distance, "unless you want to walk up the highway for two days in the rain." But it turned out that, if I came back to Ernie and Mae's house around six, I could hitch a ride up there with them.

For now, it was as far as their hospitality went. They directed me up the highway. I walked along the shoulder for twenty minutes or so, until I came to a place where out of the forest someone had carved a mall, much like those we had at home. There was a café, and as I was wrapping myself around a hot chocolate and a bacon and egg sandwich, my phone rang.

"Where the hell have you been?"

I couldn't remember if I'd had the chance to tell Meghan about *Sorcerer*.

"I'm back on the ground."

"Finally. I'll pick you up after school. We've got —"

"I'm not in school. I'm not even in Hamilton. I'm not even *near* Hamilton."

I told Meghan I was on the west coast visiting my grandfather, and that this could have a lot to do with the Great Old Ones, and that somehow it could be important.

"That's just great," she said. "Meanwhile, this town's going down the tubes."

"I can't be everywhere. There are a lot of, uh, factors."

"Do you have a phone number for Howard?"

"The same one you have. I gave up calling it months ago. And it's not like he's called me. Meghan, I'll get back as soon as I can. But if anyone can handle the Church, you can. After all, you've got the Furies. I'm sure you guys are awesome."

"Get your ass back here," Meghan said. "Sometimes even Furies need help."

CHAPTER 20
MAGNUS

For the rest of the afternoon I drifted from place to place in the Wilson Creek Plaza, killing time and drinking too many hot caffeinated beverages. The coffee place had Wi-Fi, so I looked around online for a phone number for Sidney Fraser. There wasn't a thing. I calculated he'd be eighty-three years old; unless he'd taken one of those hub-rim trips on *Sorcerer*, he'd have gone through a lot of wear and tear in eighty-three years. I wondered if my mother had considered the possibility that her dad might no longer be alive.

I pulled the copy of *RainVisions* out in the café and took up where I'd left off, but I was having trouble keeping my mind on the story. In space, it turned out, something had got into Magnus – something alive, but a different kind of life, something that had beamed through the steel hull of the *Oberth* A-7 like moonlight through window glass, and had chosen Magnus as its host.

As my granddad told it, two days after the rescue, the *Mary Maquinna*, its German castaways recovering on board, was ready to go back to hunting whales. But it was being followed. One night, a mooring rope snapped taut. Snorting and dripping, something pulled itself up the rope, flopped over the gunwale, and pulled itself upright on the ship's deck.

Barely human, it was still recognizable as Magnus, impossibly transformed. He had climbed up out of the ocean, where he seemed as comfortable and at home as any ocean creature, and "in a voice like splintering bones" tried to convince a horrified Inge to return to the water with him. Inge wasn't having any of it. She fled below decks, calling for help.

The captain had given up his cabin, and the floor was stacked with blankets and sleeping bags that we'd gathered for our guests. With Magnus on her heels, Inge didn't have time to barricade the door. Alerted by her cries, all of us – the *Mary*'s crew, and the *Oberth*'s – got to Thiessen's quarters at about the same time. There was much shouting in German, and gesticulating at Magnus – indeed there was something terrible in his look. I understood what they were saying because as it happens, the word "monster" is the same as in English. So far no one had carried out these threats, because no one wanted to go anywhere near Magnus, but outnumbered by a hostile crew, Magnus turned and in a few swift movements, unlatched the dogs that sealed the room's one porthole.

As he did so, Wolf pushed the others aside. He was brandishing one of our killing lances.

Just then, Captain Thiessen arrived. "What the hell?" He bellowed at the Germans to move aside, but before anyone could stop him, Wolf plunged the lance into Magnus's torso.

Magnus bellowed, reached down and pulled on the lance. Thiessen rushed through the crowd, squinted his eyes shut and pulled out the lance, releasing a gout of blood and torn flesh. In the next moment, I expected Magnus to collapse to the floor. I was sure he was gone. But instead Magnus pulled himself head first into the open porthole. With a cracking of bones, his shoulders collapsed, and like some tidal mollusc or bottom-dwelling cephalopod, his torso bulged out of the porthole, an escape window no bigger than a man's face.

"What the hell is going on here?" Thiessen whispered. Magnus was breaking every bone in his body to escape. Suddenly his hips were through, and then his legs, and then a few shreds of bloodied clothing dropped to the floor of the cabin. Magnus – no longer a victim to be rescued, but a ruthless predator to be destroyed – fell out of sight and splashed into the waters of the sound.

Yuck. After my exploits back in Hamilton, and what I'd seen and heard on board *Sorcerer*, I felt like kind of an expert on the Great Old Ones and their kin and their creatures and their human fans and supporters. But I'd never run into anything like this. Still, my mother wouldn't be recommending this to me, and urging me to see Sidney Fraser, unless it had something to do with the Great Old Ones, and the Resurrection Church of the Ancient Gods, and *Sorcerer*.

"Can I get you anything else?" School was out for the day, and the place was filling up with students with cellphones and backpacks. I headed out into the parking lot and shrugged into my coat as I looked out at the grey sky and the distant water, people going here and there in brightly coloured rain jackets. The weather here on the coast was wet, but I was dressed for an Ontario snowstorm. I'd be nice and warm just about everywhere as long as I didn't actually fall into the ocean. I headed back down the highway toward Ernie's house.

ALTHOUGH I'D just travelled halfway across the continent in an antique airship, its enormous propellers powered by a cellar full of flesh-eating alien fungus, I was still not fond of motor vehicles or particularly used to them. I nervously climbed into the crew cab of Ernie's pickup. Tonight Mae was driving, with Ernie beside her and Lena and me in the back.

"See, it's fate," Ernie said to Lena. "We're meant to go up to Egmont. We're not just doing it for you and your poetry. We're helping a stranger, this innocent lad who is alone in the world, friendless, without . . ."

"Dad. Enough," Lena said quietly. "You're not making me feel guilty or anxious at all."

The winding highway forced each of us to lean into the curves or push back in our seats as Mae slowed for a bend or took off along a rare straight stretch, with glimpses of ocean and beyond the ocean, mountains. We started up a long hill. Mae pulled out to pass a semi-trailer.

Lena said to Ernie, "You're talking like Phyllis."

Feeling I should join the conversation, I said the first thing on my mind. "So many trees here."

"Where you from?" When I told him, Ernie shook his head in pity.

"Too built up out there for me. Can't breathe. Especially a place like Hamilton – that's the big steel town, isn't it?"

"Not so much a steel town as it once was."

"So . . . this story about how you came to fall out of the sky, carried by that big flying thing?"

"Everything I told you is true."

Ernie shook his head. "If I hadn't seen what I seen, I'd say you were outta your head. But what I didn't see was this airship, *Sorcerer*. And it was a pretty nice day; Phyllis and me, we had a good view of the sky."

"*Sorcerer* has a kind of cloaking device."

"Of course it does." Lena looked up from her phone, smiled and looked back down at it again.

"It's not one hundred percent Earth technology. Anyway,"

I said, "I've got a grandfather up in Egmont, and I gotta to go see him."

Ernie and Mae discussed the name Sidney Fraser and whether it was anyone they knew. "Has he lived there a long time?" Mae asked.

"I think so. He's real old."

"Hmm . . ." Ernie thought for a moment. "I wonder if that's the old guy who lives 'round the point. If so, you'll have to get creative . . . see if someone'll give you a ride."

"I've been lucky with rides so far."

"I mean a boat ride," Ernie said. "If he's the guy I'm thinking of, he lives on the shore of the sound there."

Hmm. A boat. How would I manage that?

"If that's him, is he the one who gets badmouthed all the time?" Mae said.

"Why would he get badmouthed?" I asked.

"For talking trash about what's at the bottom of the sound – down in the Deep."

"That might not be trash," Ernie said. "Some of the elders talk about that. When Vancouver first came up here, two hundred years ago, the people told him that place was called 'M'trusa.'"

"What kind of word is that?" Mae asked. "My Sechelt isn't that good."

"That's the thing, it's not she shashishalhem – not from Sechelt, or Squamish, or anywhere else in Coast Salish. The word, they say it comes from someplace else. From some other language, an old language. Because that deep – for a long time there's been something down there, that's also from someplace else."

We all fell silent. I saw a sign that said EARLS COVE, and another sign pointing to the right read EGMONT. Mae slowed to make the turn.

"It's still our land," Ernie continued. "He leases it from the band. There was a village on the shore there for years – a community – and that was what they did. They watched. Something bad was in that deep, down there in M'trusa, and it was their job to make sure it stayed there – to raise the alarm if it ever surfaced. Then one day, during the war or maybe just after, something happened. They were gone."

It was almost sunset by the time we had turned off the highway and taken a long, curving road through the trees to the parking lot of a pub.

"Lot of stories about that place." Ernie was talking about M'trusa, not about the pub. It so happened that I seemed to have fallen into this area, which was called the Sunshine Coast, on the day of the pub's weekly open mike. Lena, it turned out, was a poet, and as soon as we parked, Mae rushed her inside to sign up. It took some persuading; Lena was starting to make excuses.

"C'mon girl," Mae said. "We drove all this way."

Ernie turned to look at me. "You coming in?"

"This old guy," I said. "If this old guy is my grandfather, he lives 'round the point'?"

"Been there a long time." Ernie pointed around the corner of the pub into what looked to me like limitless dark, a few lights strung below us at the bottom of the slope where I guess was the ocean. "He stands guard. I've been past there in the boat. Got an old harpoon gun set up on a boat, ready to go. Some folks say he's got a hoard of dynamite. Old Sid's ready to go into battle."

"So . . . he might not like visitors."

"No, he's a friendly old dude. So I've heard. He's not one of these old bastards who holes himself up in the bush and gets cabin fever. He's armed for a purpose. He's armed because he says, one of these days, something bad is going to come up out of the water there." Ernie shook his head. "But let's not think about that now. Tell ya what, Nate, let's go in, you can buy me a coffee, and let's hear some poetry."

CHAPTER 21
MARCH 1937:
PROVIDENCE, RHODE ISLAND, USA

Visitors often showed up around this time. Late in the day, when darkness had settled over the Jane Brown Memorial Hospital; when dutiful adults who, for one reason or another, did not really want to visit their parents in the terminal ward, came to the terminal ward to visit their parents, knowing they'd soon be asked to leave.

So when the last visitor – "Keep your eye on the clock, you've got twenty minutes" – closed the door on his way into the ward, the night nurse and the orderly weren't surprised.

"What an oddball," said the orderly, who should have been doing laundry or rinsing bedpans, not hanging around the front desk.

"He came by earlier," the nurse said, "with a whole passel of oddballs. I teased Howard afterwards – I told him he must be quite the writer, since here in his illness, characters out of his storybooks are coming to see him."

"He told me he didn't really write books," the orderly said. "Just short stories. I got him to autograph an old magazine for me. *Weird Tales.*"

"One way or another, they say truth is stranger than fiction and these were quite the bunch. Some stuck-up foreigner with an accent, a girl right out of Africa with gold-rimmed glasses and a great crown of black hair, some awful-looking tramp wearing a coat like a pup tent. And then this feller who's, I swear to god, a genuine Red Indian."

"They must be good buddies," the orderly said. "Only old ladies ever come to see Howard."

They shook their heads. They knew H. P. Lovecraft wouldn't be with them much longer.

"He told me the most awful story," the nurse continued.

"This Indian?"

"No, Howard, just yesterday. It seems that when he was little, his mama always told him he was so ugly. Even when he was only six or seven, he would sneak out of the house at night, without his mother or his aunts knowing, and walk the streets, and explore the old town. He'd hide in the shadows when anyone came. He thought he was so ugly that if they saw him, they'd be scared.

"He lives over on College Street, but his family lived for years on Angell – in the nicer part, at first, though later they had some setbacks. He told me that on these night walks, he liked to go to Prospect Park, but that one night something was there in the park, waiting."

"Bullies?" The orderly nodded. "Worse yet, a buncha perverts. Damn them anyway. They should round them all up and –"

"I told you this is the most awful story. Howard says that crouching in the shadows of the big statue, there were *things* waiting for him and these things, they scooped him up –"

"Perverts. I knew it."

"– and took him into the darkest bushes, and they – mind you, this is what he told me – they *planted* something in him . . ."

167

"I'll bet they did." The orderly smirked.

It was late, and the nurse was used to these conversations with the orderly. If you didn't find a job you could send him off to do, he'd keep talking and what he talked about would get more and more dark and creepy. But there was something about Lovecraft's story that had really got to her. The way the poor man had told it – it had touched something inside, given her a chill. So she ignored the orderly's drivel.

"This thing, this *seed*, he says it's been growing in him all his life, and now it's ready to hatch. He insists that we cremate him. He says it's for safety – for the safety of everybody, he wants to be cremated."

"Well, that's for the family to decide, isn't it? When they make the arrangements."

The nurse shuddered. "That's what's so eerie. He wants to be cremated *now*. If we wait until he dies, he says, it might be too late."

"So who were these characters? This was a long time ago, eh? You could never track them down and press charges, not now."

"Howard says they weren't human. I tell you, the way he described them, you won't ever get me near Prospect Park at night, not with a ten-foot pole."

"What kind of creatures, like boogeymen or . . . ?"

"Howard says they weren't human. He still has nightmares about them. He's terrified that when this thing hatches, whether he's dead or alive, they'll come back, and rip it out of his body, and claim it for themselves, and take it away and raise it for their own. And then . . . Anyway, the name he has for them is night-gaunts."

They sat in silence, then the nurse pointed to the clock. The orderly headed for the door.

"If I ain't back in five minutes, send a posse." He snickered. "Night-gaunts!" He opened the door of the terminal ward but the nurse noticed that when he went inside, he left it open.

Night had fallen outside the terminal ward's barred windows (in the grip of delirium, despair and opium, patients occasionally made a break for it). The long, clammy room, smelling of sweat and sickness, was full of whispers; there were no visitors tonight besides Lovecraft's friend, but in the terminal ward people lowered their voices, as if afraid to awaken and goad into rage the death that slumbered and yawned and waited there.

The squeak of bedsprings, the moans of patients too sick to speak, and there was Lovecraft's cot. A benefactor had just donated new curtains to circle each bed, heavy linens patterned in the art deco style, all bold lines and bright colours. Around Lovecraft's cot, the curtain was drawn. The orderly approached.

"Last call, gents," he announced. He drew back the curtain. "Time to . . ."

The cot was empty. And so was the chair beside it. The blankets had been thrown hastily aside, and Lovecraft's robe and slippers were gone, as was his tiny stack of books.

The old man in the next bed looked up with wide, astonished eyes, and raised a shaking arm to point at the window. The orderly felt a draft of cold air.

The window shouldn't be open. The orderly went to close it – and saw that the bars were gone from the outside. Ragged splinters of wood and paint lined the frame, and he could see the outline of the heavy iron grid against the grass below. He looked up. In the night sky, something like a cloud crossed the darkness, an invisible vapour that distorted the stars and then spread out and away. Beyond the tidy lawn, the line of trees waved as in a winter gale, and the orderly heard a tremendous hum, like the engines of the night itself, swelling and fading into the sky.

He went back to the old man. "Where's Howard?" he asked. "Your neighbour there. Where the hell did he go?"

"Somethin' ripped off the bars," the old man gasped. "Somethin' like a big octypus – pulled 'em off like they was stuck up there with thumbtacks."

The orderly sighed. Half the people in this place had lost their marbles, and weren't ever getting them back. He repeated his question. "Where'd he go? And the guy who was with him?"

"Up the rope ladder." The old man pointed to the ceiling, and fell back on the bed. "I'm tellin' ya, it had the arms with the big suckers. An octypus, and that Indian feller. They took Howie up the rope ladder. It's a rope ladder to the moon."

CHAPTER 22
LOVECRAFT ON THE SKOOKUMCHUCK

Up until now, I'd never been anyplace but Hamilton and Toronto, and I felt like I had changed planets. As I faced the pub, behind me the sun dipped out of the clouds to draw a line of fire along a horizon of trees; its last rays gold-anodized another range of low mountains over to the west, across a broad, flowing body of water.

"What river is this?"

Ernie said, "It's not a river. It's the Skookumchuck. The entrance to Sechelt Inlet. It's narrow, so it gets rapids when the tide goes in or out. It's a real big, strong body of water."

"'Skookumchuck' – what's that mean?"

"A real big, strong body of water."

Flecks of white fluttered along the opposite shoreline: a flock of gulls heading back to their roost for the night. I felt like I was at the utter edge of civilization, on the brink of a bigger world.

"I can't believe this place," I said. "So you *live* here?"

"You're a funny guy." Ernie pointed to the pub. "Lena's nose will be out of joint if we miss her reading."

Inside, I headed to the bar and got myself a ginger ale and Ernie a coffee. The place was crowded: out here on the edge of the world, poetry seemed to be a popular item.

171

The emcee introduced Lena, and she began to read, her voice shaky at first.

"I am the invisible girl – that is my superpower.

"No one sees me in real life, they just see their fantasy."

I handed Ernie his coffee.

"No one sees me on TV, 'less it's a security camera.

"But if I stick my thumb out long enough, sure – someone will pull over."

She took a breath, and her voice steadied and got louder.

"But who's that behind the wheel.

"The wheel of history.

"The wheel of destiny.

"The wheel of the first peoples' fate and the white man's law.

"I see the key that locks the door, I reach for the key –

"Can you see me now?"

Lena ended the poem and, as people clapped, hopped off the riser and headed for her family's table, passing me in the dark club. I leaned toward her as she passed. "That was great."

She smiled and thanked me.

"I can totally relate," I said. "That's just how I feel sometimes."

"Ya think?" Lena laughed and headed back to her family. I was left with the feeling, so familiar to me from previous girl-encounters, of having said exactly the wrong thing. I decided to head back toward Lena and see if I could overcome the feeling of being a goof. I sat down next to Ernie and pulled out *RainVisions*.

"I was just reading the Sid Fraser story in here – and thinking it was hard to believe, then I tell you my story, which *you* find hard to believe. Meanwhile, whoever you tell about seeing me fall out of the sky, hanging onto the thral's legs – they will find that hard to believe."

172

"Stop messing with my head."

As we talked, I was dimly aware that at the end of the room, the next reader was threading their way through the tables and climbing onto the riser. This time, a man's voice came over the sound system.

"Am I on?" He coughed and tapped the mike. "Once again in the spotlight. Begging your indulgence, my friends, here's the draft of a work – very much in progress – that I've composed while staying with some very generous new friends who have kindly, uh-huh, taken me in. I can only hope that the illuminations of their, uh, research, and others' will, uh, help ameliorate or even – who knows? – utterly curtail and circumvent certain, uh, threats that loom over this fairest – well damp, dark and chilly, this time of year, but . . ."

I stopped in my tracks. That voice. I know that voice.

"Come on, Howie," a man barked from the crowd. "Shut up and read!"

"Yes, Brad," the reader replied. "So right . . . my apologies. Let me begin." He cleared his throat and began to read.

"From boyhood dreams inviolate

"Of Faerie Queene & Kubla Khan

"One midsummer night did pilot

"To fate befelled no other man."

I stood on tiptoes and looked. What the hell was he doing here – the man who called himself H. P. Lovecraft? I had last seen him back in October, during that final ceremony in the stadium. That was six months ago.

"'Twas kidnapped, I, while but a child

"To please a stern and savage god

"To leave this world so green and mild

173

"For distant starscapes yet untrod."

At the same time, I hadn't been particularly eager to be in touch with Lovecraft, a.k.a. Timothy Kerwin. At first I assumed he had gone back to his family in Cleveland, Ohio; perhaps even given up his job as "consultant" for the Lovecraft Underground – "on the front lines of defending Earth from the Great Old Ones" – and gone back to his everyday life and work, whatever that was. Tonight, however, here he was, sounding as Lovecraftian as ever.

"To savage kings of alien mien

"A helpless boy is but a pawn

"His terror tantalizes when

"His nighttime fears survive the dawn."

"I know that guy." I signalled to Lena and her family. "Howard."

Lena nodded. "Everybody knows Howard. All his poems are about gods and monsters and outer space and galaxies. The old hippies love him."

I was missing the intervening verses. After meeting Lovecraft/Kerwin, I had checked out some of Lovecraft's writing online. The poems, I thought, were pretty bad. Some of the stories had seemed okay, a couple of them really good. Sam had brought me a few of Lovecraft's books when I was still in the hospital. They gave me bad dreams. Chanting death cults, tentacled monsters, mind control by hideous giant crustaceans, vast sunken cities under the Pacific Ocean – all this was a bit too close to home since the Resurrection Church had come into my life.

Now Lovecraft's voice was changing.

"In fevers, and polluted dreams,

"Awash upon the midnight tides . . ."

Lovecraft straightened his shoulders and looked out over the audience. "Those dreams," he murmured, "and those tides."

He smiled shyly, as if he'd totally forgotten why he was there, and was trying to keep up appearances until it came back to him. Then the smile faded. He leaned forward, and whispered into the microphone, "Something, *something is coming . . .*" and then threw out his chest, and his voice rose.

"Yig sun y'igit yath Nyarlathotep

"Chn'g R'lyhnygoth rng Wrryetkosh

"Chn'g R'lyhnygoth rng Wrryetkosh

"Ph'nglui mglw'nafh Nyarlathotep M'trusa wgah'nagl fhtagn!

"PH'NGLUI MGLW'NAFH NYARLATHOTEP M'-TRUSA WGAH'NAGL FHTAGN!"

As he weaved unsteadily back and forth, Lovecraft remained hopelessly off-mike, but he had summoned a lot of lung power, and his voice filled the crowded bar. Finally he stumbled against a guitar amplifier and stopped mid-sentence.

The crowd exploded in applause.

"Far OUT!"

"Howard, yo da man!"

Lovecraft sat down on the amplifier, blinking dazedly as the applause died down. I threaded my way through the audience, and hopped onto the riser and leaned over Lovecraft, putting my hand on his shoulder.

"Howard. You okay?"

He looked up at me, as if trying to identify the source of this familiar voice. Then he blinked nearsightedly.

"Perhaps . . . some air."

This, I reflected, was how I'd met him, what seemed like a lifetime ago. After a friendly enough introduction to Meghan and me, and what I remember as a life-saving hot chocolate and muffin, Howard had almost passed out when I'd told him about finding Dana's body in the basement of the gradually-being-demolished Prince of Wales Elementary School. My story, he said, was evidence that the Hounds of Tindalos had been summoned to appear, and it took a lot of power to summon them. At the time, I'd thought he was overreacting, but since then I'd met the Hounds.

Seeing me helping him, an audience member appeared on the other side of Lovecraft. With my attention mostly on Howard, I had the impression of a rickety denim-clad figure topped with wisps of white hair. He talked non-stop as he helped Lovecraft and me toward the bar's outside deck.

"That was great, man, it touched on some very relevant topics. In fact, maybe got too close to the bone. It was like something got into you, and I have an idea what it was. Don't know how you did it . . ." Still talking, he reached forward to push the crash bar, and together we helped Lovecraft out onto the deck. Gratefully, he draped himself over the rail and took deep breaths of the coastal air. I let go of him, and so did our helper.

"I don't know what happened . . . well, as for something 'getting into me,' that's another story, a very old . . ." Lovecraft stopped. He looked hard at me. "Nate. It's you."

"Feeling better?"

"As I live and breathe – you've tracked me down. You must have hired a Pinkerton's man." Lovecraft looked around, as if there might be a SWAT team backing me up.

Meanwhile, around us was a blackness deeper than anything I'd ever seen. As we faced the water, over on the right, a string of lights led up into the night sky – a road, or a power line, I guess, on invisible mountain slopes, their upper flanks streaked with grey bolts of snow. There were a few glimmers of light down on the waterline; besides that, the black sky, the black curtain of forest and mountain, nothing but the black, fertile smell of the ocean creeping up from the tide line.

"Howard. What the hell?"

"I'm just doing what we all do in life, my friend: piecing together the great puzzle."

"When you piece a puzzle together, it's supposed to get *less* confusing."

"Anyway," said the white-haired guy, "you got the spirit in you tonight, my man . . ."

Lovecraft turned, nodded. "Thank you, sir, though it's strictly first-draft stuff. Not at all publishable, not yet. Toward the end . . . I don't know what happened."

"You don't remember anything?" I asked. "It was kind of scary . . ."

"Let me introduce myself," the old hippie huffed. "My name's . . ." He stopped, and held up a finger. "What's that?"

"What's what?"

A white cloud of gulls burst up from farther down the shoreline and flew over the pub, almost skimming the roof.

"Can you hear it?"

The cries of the gulls receded in the distance. In their place wafted a sigh of wind that could have been the echo of thunder, maybe an avalanche down one of those rocky slopes across the channel – but as it echoed off the black waters of the inlet, I began to hear words.

"Y-I-G S-U-N Y'I-G-I-T Y-A-TH N-YAR-LA-THO-TEP"

"It's a voice," the old hippie said.

"CH-N'G R'LY-EHN-GO-TH R-N-G WR-RYET-KOSH"

"Nonsense," said Lovecraft. "It's the roar of the rapids at the turn of this coast's notorious tide. Or a ferry horn – echoing off the walls of the inlet."

"Dude, the rapids don't sound like that; the ferries don't either. Listen. I hear words."

"Howard," I said. "He's right. In fact . . ."

"PH'N-GL-UI MG-LW'NA-FH N-YAR-LA-THO-TEP M'TRU-SA W-GAH'NAGL FH-TAG-N."

". . . it's the words of your poem, the one you just read."

The voice was deeper than the bass electrobeat that would shake the Westmount auditorium during a school dance . . . and hoarse, as if it bubbled up . . .

"It sounds like the ocean itself talking," I said. "Where's it coming from?"

"You just answered your own question," the old guy said.

More mysteries. The deck had filled up with people from the bar, coming outside to hear the night vibrate with the strange voice from the darkness. They were shaking their heads and whispering. Behind us, cars and pickup trucks revved up and spun gravel as they rushed out of the lot.

"He's right, Nate," Lovecraft said. "If what you tell me is true, then something outside of me – something *out there* – took hold tonight. Do you understand the words?"

"Of course not. It's some kind of . . ."

I wanted to say "gibberish," but there were parts I recognized. They were variations of a line I had heard repeated at gatherings of the Resurrection Church – a line I had read and reread when I was still convalescing, and had started to study Lovecraft's books.

"I heard something like that at the cult's ceremonies in Hamilton. I can't pronounce most of the words. For example, the original mentions 'R'lyeh,' that's the underwater city where, supposedly, Cthulhu is submerged. This version – I think I heard 'R'lyhnygoth,' the Great Old Ones' home planet."

For the first time since he had collapsed onstage, Lovecraft showed signs of enthusiasm.

"Well, young Nathan, we'll make an eldritch scholar of you yet! Very good. The line from the original chant goes, 'Ph'nglui mglw'nafh Cthulhu R'lyeh wgah'nagl fhtagn.'"

Lovecraft pronounced the words so quickly that the syllables sputtered from his mouth like spurts from a garden hose.

"What isn't good is the complete meaning of the words. The chant is, as I recall it – and I have no recollection of reciting it tonight:

"It is the end of the long voyage of Nyarlathotep.

"From R'lyhnygoth to planet Earth.

"From R'lyhnygoth to planet Earth.

"Now in his house – and I've never heard the name, it's 'M'trusa.' What can that be? Oh well. Now in his . . ."

Our hippie friend cleared his throat. "I can help with that."

"Really?" Lovecraft peered at him suspiciously. "How would you come to speak the language of the Great Old Ones?"

"That's an overly polite term for those soul-sucking imperialist alien dungheaps, but I've picked up a bit. For example, 'M'trusa.' That's a very old name. Not Coast Salish, as far as I know, but it's a proper name that the local First Nations gave to the centre of the sound. Or that they picked up from some other language." He pointed out into the dark.

"We erased the native names, and wrote over them with

names from our legends, our culture. Well by 'we,' I mean Vancouver, Malaspina, Cook, all those explorers that came here from Europe, and the nuns and priests and church scholars who thought they had to make this a better place by moulding its people into European ways. On the left here is Agamemnon Channel. On the right, heading up into the mountains, is Jervis Inlet. Out there is the sound – Hotham Sound, we called it, and at its mouth is a marine abyss. An anomalous deep – there's no other quite like it. It had a bad reputation – when they canoed along the coast, the Salish would go a long way to avoid that deep, and their name for it was M'trusa."

Lovecraft waved a hand dismissively. "That the local language would share a word with the language of the Great Old Ones could be sheer homophonic coincidence."

"Maybe, my friend. *Or . . .* when Vancouver got to this coast, all the way from England over two hundred years ago, he moored in the sound, and he didn't like the deep either. He said it was hard to navigate – which a broad, open body of water shouldn't be, but he said it had freaky, unpredictable winds and currents – and that if they moored anywhere near it, he and his men got nightmares. He adapted the local name for it, and again he transformed it into a name from his legends, from his nation's literature, which often looked to ancient Greece for its sources." Lovecraft, I noticed, had returned to the stunned silence we'd been trying to coax him out of.

"He used the name of a creature so damned, so appalling, that one look at it would turn you to stone. Something with piercing eyes, and snakes for hair; something totally malevolent and negative. And that deep is where that voice came from tonight."

Lovecraft spoke up, his voice weak and shaky. "As I was saying, Nate, the line goes:

"It is the end of the long voyage of Nyarlathotep.

"From R'lyhnygoth to planet Earth.

"From R'lyhnygoth to planet Earth.

"Now in his house at M'trusa, dead Nyarlathotep lies . . ."

"Frankly," the old man said, "that voice, coming right after your poem, freaked me out. If Nyarlathotep is one of these Great Old Ones you talk about, then I don't believe he comes with good intentions. And the fact is, there's something in that deep, something that's been waiting a long time to resurface. So what that sounded like to me was, Nyarlathotep is about to rise. And when he rises, it won't go well for us. The voice said that Nyarlathotep has come a long way to cause us harm, and now he dreams and waits, and soon he will rise – rise into this world. From his underwater grave in the Medusa Deep."

CHAPTER 23
A VOICE FROM THE DEEP

So *that's* where I was. "The place where it all ends – any chance to become better, any redemption for pain suffered or inflicted, any chance for love, hope or evolution, gets sucked into the blackness through that void in the ocean that the maps call the Medusa Deep." My grandfather's story had made it seem like a place you wouldn't want to go for a holiday. Now I was right around the corner from it.

"You going to be okay, Nate?" Ernie and his family had come out onto the deck. "You got connected with some friends here?"

Lovecraft said, "As far as accommodation goes, I'm sure we can find space for you aboard the *Pacific Odyssey*. PIPS has lots of room."

"Uh . . ." Actually, I would have liked to stay and get to know Ernie's family better, especially Lena. But it sounded as if PIPS, whatever that was, was closer to where I had to be.

"I think I'm good." I thanked him and his family, we traded phone numbers, said our goodbyes.

"Where'd our new buddy go?" I asked Lovecraft.

He gestured over the deck's rail into the dark. Below us, a boat engine roared to life and idled, making gross glup glup sounds like a pig rooting for food in the ocean.

"He said he had urgent business. Now he's headed home."

Commuting by boat, I thought. That's so cool. "We should talk to him again," I said. "We seem to have some things in common."

Lovecraft nodded. "Seems like an awfully nice chap. Sid."

"So where do we head . . . Wait a sec. *Sid?*"

I had forgotten about asking around for my grandfather. Was it possible that old guy had been Sidney Fraser? I did a quick calculation. I guess it was possible he was eighty-three. You're always hearing about people who were ninety-five and still growing their market garden or a hundred and running marathons, so I guess you could be eighty-three and still hang around in bars and drive yourself home in a motorboat.

"How do you get down there?"

Lovecraft pointed, and I ran down the steps to a series of floats with boats tied onto them: sailboats, boats with cabins and stuff that looked like fishing gear on deck, little open outboards with gas tanks and life jackets strewn around.

I ran out onto a float. All I could see was a tail of white foam a hundred metres out, slowly shrinking. I shouted and waved as Sid put distance between him and the dock, but he wasn't listening or looking back.

Some of the patrons from the pub had gathered by the side of a big life raft–type thing that was tied up to the float.

Lovecraft caught up with me and introduced me to an older woman with long, untidy brown hair, who looked at me and frowned, as if I was some kind of swamp eel that Lovecraft had caught and was asking her to fry up for dinner.

"Cynthia," Lovecraft said. "Look who I've found, or who found me up in the pub. A young friend of mine from Hamilton – a central player in the latest battle there. Might we find him a berth on board the *Odyssey*?"

Cynthia peered at me doubtfully, and in a moment another face appeared over her shoulder, a man with a grey moustache and goatee. He leered at Lovecraft.

"I told ya, Cindy. Something like this would happen with Howard sooner or later."

"Pleased to meet you," I said. "My name's Nate Silva."

"Howard . . . ?" Cynthia gestured and she and Lovecraft had a whispered conversation. I managed to catch a few words: "Church . . . Therpens . . . Interlocutor . . . runes." I heard that last word several times: "Runes . . . Hounds . . . Tindalos . . ." Cynthia waved Lovecraft away and strode over to me.

"Is this true? Were you involved in the debacle in Hamilton?"

"Debacle?"

"When the stadium was destroyed, and a senior Interlocutor was killed. We've heard there was human sacrifice involved."

I had never heard anyone use the word before, though I'd seen it in print. "Debacle" – in other words, somebody screwed up, big time.

"Ma'am, if you mean when the Resurrection Church of the Ancient Gods tried to bring Yog-Sothoth through a continuum threshold, and we stopped them, and whipped their asses, yes, I was totally involved." I gestured at Lovecraft. "Howard was a big part of all that too. He managed to give us some idea of what was going on before it was too late. That Interlocutor too. She was totally on the front lines with us. A kind of gross-looking creature, but I would say heroic. We all owe a lot to her. If that's what you're talking about, yes, I was involved in that."

"You're Nathan Silva?"

"It was not a debacle," I said. "Unless you're one of Yog-Sothoth's worshippers, who want to bring the Great Old Ones back to Earth. To turn over the planet to Yog-Sothoth, and Cthulhu, and the rest of those slimebags. It was a debacle for those guys, for sure."

Lovecraft heard the annoyance in my voice and rushed to intervene. "Nate," he said. "All Mrs. Dampier is trying to establish, is —"

"Your scars," Cynthia said. "I want to see your scars. I understand that you're the only living human —"

"Sorry," I said. "Not presently available to the public."

"If, as Howard says, you're a bright and inquisitive young man, perhaps you can understand how important our work is. You've heard, of course, of PIPS."

"The hard candy they sell at corner stores?"

Cynthia paused to let me know her patience was running out.

"The Pacific Institute for Paranormal Sciences. If there's any so-called 'front line' between the extraterrestrial Great Old Ones and the people of Earth, it's not some vigilante fan page in Hamilton. Hamilton — it seems unlikely that an extraterrestrial force wanting to make a major foray onto this planet would pick Hamilton, Ontario, for god's sake, as a port of entry. Anyway." She leaned forward.

"Even a minute's perusal, one or two photos, and a few measurements of size and depth to facilitate discriminant function analysis could provide information that could launch a major breakthrough. I can't force you — it's your body — but I can make you an offer you can't resist. We've built a fortified research centre at our headquarters, and we've got a project underway to conjure the Hounds of Tindalos. In rigidly caged, absolutely secure conditions."

I couldn't think what to say; was, in fact, speechless.

"Although there seems to be a kind of folkway, or ritual protocol, that creates, or replicates, a dimensional shift through some incomprehensible, arcane use of ancient runes, we're sure that we can improve on the process by using engineered sound waves, an oscillating magnetic field and a rigorously medicated test subject."

I laughed. "Lady, you people are *so* screwed!"

She smiled at me. "The perfect test subject would probably be young and male." Howard sighed. Cynthia turned to him. "I'm not warming up to your young friend here."

"Talk about a debacle," I said. "Anyway, do you think you can put me up tonight, or not?"

"Not if you're going to be like this."

"Cynthia," said Howard.

"Oh, all right," she said. "We'll find out if he's worth the effort. In fact, Howard, why doesn't he ride back with you?"

"You're not travelling together?" The rest of her party were climbing into the big life raft.

"We could all fit in the inflatable," Cynthia said, "but the outboard motor makes Howard nervous."

Everyone else had seated themselves in the inflatable (Lovecraft made me stop calling it a "life raft"). The man with the goatee guffawed when he saw Lovecraft and I turn toward our transportation, a rowboat looking pale and fragile in the dark water.

"That man," Lovecraft sighed. "Brad – Cynthia's husband. The vulgarity is so unnecessary."

"They're both total dickheads."

"Nate, they mean well. And they have resources you and I don't have, and that someday we might need."

Lovecraft gave me instructions for getting in without literally rocking the boat, and showed me how to mount the oars. His help in strapping me into a wet life jacket reminded me of my mother's parachute instructions, just a matter of hours ago (now *that*, I thought, was what you'd call a debacle). I looked around nervously. The only boat I'd ever been in was the Toronto Island ferry.

"I feel like I'm in a submarine that's about to dive."

"You'll feel better if you do the rowing. Don't worry," Howard said. "You'll find that this little vessel is amazingly hard to tip, much less sink."

He coached me on rowing – it was really pretty easy – and we left the dock. The rowboat rocked in the wake of the inflatable, which soon left us behind. It was heading toward a vessel moored offshore; from here it looked like a good-sized boat – a ship, really, I guess.

Lovecraft pointed far out into the night, where a distant pinpoint of red light hovered just above the waterline. "That's where your friend Sid lives. Just around that point."

"It doesn't look very far."

"It's not."

We didn't avoid the inflatable's wake, but steered into its calm middle, following directly behind the inflatable's stern and making, I thought, pretty good time. Soon, however, the larger boat left us far behind, and I glanced backwards to keep my bearings on the distant ship. I was doing pretty well, I thought: despite my inexperience, I soon had us skimming smoothly through the gentle swells coming in from the Salish Sea.

"Howard, let's go there."

"What's that? Cross the inlet – up into the sound – to the mouth of the legendary deep?"

"You said it wasn't far."

"'Far' is a highly relative term when you're in a rowboat."

"I never asked to come out here," I said. "I should be home, and now that I'm here, the only thing I've got to do is talk to my grandfather. My mother told me this was important. Once I do that, I can go home."

"Really, Nate. I think it's important that you try to get to know Brad and Cynthia and get an idea of the research that PIPS is trying to do."

"Like summon the Hounds?"

I heard Lovecraft catch his breath. Last year, the mere mention of the Hounds of Tindalos was enough to make him hyperventilate and pass out. Somewhere in his past he'd had a run-in with the Hounds, maybe bore scars that ran deeper than mine.

"All the more reason that you spend some time with them," he said. "So far they've had no direct contact with any creatures that are, like the Great Old Ones or the hihyaghi, from outside of this planet – and certainly not with any creatures who, like the Hounds, are from another material dimension. I think they'll respect your experience."

"I didn't really get that vibe off them."

We were now far out into the middle of the channel. I saw a flash of movement to our left where the water between the mountains led out to the Salish Sea; once you got there, you would have to get around Vancouver Island, which, as I understood it, was pretty humongous, to get out to the vast Pacific Ocean itself.

There was, in fact, something coming up the channel toward us from – it took me a second to estimate – the southwest. The water around us was calm, with just a bit of a gentle swell. Here and there along the dark shorelines on each side of us, white ribbons of bubbling streams flowed and vanished into the ocean. But coming from the southwest I could see a sort of churning, as if somehow one of these streams – in fact, a whole turbulent mountain river – had slithered like a living thing into the sea and was frothing its way toward us.

"Howard? What's this?" I kept rowing and craned my head in the direction of the disturbance. "It's like rapids, except . . ."

"I believe it's something alive," Lovecraft said.

This sounded worrisome. Somewhere in the dark, freezing-cold depths below us, wasn't there a long-dormant alien supermonster? But Lovecraft didn't look worried. He pointed.

As the first lines of foam reached our bow, extending ahead of the white mass, they changed course to go around us, and I saw dark, backward-pointing fins arc and submerge. Another fin, and another, until the "rapids" that arrived to embrace our little rowboat on both sides were dotted with black fins racing and submerging and surfacing as they passed.

"Dolphins," Lovecraft said.

All around us the rapids foamed and spread but even amid the silence of our passage, I only heard the faintest hiss of foam or the tiniest plop of a splash as these creatures moved, so sleek and slick, through their natural element.

"Jeez. Howard. It's like we're in MarineLand."

"Well, Nate, it *is* the Pacific Ocean."

The pod was passing, and I looked over my shoulder and went back to rowing in earnest.

"Ahoy, mateys, thar she blows," I said, putting on my best pirate accent. "'N' sure and begorra we'll follow them dolphins across the seven seas . . ."

"If that's a Long John Silver imitation," said Lovecraft, "let's keep it down lest there are any Robert Louis Stevenson scholars among these creatures."

". . . and we'll set a course for the lost isle of ye Medusas! Yarrr!"

"Or in case any of them are Irish or from Bristol – two idioms you seem to be mingling to egregious effect."

"I can't help it, Howard." The last of the dolphins was just passing us, and the water calmed. "This is the most amazing thing I've ever seen."

"If you say so, my friend." Lovecraft laughed – a sound I had not heard from him very much – and I laughed too.

Lovecraft looked out into the expanse of night on every side of us, blackness speckled with little needle-points of light: the windows and mooring lights of the *Pacific Odyssey*, the windows and beacons of Egmont behind us, the red light that – like Hansel and Gretel's trail of crumbs – pointed the way to my grandfather's house.

"Did you hear something, Nate?"

All I could hear was the splash of the oars.

"Can you feel that?" he asked.

"Yeah. I think."

Actually, I knew what he was talking about: through the rowboat's thin hull I could feel a kind of sub-audible hum. A sound sighed hoarsely over the ocean around us, and for a moment I feared that, with the dolphins' passing, whatever lay in the depths had found a way to rise and engulf us. A dull subwoofer thudded off the cliffs of the surrounding islands, and for a moment, I thought the lights of the *Pacific Odyssey* had brightened – perhaps they'd turned on a searchlight? – but when I turned to look, the ship was still quietly moored. The sound was coming from the other direction, from the south where a wide channel spanned the dark shapes of islands. Another ship had appeared: one much bigger than the *Pacific Odyssey*, lit up like a Gore Park Christmas display, and headed right in our direction.

Riding up with Lena and her family today, there had been some mention of the Powell River ferry that left from a place called Earls Cove and . . .

As we looked, I stopped rowing, and the boat started to swivel in the waves, following wherever the tides and current wanted it. The ship was drawing nearer. It was going much faster than you'd think.

"Nate, hand me the . . . forget it, there's no time. Row for your life. That way!" He pointed toward the moored *Pacific Odyssey*.

Now the approaching ship was a mountain of light. A ferry ten times as big as my high school was bearing down on us, moving much faster than something that big should move.

I pulled hard on the left oar and it slipped out of its lock; as I fumbled to get the metal pin back in its little hole, the ferry sounded its horn. I pulled one oar, then the other, trying to wheel the boat around, and then pulled as hard as I could on both oars. The ferry was getting closer, but in a few moments we'd drawn alongside the *Odyssey*.

"Around the stern," Lovecraft said. "Quick!"

Then the rowboat tilted so acutely that if I hadn't grasped hard onto the oars, I would have somersaulted into the ocean. I smashed hard into the seat, water splashing over my head. The rowboat careened in the wrong direction, and then we passed around the stern of the *Pacific Odyssey* and suddenly we were bobbing in the midst of inexplicable calm. Around us, waves from the ferry rushed past like surf in a storm. My head smacked into something, and I grabbed it. It was a taut, heavy nylon rope – one of the *Odyssey*'s mooring lines – and I held onto it. If we could keep this position, the ship would shelter us from the ferry's wake.

Feeling as if I had just dodged a toppling skyscraper, I watched the lights of the ferry slowly fade into the distance. I opened my mouth to speak to Lovecraft, but he put a finger to his lips and held up his hand: listen.

The man from PIPS, Brad. We could hear his voice from the deck overheard. "If you're seasick, you can barf over the side."

"I'd like to know where Howard went," said Cynthia. "I don't see the boat."

"It's a little boat, and it's dark. They'll get here soon."

"I get weary sometimes, of people who have had contact with these creatures. Just because they're so different, so alien, they insist that they're evil. I'm sick of that word. Evil evil evil. It's provincial and it's counterproductive."

"Cindy, if these beings, or aliens, if they're that much different from us, they might have their own notions about, you know, what's right and what's wrong."

"All that could be negotiated if we could just make contact. *Othering* them like that is no help. Evidence: that's what we need. I'm hoping . . ."

The voices shrank and faded as Brad and Cynthia walked down the deck.

"Evidence," I said. "Is that what they're looking for?"

"Tomorrow, they're undertaking a dive to the wreckage of the ship that's claimed to be in Hotham Sound," Lovecraft said.

"A marine abyss – the Medusa Deep itself. I'll tell you what, Nate: Are you up for some more rowing?"

"I guess."

"Let's go with your original idea: let's find Sid. Let's go to your grandfather's house."

CHAPTER 24
MALIGN AND DEMONIC MONSTERS

Lovecraft offered to take the oars. We pulled away from the *Pacific Odyssey*, past its floating dock. Tied up there was the big inflatable and another vessel, dull yellow in the dim light. As we passed, I saw it was some kind of mini-sub that didn't look like it could fit more than one or two people. We headed toward the red light that hovered in the darkness across the water.

After a while I observed to Howard, "You're a better rower than me."

"Just experience, Nate." Ever since last October, I had been recovering in the hospital, groaning whenever I had to flex my mangled shoulder, getting on and off painkillers, trying to catch up in school, and meanwhile Howard had been happily rowing back and forth across these green and peaceful fjords.

"Howard, where have you been? That night at the stadium . . ."

"I'm sorry, Nate. Perhaps I could have stayed and been some help . . . but I had to go."

"You said things were even worse than you dreaded. And then off you went."

"I should explain . . . " Howard fell silent. Behind us, there was no one on the deck of the *Pacific Odyssey*, and as I watched, a cabin light went out. Howard kept rowing. I waited for him to start explaining.

"Didn't you say we had to go to the left of the light? We're

194

heading straight for it." Howard adjusted the course, but still had nothing more to say. I tried to prompt him.

"So at the stadium . . . you took off . . . and *Sorcerer* appeared . . . and then Yog-Sothoth faded away . . ."

"*Sorcerer.* Nate, you know about *Sorcerer?*"

"How do you think I got here?"

I told him about my search through the North End in a spring blizzard . . . my unwilling induction into the crew of *Sorcerer* and learning their bizarre history . . . about meeting my mother ("Nell's your mother? *Nell?*") and Tobias and Agnes. I was leading up to my grand climax (I knew he'd be dying to hear it, who wouldn't be?), about how I got off *Sorcerer* and safely onto the ground, but Lovecraft couldn't get over the part about Agnes being on board.

"Agnes? Really? How is she?"

"Wondering where you are, Howard, like everyone else."

"I suppose so . . . unfortunately . . ." He sighed.

"I've got her number. I talked to her just today."

Lovecraft remained silent. I looked at the red light. It looked like we were on course.

"So, Howard, is Agnes, like, your girlfriend?"

"Look over the horizon." Lovecraft pointed. Sure enough, draped in the night between sky and ocean, silhouetted over black islands like the shapes of sleeping bears, a yellow moon was rising.

"I remember a night . . ." Lovecraft sighed.

"Yes?"

"Agnes and I went to the opera outdoors – a theatre under the stars outside Mexico City. It was a warm evening, the stars over the hills and the scents of roasting food and the perfumed trees . . . I don't even remember the opera. Something Italian:

Verdi, Puccini. And I was there with Agnes – it was a way of life I'd always wanted to live but never managed – I never knew how to get to it, and there was never any money. I couldn't afford to become a man of the world. But for a moment in time, Agnes helped me."

I couldn't tell if Howard was evading my question, or answering it.

"And the sun went down, and the performance started. It was exquisite. I'd never heard anything quite like that before. After the intermission, the house lights went down for the second act, and the amphitheatre was suffused with this warm, rosy glow. The moon had risen, and before the performance resumed, the lead tenor came out from the curtains and pointed and led us in a cheer. *'Bravo la luna!'* he called, and there it was, hanging over the hills like a festival lantern, this giant golden disc, a planet of dreams. *'Bravo la luna!'* – we gave the moon a standing ovation, and had some wine, and the performance carried on."

"Sounds pretty nice."

"It's the sort of experience I've had with Agnes, and no one else."

"Howard – look there! D'you think . . . ?"

Now we'd rounded the point; the red beacon had vanished. Then I saw not one light, but a cluster – what looked like a distant community or way station. Whether that was the Fraser place or not, I was wet, hungry and tired, and lights meant – I hoped – buildings, warmth, people, food. It was so dark that distances were hard to estimate. With luck, these lights were no more than a kilometre or so away.

"How far do you think –" said Howard, and suddenly the prow of the boat crunched into coarse gravel. Howard shipped

196

the oars and twisted to see. I put a hand on his shoulder to steady myself and climbed over the prow onto the beach. The clouds had thinned a bit, and somewhere through them peeked a sliver of moon. Now I could see the curved avenue of a rocky beach, leading along the shore to a shape that might be a dock.

Howard and I took hold of the mooring line, pushed the empty boat off the gravel and towed it along the shore until we could tie it to the dock, which was not much more than a boat-sized wooden platform between a couple of pilings. There was a bigger boat there, this one with a steering wheel and an outboard motor.

"That's his boat, isn't it?" I said. "Sid's?" What did I know – I was in a steep learning curve as far as boats were concerned.

Lovecraft shivered. "Let's find shelter. Wherever this place is."

Now I could see a house off in the darkness, thirty metres or so from the shore. As for the lights I'd seen – I walked toward them. They were a cluster of solar garden lights. They hadn't been a kilometre away, but a stone's throw, across the beach and a strip of ragged grass.

It was getting toward midnight. Whether or not this was Sid Fraser's place, I was about to freak someone out. I walked up to the house – an old cottage with cedar shakes covering the outside, and slippery wooden steps leading up to the front porch. There was no little glowing doorbell that I could see.

I peered through the window set into the door. Everything was dark inside. I was about to knock, when the landscape around me exploded in daylight. Lights on poles illuminated every inch of the lawn, the weeds, some kind of gazebo near the dock, the rocky beach. The front door flew open. I squinted against the glare. Outlined against the dim radiance from inside the house was the man that Lovecraft and I had met earlier in the evening.

"Who are you?" He squinted at me and Lovecraft, who, a bit unsteadily, was climbing the path behind me. "What are you doing out here?"

Before I could explain he said, "Goddammit, come in out of the cold."

He gestured us in and shut the door. We were in a living room that extended the width of the house, on one side leading to a kitchen from which shone the only illumination. I introduced us, although in a moment he'd recognized us.

"Why are you soaking wet?"

"Because, uh, it's wet outside, and I rowed here – we rowed here – from Egmont, and just about got swamped by a humongous ferry."

The old man just kept staring.

"I didn't know," I continued feebly, "that boats made such big waves."

He kept staring. It was getting a little creepy. When he finally spoke, his voice had dwindled to a harsh whisper, as if he was having trouble negotiating the words.

"Are you Nell's boy?"

"So is this Sidney Fraser's house? You're him?"

At this point, I didn't give a damn if he was Sidney Fraser or not, if I could just get warm and dry out my phone.

"Nathan," he said. "Nell's boy. Nathan Silva."

"Everyone calls me Nate."

"I hope you don't mind . . ." Lovecraft said. He collapsed into a frayed armchair that faced the front window.

"Take your coats off," Sidney said. "I'll build up the fire."

At one end of the room was a stone fireplace, embers still

glowing through the glass window of a cast-iron stove set inside it. Sidney pulled aside a mesh curtain, opened the front of the stove and, with a sheet of newspaper and a few pieces of kindling, produced a great deal of white smoke. He blew on the mixture until it burst into flame. Coughing into his sleeve, Sidney threw in some more bits of wood, and peered at us in the growing light. I took off my boots, dropped onto the floor and held my hands out toward the heat.

Sidney peered at me curiously, as if some indecipherable foreigner speaking an unknown tongue had just washed up on his private shoreline. He turned to look at Howard. "Explain to me how you can be H. P. Lovecraft, for Christ's sake."

Lovecraft smiled weakly. "Actually, I'm what you would call a Lovecraft proxy. It's a novel system that they use – a group with whom I'm affiliated, the Lovecraft Underground. When the need arises they delegate a sort of avatar, or proxy, in order to –"

"Give it up, Howard," I said.

"You sure look like the real deal. Never met him, of course, but I've seen his picture in books a hundred times." Sidney Fraser grinned at me. "This guy's Lovecraft all right."

"Come now," Howard blustered. "How would such a thing be –"

"Seriously, Howard. Forget it," I said. "The whole proxy thing is a scam. This guy . . . uh, Mr. Fraser, uh, my grand . . ."

"Call me Sid. Everyone does."

". . . Sid, here, is right. You're the real thing."

"He would be, let's see," Sid admitted, "123 years old." He looked at Lovecraft, raising his eyebrows.

"Exactly. You see, Nate?" Howard chuckled. "I'm already a venerable elder, so there's no need to exaggerate."

"Howard, I know about the hub-rim differential. Obviously, you didn't die in nineteen thirty-something like the books say, so let me guess. Somehow you got hooked up with *Sorcerer* . . . went through this continuum threshold to . . ." I always had to take a run at this word ". . . R'lyhnygoth? . . . and then because of the hub-rim differential? . . . C'mon, Howard, help us out here."

Lovecraft held up his hands as if to concede defeat. "Nate, I'm sorry to dissemble. I want you to know it's not my nature. But I need to warn you: Do you really want to know? The more you know, the deeper you'll get into a world that once entered, might not let you out. No matter how much you want to leave."

"I think that boat sailed a long time ago."

Sid handed me a flashlight and a paring knife. "Take this," he said, "and go slice a handful of chives from the base of that whirligig in the garden – the one nearest the boathouse. It's about twenty steps in front of the house. The raised bed on the right."

Sid had switched off his outdoor lights, so his front yard was a darkened theatre where anything could happen. Something was squeaking so I headed toward it: the whirligig in question, some kind of wolf figure, bravely pedalling its painted haunches in the misty beam of the flashlight. I took a minute to look around, impressed with the difference between March in Hamilton – where snow had been falling just a few days ago, and for all I knew still was – and here on the west coast, where buds and wildflowers were coming out and the only snow was way up the sides of the mountains.

The knife in my hand had a cracked wooden handle and the blade, honed over many years, was pencil-thin. I sliced off some chives and looked around the foggy dark. I could smell the wind off the sea, the fermented muck of the shoreline and the freshness of the surrounding forest . . . The front door of the house opened and Sid yelled for his chives.

Back in the house, Sid put me to work slicing potatoes. Over a gas stove he heated up two frying pans, got my cubed potatoes sizzling in oil in one of them, then started mixing up eggs.

Introductions had been awkward – granted, we'd busted in on Sid out of nowhere in the middle of the night. For a while, I wasn't sure that Sid and Lovecraft were going to get along. By the time we started eating, however, it was all I could do to get a word in edgewise. For having just met, each seemed to know a lot about the other. Sid asked Lovecraft who the hell were these PIPS people.

"Well, they have money," Howard said. "They're not devotees of the Great Old Ones, but researchers who are collecting evidence, so they've funded – or someone has provided the funds, I'm not quite sure – an oceanic institute here on the coast. PIPS: The Pacific Institute for Paranormal Sciences."

"If you ask me –" I started.

"Nate, listen. They're talking about an internship where students can get high school credits by taking courses and working with the institute. On-site. They're looking for young people who've had contact with the Great Old Ones and their followers and who have the ability and the inclination to do further research. Nate, instead of gasping through your teens in a dank, exhausted steel town you could be –"

"Hey – that's *my* dank, exhausted steel town you're dissing!"

"Suit yourself. They're here now because the institute has a sort of undersea vehicle – a high-tech submersible – and they've enlisted experts. They're planning to explore the wreck of the *Mary Maquinna* tomorrow morning. They have an idea about, in the long term, raising it to the surface by attaching a network of inflatable bladders."

I glanced at Sid. His expression took on a glazed look, as if his mind was far off somewhere.

"Raising the wreck," Sid muttered. "Let them raise the wreck. *Experts*. They'll raise *it* too. I'll be ready. I've been ready for thirty-five years – since 1978, when I left the outside world and set up here. If they raise it from the deep, I'm ready. I've spent decades cleaning and reloading and keeping my powder dry. Experts, schmexperts. I'm the world's foremost expert on this subject."

"What subject is that?" I asked. "Raising sunken ships?"

"The subject of killing malign and demonic monsters of the deep," Sid replied, "using a deck-mounted cannon that launches grenade-tipped harpoons."

CHAPTER 25
THE LAST STAND OF
THE *MARY MAQUINNA*

When I woke up in the morning, life, at least for a minute or two, was normal again. I was sleeping on a couch in a room in a house built on solid ground, instead of on a bunk in a metal cabin thousands of metres in the air. Outside the window was not clouds, jet trails, thrals and the wintry upper atmosphere, but trees, rocks and ocean. My clothes, strewn over a book-covered coffee table, could use a wash, but at least they were dry. I was wearing a frayed set of long underwear that my grandfather had probably worn on board the *Mary Maquinna* when he was sixteen. There was coffee on in the kitchen, and the CBC crackled from a radio on the counter. There was cereal and stuff in the fridge. My phone rang and I pulled it out.

It was my mother.

"That *thing* knocked me over, I was fighting to get it off, there were gunshots, suddenly all the thrals were gone and I was bleeding. Once I got patched up, Agnes told me a story that's so ridiculous I don't believe her. You got *pulled out the door* by a thral?"

"It all happened in about two seconds. I pulled it off you, and next thing I knew . . ."

"How did you not get mauled to death?"

"It couldn't maul me to death and fly at the same time. We

were thousands of metres up. It had to keep flying to save itself. As soon as we hit the ground I let go, and it took off. It was pretty freaked."

"*Freaked?* What about you? I got attacked by that same thral, and I'm bandaged like a mummy."

"Well, I got scratched up by branches quite a bit."

"Branches? Do you realize –"

"Mum, I did what you asked. I found your dad."

Over the phone, my mother's voice faded in and out against a dull roar in the background, as if she was being swatted by the gusts of a storm.

"Where are you?" I said.

"I'm on my way."

"In *Sorcerer?*"

"I've been up half the night. *Sorcerer* landed at the Georgia Hangar and before Eadric and Tobias could lock it down I jumped off, ran to the dock and stole one of their boats. I'm just passing a place . . . the sign on the dock says Earls Cove."

I remembered driving up with Lena, Mae and Ernie the day before. Earls Cove was where we'd turned off for the pub at Egmont, and the terminal for the ferry that had just about whacked us last night.

"That's close."

"Nate, listen to me. It's got to do with this thing the Great Old Ones have. Neural suasion?"

"You told me all about that. I don't get the whole thing. I wonder if my scars . . ."

"It's more than just transmitting thoughts and feelings. It's the gateway to some other level of physics – some entry into matter and existence that I don't understand. I don't know if anyone on Earth really understands it."

"Not me."

"Exactly. I've got to warn you. Look, nothing against Tobias, but he's desperate —" A gust of wind wiped out her voice.

"Having a hard time hearing you, Mom."

". . . he wants you back on board . . . the only way he can get to Max . . ."

Her signal was breaking up into static, so I hung up. After all, she'd be here soon.

When I stepped outside, things were less normal. I had never been anywhere like this, where everything was rock and trees, and nothing much was level except the ocean. It was strange to look out a window and across a grey sea to the green flanks of snow-capped mountains. Where were all the parked cars, hydro poles, phone wires, pigeons, Ticats banners? Talk about an alien world.

The gazebo-thing I'd noticed last night was some kind of open boathouse, and my grandfather was working on a very strange vessel: an open boat, long and wide, and in the middle of it an even stranger contraption that he was polishing and squirting with a can of WD-40. A steel deck mounting raised it to eye level, and Sid could turn it on a swivel, like an astronomer's telescope. Sticking out the front was a metal thing like a model rocket ship — except that its barbed tip and metal vanes looked sharp as razors, and gleamed in the morning sun with the buffing that Sid was giving its long shaft and sharp edges.

"Is that . . . is that a harpoon gun?"

Sid stood back, regarding his work. "That's what I'm going to whup the monster's ass with if I'm still alive the day that bugger

– go ahead, call it Nyarlathotep, I call it Magnus – emerges into the light and air. After his long prison sentence on the bottom of the saltchuck." He pointed out into the sound. "That cursed abscess on the ocean's floor that some of us call the Medusa Deep."

I'd brought out the copy of *RainVisions*.

"Where'd you get that?"

"My mother gave it to me. I got shanghaied by *Sorcerer*, flown across the country from Hamilton against my will and ended up here. When I just wanted to go home. I mean, I'd like to finish high school someday. But my mother seems to think it's important that I *not* go home. That it's more important to come here."

"Maybe she's right." Sid stared intently at the housing of the harpoon gun, as he polished it between shots of WD-40. "Dunno for sure."

"Maybe you can help me link up some facts. For starters, what does your story in this old book have to do with my story? Last fall, I snuck into some ceremonies in the local football stadium that were run by an outfit called the Resurrection Church of the Ancient Gods . . ." I gave him a recap of pretty much everything I'd gone through to get here.

"And now," I finished up, "though I thought we'd put it down for good, the Church seems to be coming back to Hamilton. But I can't figure out what that has to do with you."

I paused, and Sid chewed his lip thoughtfully. Would I have to rephrase it as a question?

"You know, back in '46, we whupped that creature's ass," he said, "and I thought it was all over. Like a horror movie: the monster is dead, the danger's all over.

"But that night he came onto the ship – and got away from us by changing his body shape to squeeze through a porthole.

206

After that, we didn't see him again for days. But Magnus stayed in the water. He kept changing and growing. He turned into something that could live there – that belonged there."

He squinted down the coast the way we'd come the night before. "For almost a week, we thought he was gone. Then from out in the strait, we heard a whale in distress. I've never heard such a cry – like a lost soul that knows it's damned with no chance of redemption or rescue. The *Mary Maquinna* steamed out there – it had been a crummy season, Captain Thiessen said it would be his last, but he was hoping for a sick or injured whale, an easy kill so he could pay some creditors and make his payroll.

"There was a young whale there all right, but something else had got to it before us. Something huge and cold-blooded, like nothing ever born in the deeps of the ocean. This was from the far greater deeps – the deeps of outer space. The thing that Magnus had become – the monster that he was still in the process of becoming." Sid shook his head. "Thiessen harpooned the whale up close to put it out of its misery, and told us not to harvest an ounce of that tainted flesh.

"Then there were greater horrors, when Magnus started coming ashore. For the people in all those isolated little villages along the coast . . . back in those days there were no phones, erratic radio reception, just weekly stops by the Union steamships . . . Someday someone will piece it together: newspaper reports of seemingly unrelated deaths, local plague outbreaks, mysterious accidents, wild animal attacks, shipwrecks – all Magnus."

Sid fell silent. Here it was almost seventy years later, Sid the only one left alive, and still it affected him, like a veteran who'd been to war and back.

"Then it came after us, after the *Mary Maquinna* itself. My god that was a sight. By this time, the thing that had been Magnus was almost as big as our ship."

"I read this in your story," I said. "I thought it was fiction. It was even weirder than the stuff I'd seen in Hamilton last fall."

"Thiessen prepared for it." Sid's voice trembled. "He ordered us into the boats, and when we were clear he took hold of the cannon and shot two harpoons into the creature. Long spears with barbs and explosive heads that sank deep into its body." He patted the shining metal of the cannon. "Believe me, they are cruel instruments. Once they're in, they will not come out. When Magnus reached the ship, Thiessen was ready for it, with a third harpoon. Then, using the rest of the explosives, he sank the *Mary Maquinna* itself. He sent the ship to the bottom of the Medusa Deep along with the monster that was now bound to her with ropes that could hold the biggest whales."

He pointed to the boat, poised at the top of a ramp that extended down below the tide line. "I can have this in the water in five minutes," he said. "All electric – I keep it good and charged up for the big faceoff. A lockbox full of harpoon heads tipped with grenades. This time the job will be finished.

"For years I've heard Magnus calling to me in my sleep – I know it's not dead down there, only dormant, folded into itself like a tree in winter, keeping at bay the ropes and the cold and the pressure that slowly drain the life from it, waiting, chanting, dreaming and straining to get himself free again. Is Magnus the Great Old One Nyarlathotep? From talking to your friend Howard, it sounds like it to me. But it won't matter this time. This time, when he breaks surface, he'll get a surprise. This time, Magnus won't get marooned on the bottom of the Medusa

Deep. This time I'll blow the bastard to bits, one harpoon at a time, until there's nothing left but mush for the prawns."

Sid fell silent. My run-ins with the Great Old Ones, and the Church, they gave me some stories to tell, but I don't know if they could top *that*. I thought about telling Sid about my exit from *Sorcerer* via winged predatory extraterrestrial. But I heard the distant rumble of an engine. I pointed down the channel.

"They're coming."

PART 4
THE
MEDUSA
DEEP

And He shall put on the semblance of men,
the waxen mask and the robe that hides,
and come down from the world of Seven
  Suns . . .
Nyarlathotep, Great Messenger,
Father of the Million Favoured Ones, Stalker.

– H. P. Lovecraft, *The Whisperer in Darkness*

CHAPTER 26
THE *PACIFIC ODYSSEY*

Sid swore. "From the institute. Those people."

Black smoke wafted from its single stack as the *Pacific Odyssey* rounded the point and entered the sound. Flanked by a smaller boat, it was towing the mini-sub I'd seen moored at its floating dock. The dock itself had been winched to deck level and was hanging off the side like a huge plastic toy.

"They better keep that juggernaut away from my dock." Sid headed for the shore. My phone rang.

It was Meghan. "Nate, where are you? We've got to get our act together here."

"Still out of town, but —"

"There was a ceremony last night. At the stadium."

"What stadium?" There was no stadium, not anymore.

"They tore through the fence," Meghan explained, "and did some kind of ceremony perched on the wreckage, hundreds of them like ants on a cheesecake."

"Did anything happen? I mean, did anything come through?"

"Don't think so. I wanted to try and go in, but Mehri and Sam talked me out of it."

"Meghan, you know you should stay away from those people." For god's sake, I thought, I sound like my dad.

"By the way, Nate, we've decided you can join. The Furies. I think we can use your talents."

"I don't know about 'talents,' but as soon as I can get back . . ."

"Where the hell are you?"

I did my best to explain, though I stammered a bit when Meghan asked what this had to do with stopping a revived Resurrection Church of the Ancient Gods from summoning the Great Old Ones.

"Jeez, Meghan, I didn't really plan this. I just got stuck on *Sorcerer* . . ."

"Right." Meghan chuckled. "This mythical zeppelin thing that only you have ever seen . . ."

". . . and now I'm caught up in a local drama that I think has to do with the Great Old Ones."

"Nate, wherever you are, really, no kidding, get back here."

I looked out at the ship, which had lowered its dock into the water. Now some kind of folding gangway was being extended.

"It should all be over soon . . ."

"Another thing. Did you ever figure out what ever happened to Howard?" Just as Meghan asked that question, the rumble of the approaching research boat stopped as the mini-sub was pulled around to the dock. I looked around and Lovecraft came out of Sid's front door, buttoning his coat as he came down the path.

"In fact, I'm looking at him now." With my free hand, I waved to Lovecraft.

"Tell him to get his butt back here. We need all the help we can get. This means you too."

Meghan hung up. Lovecraft waved back at me. In his long grey overcoat, a black toque pulled over his bony head, he looked like a tourist from another era, out of place both in this rough overgrown yard with its mountain background, and against the shiny fittings, blinking LEDS and modern gear of the approaching research vessel.

He was a lot more than a tourist, but I thought about what my mother had said, that this nervous, eccentric man (I had to admit, I liked Howard, although the moment he showed up, my life became much more scary and dangerous) was an alien fiend in human form, a menace to life on our planet who had to be eradicated. I would have to ask him, one of these days, when things settled down a bit.

An open boat was on its way from the *Pacific Odyssey*. Sid puttered around his dock, making room for the boat and muttering about stowing anything valuable that these bastards might walk off with. I borrowed his binoculars and tried to get a good look at the mini-sub. As I watched, a human figure climbed onto it; someone petite and slender in a form-fitting outfit, maybe a wetsuit, black trimmed with electric blue.

"Can we go out to it?"

"Not on your life," Sid spluttered. "In the past, I've told these guys that I won't co-operate with them, much less help. If that sub makes it to the bottom, watch out. Any contact they make, that creature that lies down in the abyss, it will just turn it to its own advantage."

"Sid, surely that thing's dead," I said. "Didn't you guys blast it with harpoons and send it to the bottom of the ocean? And wasn't that like, back in the last century? Don't you think it's dead and rotted away by now?"

Sid had just finished retying a loose bumper to the wooden dock. He stood and glowered at the approaching boat. Then he turned to me. "I can't picture what you went through back east – I guess it was quite something. But you've only scratched the surface of the attempts of the Great Old Ones to make their moves on this planet. You know that thing is still alive . . ."

"How would I know that?"

"You know it because you heard it last night. Something in Howard's reading, something *alerted* it, and it called up to us from the depths. You think it's dead? Come off it."

The float we were standing on began to rock alarmingly. Sid didn't seem to notice, so instead of running onto the shore, I mirrored his moves and stood my ground, hoping this sort of thing was normal. The open boat from the *Pacific Odyssey* edged up to the float. Sid caught a line from it, and signalled to me to grab one from the stern. I pulled it against the bumpers, regretting that I'd never learned any fancy sailors' knots, and tied it like I'd tie a shoelace, pulling the knot as tight as I could. The pilot climbed out onto the dock. There were introductions all around.

"What we're going to do here today," the pilot, Raymond, began, "is –"

"Howard, what do you think?" Sid said. "Young Nate here has read my story about the *Oberth* A-7 and the *Mary Maquinna*, but he's not convinced that the thing at the bottom of the deep isn't dead."

"It's been years," I said. "The cold. The pressure. And doesn't it have to breathe?"

"That thing," said Sid, "thousands of years ago, launched itself from its home planet, light years away. It travelled through space powered by a kind of technology we can hardly dream of; kept alive by a kind of patience, and *stillness*, inconceivable for a human . . ."

"If you can get into the boat," said Raymond, "you're invited out to the *Odyssey*."

". . . then it hovered in orbit for who knows how long, in a form we can't even imagine," Sid continued. "I don't know what to call it – plasma? aether? stardust? Kept at bay by the barrier of gravity and air, hung around maybe for *centuries* – until it found a vessel that would bring it to Earth. In fact two vessels – first it entered the German spaceship, and then it entered the body and heart and mind of Magnus, the captain of the *Oberth* A-7. It took him over, possessed him like a demon in a fairy tale."

"The Great Old Ones can be huge, predatory and danger-ous." Lovecraft nodded. "But they hunger for the souls of their human victims, as much as for their flesh. Your grandson here has a singular sensitivity to their power over the mind – you said, Nate, that your mother told you about the Great Old Ones' capacity for neural suasion – but he also has, as far as I can tell, a great ability to resist."

"Whatever you say, Howard. That thing scares the hell out of me every which way. It's alive and I won't accept the conse-quences of pretending that it's dead, when it's not – when it's actually just *waiting*. Biding its time."

"Like I say," Raymond began again, "if we can get started –"

"My theory is that the creature in the Medusa Deep is one of the original Great Old Ones," Lovecraft said. "A lesser god, mind you, but a particularly mendacious and destructive one, a creature often at odds even with Yog-Sothoth and Cthulhu themselves. I believe that it is none other than the entity known as Nyarlathotep."

"Now here I'm inclined to agree. Nyarlathotep is what called to us last night, out of the ocean. I understand that it's a being that can take many forms?"

"Exactly, Mr. Fraser –"

"Call me Sid."

"– as you yourself saw in that dangerous encounter so many years ago. No astrobiologist myself, I can't tell you if such a creature has an innate need to constantly change, or if Nyarla-thotep's personality – or its destiny – is such that it must con-stantly deceive. It assumes the camouflage of a master predator, a master manipulator of truth. Savage and ruthless, Nyarlatho-tep is not the most powerful of the Great Old Ones, Sid, but it is in some ways the most frightening."

While they spoke, Raymond had been glancing at his phone, and furtively texting. "I hate to interrupt," he said, "but I un-derstand that we're here to look for the wreckage of a historic west coast whaling ship, the *Mary Maquinna.*" He pointed to the shelter on the shore. "Mr. Fraser – what's that you've got there?"

"It's a kind of heritage monument. An authentic west coast whaling harpoon gun. Completely non-functional, just set up there for display." My grandfather was lying through his teeth.

"There's been some talk that you're, uh, resistant to outsiders."

"I try to be friendly, if that's what you mean," said Sid, "even to tourists and other visitors who think the whole coast is some kind of theme park set up for them to look at. The real outsiders – that is, those who come to this planet looking to pillage and prey and rule – those are the ones who really shouldn't mess with me."

"So the rumours aren't true?" Raymond looked genuinely relieved. "You don't order in explosives, and test this harpoon gun every year or so?"

Sid smiled. "When you live off by yourself in a community like this, people gossip. I occasionally bring in a bit of dynamite to blast a stump, but that's just business: I'm a licensed operator. These days, get your blaster's ticket, and the next thing you know, you're a dangerous crackpot or terrorist."

"I hear ya," Raymond said. They shared a few seconds of funless laughter, as if having this conversation was actually something they both wanted to do.

"Can we watch the dive?" I asked.

"You'll be able to see pretty much everything from here."

"I mean, on board the research ship. Where we can watch the dive as it takes place."

"Sorry," Raymond said, "Cynthia and Brad told me you're not allowed on board under any circumstances."

I groaned.

Sid rolled his eyes. "Screw them."

Lovecraft said, "What can we possibly have done to merit this censure?"

"Stole that boat for one thing." Raymond pointed. "But they don't mean you guys. You guys are fine. They mean this one – you're Nate, right? I mean, no offense, man."

"If you can excuse us for a few moments, Raymond," Lovecraft said. "Before I join you, I just need a moment's confab with Nate and Sidney."

We walked back to the house and stood on the porch, where Sid shivered in the wind off the inlet. Not for the first time, I was glad I was still dressed for an Ontario snowstorm.

"Those people are such dickheads," I began. "If I could actually be on board for this, to see what happens, I could maybe –"

"Shut up," Lovecraft said.

"What?"

"We don't have time to complain," said Lovecraft. "I need your help. I can probably keep my phone in my breast pocket, so you can at least hear what's happening."

"Just in case worst comes to worst, I wouldn't want to be on the ship," Sid volunteered. "I can do more good here."

Lovecraft pulled out his phone and held it in his palm gingerly, as older people often do, like if he touched the wrong icon it might blow up in his face. I showed him what to do so that I could hear whatever he was hearing without anyone at his end being the wiser.

Sid shook his head. "After all these years," he said. "Diving to the wreckage of the *Mary Maquinna*. A bad idea." He turned to me. "Nate, if the kelp hits the fan around here, I might have to go into action tout de suite. *We* might have to."

I wasn't quite sure what kind of "action" he had in mind. "I'll listen for breaking news."

"Alert me if things go bad, and we can have that boat in the water in two minutes."

"Uh, have the boat in the water to do what?"

"When that happens, I'll need you to do whatever I tell you to. I won't be asking. I'll be your captain."

I gave an exaggerated salute. "Sir yessir."

"Get serious."

"Just what is it we'll have to do, that is, with the boat?"

"There won't be any please and thank you. Just so you know." He handed me a key. "There's a cellar door in the kitchen. Down in the cellar you'll find a steel cabinet. Go into that cabinet . . ." He gave me a short list of things to fetch.

The house smelled of bacon, woodsmoke and the seashore.

Sid seemed like an okay old guy. I paused in the kitchen and thought maybe someday it would be nice to spend some time there. Splitting firewood and doing, well, whatever people do when they live out in the bush: Mend fences? Raise chickens? Practice axe throwing? Go fishing? I didn't have a clue.

I found a light switch. The cellar ceiling was low. When I unlocked the steel cabinet, the door bumped against a ceiling timber. Inside, a few hunting rifles leaned in one corner next to a net bag full of ammunition. In the other corner, what I figured were whalers' flensing knives, in all shapes and sizes: ones like kitchen knives with oversized handles, to hook-shaped blades, to curved machetes, to big long things that were like hockey sticks – if in hockey you scored points by beheading the other team.

At the back, spears, broad shiny heads narrowing to sharp points, at the end of long wooden shafts. Sid had called them "lances." Harpoons were what whalers used to injure and tether a whale and then, with it hurt and exhausted into immobility, they would climb onto its body with these lances and . . .

I didn't want to think about it. I gathered up six lances, locked up the cabinet and reported back to Sid on the beach.

CHAPTER 27
THE DESCENT

I felt bad for Raymond. His job was simply to stop at the dock; pick up Lovecraft, Sid and the rowboat; and get back to the *Pacific Odyssey*. But to do this he had to sit through me complaining, Lovecraft speculating and my grandfather ranting. By the time I got back with the lances, Raymond was patiently tying the rowboat onto his launch – presumably at Sid's insistence – so it could be towed to the *Pacific Odyssey*. Sid, meanwhile, had built up quite a head of steam.

"Curse these people and curse their goddamned mini-sub. Good people died decades ago so that creature could remain, as it should, slumbering forever in the cold and blackness of the Medusa Deep. If that Magnus-thing re-emerges, I'll send it right back where it came from. And I don't mean outer space, I mean hell itself, the burning depths of . . ."

I made a mental note, should this meeting between Sid and Magnus ever occur, to stay as far away from it as I possibly could. Fortunately for us (I was afraid what Sid would do if they came close to his dock), the *Pacific Odyssey* had moored several hundred metres offshore. The submersible ("it is *not*," he admonished me, "a 'mini-sub'") was about to be launched, Raymond announced, as he hustled everyone except me into his boat.

"No way I can go," my grandfather insisted.

"We're heading down to the wreckage of the *Mary Maquinna*,"

Raymond said. "You're the only living survivor – maybe the only person who, when we find the wreck, can tell us what we're seeing."

Finally Sid relented. He took me aside and handed me a key ring.

"Finding the wreck is one thing; it'll be days, or weeks, before they're ready to raise it. I guess I can lend a hand. After all, once they get a good look at the Magnus-thing, with their TV cameras, they might think twice."

However, in case he needed his well-armed whaleboat, he told me how to launch and start it up. We stowed the lances under a seat, and Sid fitted grenades onto his stock of harpoons. I saw the manufacturer's name was the same as on the lances.

"Nianzhen Marine Supplies," I read aloud. "White Rock, BC. They make explosive grenades?"

"That's An's company. The cook on the *Maquinna*. After that mess, he retired from the sea and started up his own business. Did real well for himself. His son Albert runs it now."

"A marine supply company? Why would they make grenades? What kind of fishermen need grenades?"

"Albert doesn't make them for the fishing industry. He makes them for me."

I stood at the shore as he and Lovecraft boarded the launch and headed for the *Pacific Odyssey*, smarting at missing out on all the action, practising the moves Sid had shown me to operate the boat and the harpoon gun, and practising saying "Nyarlathotep" under my breath. I was getting better at it.

Sid's house was an amazing clutter of the old and new. A rusty old hand drill beside a shiny new laser level; an internet modem sitting on a stack of old *Popular Mechanics* magazines (Color TV is Here! / Will Monorails Ever Get Off the Ground?). Next to a Brownie Hawkeye camera I'd found, of all things, a phone charger, so before going to bed, Lovecraft and I had both made sure to charge our phones. Sid acted appalled ("Being connected – the modern obsession!") but I was glad we'd done it.

Already, Howard's surreptitious audio feed was keeping me updated. I could see they were all on the floating dock next to the *Odyssey*, clustered around the yellow submersible, and I was able to hear a lot of the conversation, most of the time – it depended on who was doing what. People were switching on and off boat motors, compressors, winches, drainage hoses, god knows how many things that roared and rattled and gushed. I had no idea life at sea was so noisy. Through the binoculars, I saw Lovecraft talking to the person in black I'd noticed before.

"Don't tell me," Lovecraft was saying, "you're the Leslie Chung-James who authored *Our Undersea Past*?"

I heard a woman's voice, but couldn't quite make it out. I could see that as she was talking to Lovecraft, she was leaning over the *Deep Range* (from here, I could read its name on the side), checking I don't know, switches or trim-tabs or watertight fittings or whatever they have on submersibles.

"I couldn't help but feel, reading your *National Geographic* piece, that you came to some highly debatable conclusions about the eldritch statuette that was brought up from the wreck of the *Zuytdorp* in 1964. I wrote to you a year or so ago – suggesting the actual location of the Great Old Ones' submerged ancient city of R'lyeh."

"I remember that email." Chung-James's voice grew more audible; I saw her turn from the sub and face Lovecraft. "I didn't answer it because it came from someone who said they were

H. P. Lovecraft. Who of course passed away many years ago."
Even through the audio compression of the phone connection,
her voice was clear, musical and confident. "Don't tell me that's
you."

The distant Lovecraft-figure bowed slightly. "One and the
same, ma'am."

"It figures. Who else would use a word like 'eldritch' — as if
that's a thing. Look, can we talk later? I'm kind of . . ."

A bearded man — Cynthia's husband, Brad — approached and
gestured, and climbed into the top of the submersible. In a moment, Leslie climbed in after him. I watched as the hatch of the
Deep Range was closed and sealed, and the little sub steered away
from the dock and vanished under the surface of the sound.

I knocked around the boathouse, checking what keys unlocked what, and hoping I wouldn't have to use them. With a
shovel I scraped barnacles off the metal rails that Sid called
"ways," that slid the boat down into the water. I could hear
Lovecraft, on board the ship, clattering up and down stairs, with
other people who were walking and talking. It was a while before
anything coherent came over my phone.

"I'm surprised the water is so murky," Lovecraft said. "I
thought it would be clearer, in such a remote location."

"It's actually very clean," Raymond's voice pointed out. "The
cloudiness is plankton: microscopic animals. But you know,
where we are really isn't remote. We're just around the corner
from a good-sized city."

Evidently the sub was staying close to the wall of the abyss
as it descended, so there were comments about rocks, seaweed,
anemones, various plantlike creatures.

"Is that an octopus?"

"A big one."

Then I heard a voice – Leslie Chung-James – thin and distorted, coming through the ship-to-ship comm system, over a speaker and through a room full of people, before getting to me via the phone in Howard's pocket. "Now we're well into the Deep," she said. "Past the two-hundred-metre mark."

"How are the instrument readings?" asked a voice, Cynthia. "Everyone feeling okay?"

"Just ducky," Brad's voice said.

"I've got my down vest," Leslie said. "But I haven't even zipped it up. Pressure, oxygen, all that looks fine. Batteries as expected."

"What's that?" Cynthia asked. "Up on the left."

"It's a smokestack," Leslie said. "There's something on the bottom: a large boat, or a small ship. Let's approach it very slowly, and figure out how long it is."

"My god, that's it." I heard my grandfather's voice. "The *Mary Maquinna*. I can tell you how long it is: forty metres."

"Brad, I mean it." Leslie's voice sounded tense, tightly controlled. "Slowly . . ."

There was an audible crunch.

"Oops." Brad chuckled.

"The smokestack is gone," Leslie coolly announced. "It fell straight into the abyss, so it's gone." She paused. "That's good, I guess. If it had fallen here in front of us, it would have raised a cloud of silt. It's hard enough to see as it is."

"It's the *Maquinna*, all right," my grandfather said. "See those lines going over the side? Follow that, and . . ."

"Brad, I need you to turn the helm over to Leslie," Cynthia said.

"No way."

"There on the deck – is that the mount for the harpoon gun?"

I heard Sid speaking up from on board the *Odyssey*. "There was a system where, after firing, the line – a rope almost an inch thick – once you'd shot it into a whale, could be snapped off the gun. One man tied it to a bollard on the deck while the other reloaded. You see? There are two ropes still secured next to the harpoon mount. Look there, they converge and go over the side."

"We need more finesse in piloting. You don't even have to move. She can pilot perfectly well off the video feeds. Switch the helm control to Leslie," Cynthia said.

"Well if that's what you want," Brad said testily. "You can take this job and . . . What the hell?"

Suddenly my phone fell silent – not the silence of a broken connection, but the aural background wash when the person on the other end fell silent. Only in this case, it was a roomful of people who had fallen silent and over their speakers, related through Howard's phone to me, the two people in the *Deep Range* had also fallen silent.

"Lookitthat," Brad whispered.

I could hear the hiss of the radio link between the *Deep Range* and its mother ship echoing through the control room on the *Pacific Odyssey*. *"What was that?"* somebody gasped, in a choked uncertain voice as if the air was being sucked out of the room. Then I heard Cynthia's voice, drained of all bravado or command.

"Brad?" Her voice quavered. "On the monitor, all we see, there's just . . ."

"What the hell is that?" It was Leslie Chung-James on the sub. "Move your head!"

"You don't wanna see this." Brad's voice sounded dreamy and detached. "It's the dark all right, but it *moves*; it's *alive*."

"I can't see that well," Leslie said, "but the wreck is perched on the edge of a chasm – who knows how deep it goes. And the dark . . . I can't look!"

"What's happening with Brad?" asked Cynthia.

"I've got the helm," Leslie said. "I'm raising our bow. The ropes lead *here*, across the bottom . . ." Then there was more silence. I could only hear the humming of machines on board the ship, and the movements of the spectators.

"So dark," Brad said.

Leslie said, "The ropes lead down the slope onto the rim of the chasm. But I'm not going to look down – I've never seen anything like that. And there on the rim – what's that?"

There was a pause, and I could hear just the static of the radio link, the sounds of people together on the ship, moving and murmuring, and then Leslie's voice again.

"Oh. My. God."

Lovecraft spoke, his voice a harsh whisper. "Nyarlathotep. Nate, I can see it on the bottom: something enormous, all bones and carapaces, some combination of invertebrate and vertebrate, cold-blooded and warm-blooded, mollusc and mammal, crab and whale . . ."

"Howard, who are you talking to?" asked Cynthia.

"Some demented sculptor's worst nightmare. Taking notes, Cynthia. Always looking for material. Is one of these things a microphone? I've got to talk to the submersible."

Raymond said, "Now is probably not a good time."

"They mustn't go any closer. They don't realize –"

"Not now, Howard," Cynthia echoed.

"They've got to stay back! Of course, this thing is an

unprecedented find from a scientific point of view, but, Cynthia, there's real danger here. You've got one of the Great Old Ones right in front of you, and I can assure you, it's still alive!"

"Howard, they know. We've got an award-winning marine archaeologist – I'm responsible for her well-being – and my husband, and we've got to get them back to the surface, you're right. But in deep-sea dives, you don't rush."

"Look at the complete absence of undersea life around this part of the wreck," my grandfather said. "There's a reason for that."

"At the very least, ask Dr. Chung-James to back away," Lovecraft continued. "I know that the wreck, and that enormous carcass, is a fantastic find, but if she could just put some distance between it and the *Deep Range* . . . until we've undertaken further observations, I for one –"

Leslie's voice came over their monitor. "We're stuck."

Cynthia sighed. "Leslie," she said, "perhaps you should back away for now. Just five or ten metres, and we'll discuss what to do next. The footage is certainly valuable, but –"

"Can't you hear me?" Leslie's voice trembled. "We're stuck. We can't move."

"Now, Leslie" – Cynthia spoke slowly and clearly, trying to sound calm, hoping to soothe the feelings of her increasingly nervous crew – "if there's a problem, let's call it a day and get you back to the surface. Is it an engine malfunction? Is that why you can't move?"

"The engines are fine. The propellers are fine. We just can't move."

"Why not dump some ballast?" Cynthia sounded as if she was working hard to stay positive. "You'll surface, and we can

229

pull you in."

"I'm trying that just now." Above the background noise of the submersible's transmission – the hiss of air, the hum of the electric motors – there came another machine-like hum.

"There," Leslie said. "I've dumped a hundred litres of water. That's like attaching a hot-air balloon. The submersible's at maximum buoyancy. But it's not budging."

"Feel around with Mickey," Cynthia said. "See if you can find whatever's snagged onto you."

"Mickey?" Lovecraft asked.

"There's two mechanical arms on the outer hull," Raymond answered. He must have leaned over, because I could hear him clearly, his voice a loud whisper. "A good old-fashioned waldo – a metal gripper, like a steel claw. That's Mickey. And on the bow, a hydraulic circular saw with a diamond-tipped blade. That's Minnie."

"What if they can't get it moving? Do they have scuba gear? Is there an escape hatch?"

"There's emergency breathing equipment, but they're almost three hundred metres down. The entry hatch is hinged to swing outward, so they could never get it open; with the water pressure down there, it would be like lifting a couple of tons. If somehow they got it open, the pressure of the incoming water would crush them. The only way a scuba diver can survive at that depth is to descend very slowly, taking several air tanks along, and then come back up even more slowly, so their body has time to decompress."

"Whatever's got you," Cynthia explained to Leslie, "must be snagged onto one of the arms."

"The arms are on top of the sub," Leslie said. "How could

they get snagged? It's not like we piloted *under* something."

"Can you use Minnie?" Cynthia continued to talk slowly. I had to admire her deliberate calm. "Maybe . . ."

"I don't think we're snagged," Leslie said. "We're *grabbed*."

A humming sound rose over the radio connection. "I'm starting up Minnie," Leslie said. "I can reach one of those ropes."

"Is it a rope that's trapped you?"

"So dark . . ." Brad whispered in the background. "How's it *that* dark down there?"

Leslie said, "I've started up Minnie. I'll sever anything in reach."

There was a rush of voices, cries, complaints, advice. I heard Cynthia Dampier's voice: "What the hell is that?"

"We're free," Leslie said. "We're ascending."

Then, before my audio connection dissolved into chaos, with the sound of people running, everyone talking and arguing at once, I heard Leslie's voice again.

"This thing is moving. It's alive. It's coming after us."

CHAPTER 28
THE WHALEBOAT

I hung up and kicked out the wooden chocks that kept the boat in place. Sid had explained that those had to go before I unlocked the chains that secured the boat. Finally, I stumbled on the right key, unlocked the locks, released a catch and the whaleboat shot down the rails into the water.

Clearly, I'd forgotten a step. I ran to the shore but untethered, the boat had already moved out of my reach. Slowly turning, it began to drift westward. My phone rang. I looked over at the *Pacific Odyssey*, hoping no one was watching. Just in case, I wasn't answering that phone.

I got to the dock just as the whaleboat drifted past it, and I ran along the dock, gathered speed and jumped, clearing the end bumper and landing on the whaleboat's gunwale. I tumbled forward and grabbed onto the cannon for balance, then I swung over the pilot's seat and fumbled with the keys until I found the one that fit the ignition. I turned the key.

Nothing happened. The force of my landing was driving the boat even farther from the dock and the shore. Unfortunately, as it bobbed in the waves and rotated rudderless, it wasn't getting any closer to the *Pacific Odyssey* either.

Then I remembered that it was all-electric and, indeed, indicator lights had come on all over the dashboard. To the right of the wheel was a kind of lever. I pulled on it and the boat moved.

I pulled it a bit more and with a rising hum, the boat went faster. This was great.

I turned and got the *Odyssey* in my sights, aiming for the floating dock along its side. I experimented pulling the lever faster, then slower, so I could bring the boat to a stop before I rammed it into the dock. Above my head, the cannon bobbed and nodded and shook its head with each change of direction. I felt very powerful. Watch out, Nyarlathotep. Nate Silva is coming and he's ready to kick some –

"What the hell is the matter with you?"

The boat was approaching the floating dock, and it was my grandfather yelling. Only he and Lovecraft were there. I slowed to a crawl, and looking over my shoulder . . . did I mention that I'd been piloting the boat backwards the whole way? Once it started moving, I didn't want to mess with anything, and I wasn't sure how to make it go forwards.

"Stop. Stop!"

That was easy: I just slid the lever to the middle position. While Lovecraft reached down, grabbed the gunwale and found a mooring line, Sid clambered in and took over the helm.

"Why'd ya back it in?"

"I thought that way, we could take off faster, going forward. To make our escape."

"Yer full of it. Howard, get in here and help Nate." Accelerating smoothly, so we wouldn't lose our balance, Sid pulled away from the dock and began to circle the *Pacific Odyssey*.

The whaleboat was a sort of catamaran with long tubular pontoons on each side, to stabilize it against the weight of the cannon that stuck up out of the middle of it like a sculpture in a city park. I braced myself against the movements of the boat and looked at this murderous machine, its gleaming spearhead tipped with the polished and barbed explosive grenade, and on deck, the pile of harpoons waiting beside tall coils of yellow rope. I thought of how, for centuries, human beings had dreamed up more and more awful ways of killing the huge and intelligent mammals we share the planet with. Until we got so good at it that they're almost gone and if we're not careful, we're next. Was Magnus, or Nyarlathotep, or whatever this creature was, so evil that it deserved *this*?

Lovecraft leaned toward me. "The sub's come unstuck from the bottom. They're returning it to the surface – but there's something after it. Sid caught a glimpse onscreen and seized my phone to call you."

Sid had piloted the boat around the side of the *Odyssey*. We were about a hundred metres out; looking back, I could see Cynthia and Raymond among a crowd scattered from the deck down the gangway to the floating dock.

"Like I said before," Sid announced, "as long as we're out on the water, I'm captain of this boat, and you two do *exactly* what I tell you to do."

Lovecraft and I looked at each other. I shrugged. "Sure. I guess."

"Believe me, it's for your own good." Sid had me take the helm. "We won't bother with putting her in reverse, Nate, since you've demonstrated your expertise in that department."

I drove the boat around the *Odyssey* to familiarize myself with steering and acceleration, and the feel of driving a boat properly, and also with changing gears. Then, Sid had me keep the boat steady while he and Lovecraft prepared the cannon.

"If this thing surfaces, it's going to be dangerous," Sid warned us. "My plan is to get in fast, and get in close, and fire, and then run like hell."

Lovecraft's phone rang, and I heard Cynthia's voice. "Keep that contraption away from my ship."

"We'll just observe, Cynthia, and only intercede if we're needed. In a clear emergency situation. Always good to have another boat in the water, eh?"

"We know what we're doing. We don't need a walking scarecrow and a teenage boy piloting some kind of a parade float exhibit to bollix things up."

"I'll pass on the message." Howard hung up.

"By the way, both of you," Sid said, "if I have to fire this thing, cover your ears and open your mouth. Protect your eardrums."

"Sid." I pointed at the ship. "I see something." A shape was breaking the surface. I was ready to pilot the whaleboat toward it.

It was the *Deep Range*. First a slender comm tower poked above the waterline, then the water parted to show the full length of the submersible as it manoeuvred toward the floating dock. Leslie Chung-James appeared from the entry hatch and climbed onto the dock to secure the sub, and gestured to crew members to help her get Brad to safety. A few cheers rang across the water as Brad was helped onto the dock, but Leslie hurried to the gangway, gesturing for the others to follow her. Although their voices carried across the water, too many people were talking at once for us to make out anything. Where was the Magnus-thing?

"That woman," I said. "Leslie Chung-James. She's trying to get everyone away from the water. Should we head in?"

"No." Sid pointed north. "We back off." At his instruction, I turned the boat and we idled slowly away from the *Pacific Odyssey*. Looking back, we could see that Chung-James was still urging everyone off the dock, up onto the main deck, the rest of the party straggling behind.

"Magnus –"

"Nyarlathotep," Lovecraft interjected.

"I think of it as Magnus. If Magnus has let the sub go, it's for a reason. Now it's down below us somewhere. It tricked the folks on the submersible into freeing it – in order to get themselves out of its clutches, they cut the ropes that bound it to the wreck – and he's on his way. Speed up a bit, Nate. Let's put some space between us and the ship."

"On the monitor," said Lovecraft, "as much as I could make out, the creature was smaller than you described, although still huge: perhaps seven or eight metres long."

"I was there and I saw what I saw," Sid retorted. "Though that was, jeez, fifty . . . sixty years ago."

"Sixty-seven," I said.

"I guess."

"Perhaps that's why it's smaller," suggested Lovecraft. "Like a hibernating animal, it's been feeding on itself all this time."

"Consuming its own body." Sid nodded. "Puttering away on a thin trickle of fuel like an old Easthope motor. Year after year after year, until finally there'd be nothing left. Until some fricking mesachie idjit shows up to set it free." He looked around. Now we were at least half a kilometre away from the *Pacific Odyssey*. "Nate, turn the boat around, and shut off the motor."

I was proud to be given the authority of piloting this little craft, but as we sat there I thought about how much I had to learn about boats. Although I tried to keep us stationary, that was just not possible. I kept having to start the engine and move it this way and that in order to keep us pointing in the direction we wanted. I apologized to Sid about this.

"You're doing okay," he said. "Even when it's calm, the ocean is not a stable entity."

From here, we couldn't see any movement aboard the *Odyssey*. The submersible was secured and everyone had gone inside. Then the ship seemed to shudder; its smokestack and comm masts swayed as if the vessel had been rammed.

"Did you see that?" Sid pointed. "Could have been a wave, a gust of wind."

Indeed, there was no movement from the direction of the *Odyssey*. Against the backdrop of the coast, the green expanses decorated with vertical slashes of black rock, grey gravel, the white foam of rocky creeks, it was as pretty as a postcard, and showed about as much action.

"We'll sit and wait," Sid said.

I could see a white ship coming our way from the north part of the sound. The same ferry, I supposed, that had almost run us down last night. Anyway, we were well out of its course; it would pass to the southwest.

So there we sat, me adjusting the tiller and running the engine to maintain our position. When I looked to the southwest, I saw a small white boat, coming our way from Earls Cove, just around the corner from Egmont and the pub where I'd had my reunion with Howard.

Everything in my life seemed to be changing very fast. That snowy night in Hamilton had only been three or four days ago. Jeez, I thought, I'd sure like to get back there. Among other things, Meghan was insisting . . .

On board the *Pacific Odyssey*, somebody screamed.

CHAPTER 29
THE STALKER OF SOULS

Sound carries across the water, I'd found out, but we were a long way from the ship. Whoever made that sound had been screaming out their last ounce of breath.

Sid turned and barked, "Get us there. Right now."

I accelerated too fast, slowed when I saw I'd almost knocked Sid and Lovecraft off their feet and then tried to get up to speed more smoothly.

"Howard, keep your eyes on the water," Sid called over the hum of the boat and the rush of its wake. "We'll watch the ship."

His words sent a chill through me. He had described Magnus – what Magnus had become – as nasty and powerful, capable of attacking on ship or shore or underwater. Until we found out where Magnus was, we had to be ready for it to appear anywhere.

I'd manoeuvred us into the shadow of the *Pacific Odyssey*. I slowed the boat and turned off the engine so we could tie up at the dock. On the way up the gangway, Lovecraft stopped us.

"Listen."

We listened. On board we heard a door slam, voices raised as if in argument, then a shout of desperation – "There's no time. It's here." – and another door slam.

"This is nothing," my grandfather said. "If anything, it's some domestic blow-up."

"It could even be a trick," Lovecraft pointed out. "Nyarla-thotep *is* known for disguise and deceit."

"Howard, let's get back on the boat. Nate, you stay here."

"But . . ."

"Remember I'm in charge."

"Okay," I sighed.

"I think Magnus is still in the water. That's its element now, that's where it wants to lure us. You and Howard stay in touch with your phones. Nate, you go to the top of the gangway and stay there. We'll take the whaleboat and circle the ship slowly. Watch the ship, but don't venture any farther onto it, just in case. Here."

Sid handed each of us one of the long steel lances I'd taken from his cellar locker. Lovecraft looked dubious. "We're going after Nyarlathotep with spears?"

"Dammit, Howard, I admit it. I should have brought my Remington, but I didn't. So now I'm winging it."

They climbed back into the boat and I took position at the head of the gangway.

"We'll circle the ship once, be back in a few minutes. Unless Magnus makes a move on us, which I hope he does. Don't go any farther on board," Sid reiterated, and pointed at the lance. "Keep that thing pointed down. These people will freak out if they see you on their ship with it. And watch your back."

They left the dock, Sid coaching Howard on using the harpoon gun, and in a few moments disappeared around the stern.

Without the hum of the boat and the shush of its wake, everything became very still except for the wind in my ears. From here, near the stern, I saw the white boat from the southwest was getting closer. I wondered if that was my mother. For a moment

I pictured her pulling up to the floating dock. I would jump in and we would navigate down the coast to Vancouver. Tie up at the Vancouver waterfront, hop on the next plane home.

From somewhere in the ship I heard someone sob, and then a voice weakly crying for help.

Sid had told me to stay put, but I ran across the deck anyway. Out on the water was the whaleboat, Sid at the helm, Howard looking uncomfortable at the big gun.

"Help!" The voice came weakly through a half-open window.

I would take a quick look, and then phone. Then I noticed something farther along the deck, about halfway along the length of the ship. I approached it, wrinkling my nose.

A fishy stink of mud and dead, fermented things wafted from the gunwale and the deck, drenched with water and stained with black muck. The nearest cabin door, smeared with mud and seaweed, slumped off its broken hinges onto the deck.

I waved at the whaleboat, trying vainly to catch their attention. Then I pulled out my phone and called. On the boat I saw Lovecraft reach for his phone, say something and pull it out, then both he and Sid looked up at the ship.

All I needed was to get their attention. I hung up, waved my arms, pointed at the door, gestured with the spear and then to make my point, jumped through the door into a dark compartment.

Once inside, this seemed like a dumb move. It looked to me like the freed Magnus had followed the submersible to the surface. But it wasn't the sub that it wanted. It had come around to the side – the side, either by luck or by design, that we couldn't see from the whaleboat – and pulled itself out of the ocean and up the side of the ship.

This was some sort of lounge with couches, tables and chairs, a dartboard and a big-screen TV where a rerun of *The Apprentice* showed some scumbag wannabe entrepreneur grovelling for the right to stay in the tower. The pale flickering light helped my eyes adjust to the dark room. But if Magnus wasn't here, something from out of the ocean was clearly somewhere on board.

The connecting wall banged and shook, as if someone in the next compartment was throwing around furniture.

From the outside deck came only the sound of the wind. Out on the water, I heard my grandfather call, "Nate? Get the hell out here! Nate!"

At the far corner, the door to the next room stood ajar, and on the floor in front of it something moved. Brandishing the lance, I stepped gingerly around a couch and a coffee table in the flickering light from the TV.

There was a man's body on the floor. I stooped over him. It was Brad, still in the wetsuit he'd worn when he and Leslie Chung-James had piloted the sub into the Medusa Deep. But there was something different about him. His face was shadowed and sunken, his hair gone straw-like and dry. The suit showed a line of bloodstained perforations along his torso, and he didn't move.

I jumped when a voice came from the corner.

"It pushed me aside to get at him. It *hurt* me." Raymond huddled in the corner. "It got him. It did something to hurt him, he screamed."

Christ, I thought, what have I gotten myself into? Now the noise next door had become a slow, rhythmic pounding, as if something was trying to get in or out.

"He couldn't hardly see," Raymond gasped. "He said it was

the dark. 'It's the dark that blinds you,' he said, 'like frostbite, so cold it burns.'"

"Help is coming," I told him, hoping it was true. "Hang on." Whatever that meant.

The hell with this, I thought. I left Brad's body, and opened the lounge door.

It was a kind of dining or serving area. Unlike the lounge it was full of light, and filled with the dripping coils, segmented like an armoured worm, of the thing that had pulled itself out of the ocean. Raising its crablike head, Magnus was throwing itself against the heavy bulkhead door opposite me. For a moment, it didn't notice me, but maybe I made a sound, or caused a draft, because the thing turned. I saw a huge mouth topping an expanse of pale flabby-looking flesh ribbed with muscles like tree roots, dripping mud and barnacles and sea water. Its torso was rimmed with writhing tendrils, tipped with suckers that braced the thing as it attacked the heavy steel door.

As it turned, the suckers detached and stopped their frantic motion, and with a curious stillness, Magnus did something: it hunched, and I felt a shock of mingled fear and wonder from my head to my toes, the kind of feeling I had when I'd encountered the vulsetchi, or when the shape of Yog-Sothoth filled the night sky over the stadium in Hamilton.

The motionless suckers framed the creature like a halo of dead flowers, and in the middle of each of these throbbing blooms an eye opened, each centred with a dark pupil, the iris shining with a spectrum of colour like oil in a puddle. The eyes locked me with their gaze like a predator that had found its prey, and I could feel the same awful suasion I'd felt at the first of the Church's ceremonies.

242

I can help you, I can lead you.

I couldn't turn away from those eyes, but like a caterpillar the thing was coiled around the room, its head and torso raised, its tail at my feet. I took a step forward and rammed the whaler's lance into the thing's rear end.

I pulled back through the door, shouted at Raymond to hide, ran through the lounge and found myself not out on deck, but running down a corridor. I looked back to see Magnus's armoured head breaking through the door, mandibles clicking eagerly as it came after me.

I burst out onto the deck close to the gangway. Leslie Chung-James was standing there as I slammed the door and fumbled to find some way to lock it after me. But the door wasn't designed to keep things inside.

Down on the floating dock Lovecraft and my grandfather were just tying up the whaleboat. I began shouting at the top of my lungs and with the bang of a shattering latch, the door behind me flew open, bouncing off the outer wall, and a flurry of tendrils burst out of the dark. Leslie backed up, raised a nasty-looking speargun and fired into the centre of that hungry mass. Barking at me to follow her, she grabbed the railings and flung herself down the stairway, landing only every four or five steps. I did the same as best I could.

"Those people on board," I said, "we've got to help them. The whaleboat, it's armed."

Something exploded like a car bomb, and my ears stung with the blast and the twanging air of a passing missile. The whaleboat cast off, churning water as it headed out into the sound, my grandfather at the till and Lovecraft hastily shrugging ear protectors over his head as he paid out line from a coil on the boat's deck. The line snapped and sang, scribing circles in the air. Above us, Magnus had emerged onto the deck of the *Pacific Odyssey*, and snarled with rage and pain at the terrible barbed spear that had sunk deep into its body from my grandfather's deck-mounted cannon. Now the boat was beginning to circle back, Lovecraft reloading the harpoon gun.

All eyes and tendrils and horned, crablike skin, Magnus scrabbled over the rail, black blood gushing from one wound, and Leslie's spear and my lance bobbing like vestigial limbs. The thing's whole length slithered like a dragon, penetrated the surface with hardly a splash and was gone.

"Let's get back up on the deck," I told Leslie, "away from the water. We can't help them from here."

"Out there." She pointed. "That's where the action is."

I looked. The whaleboat was heading farther out into the sound, and behind but gaining on it fast, Magnus's spiny back undulated through the water.

"We've got to do something," Leslie said. "If they can't stop it, with that little boat, it will kill them. Then it will come straight back here to the ship."

She ran to the side of the dock, switched off an extendible charging post, then leaned over the fuselage of the submersible and pulled a cable out of an on-board socket. I followed her and she threw the lead to me.

"Roll this up. Secure it." I obediently looped the cable around its bracket as she sealed the charging port and then unsealed the entry hatch. "Untie the sub," she said. "I'll cast off."

Events were moving very fast, and so was Leslie. I could see I'd have to work hard to keep up, though her plan didn't seem to include me. I untied the mooring ropes, pushed the submersible away and jumped onto it as it left the dock.

"What are you *doing*?" I could see Leslie calculating the time she would lose starting the sub, taking it back to the dock, persuading me to get off . . . "Dammit, get in!"

I dropped into the hatch and Leslie, still fuming, reached back to seal it. "Fasten your seatbelt, don't touch anything or say anything." In the cramped space, I started to take off the life vest I'd been wearing since I'd got into the whaleboat but Leslie snapped, "Leave it on! At this rate, we'll have to abandon ship before we accomplish a damn thing!"

Smarting at her attitude, and the implication that in an emergency I would need a life vest but she wouldn't, I fumbled with extending the seat belt and snapped it shut. Around us, a profound hum arose as Leslie pushed the submersible to its maximum speed in pursuit of Magnus and the whaleboat.

At least, I assumed that's where we were going. The ceiling was a kind of Plexiglas, but as we increased speed all I could see were bubbles and froth. From where I sat behind Leslie, there was a rectangular video monitor that showed more froth and bubbles. Another screen, with spots of light on a green background, I couldn't decipher. It was starting to feel like Leslie was right: on this mission I was dead weight.

"That thing," she gasped. "It came up with us, followed us. Pulled itself up onto the ship. People were hiding, locking themselves into cabins. I was looking for some way to drive it away or decoy it . . ." She shivered, still in the wetsuit she'd worn for the descent, and barefoot as if she'd been preparing to dive off the ship.

"Do you want a blanket?" I scanned the transparent fronts

of the compartments and read labels on some of the drawers around me.

She shook her head.

"My name is Nate, by the way."

Leslie was scanning dials. "Damn, that thing is fast. What is this thing? Do you know?"

"It's a kind of extraterrestrial."

I looked at her sitting and fretting over the instruments. She pulled a lever and the hum of an electric motor came from the bow, adding to the buzz of electronics that already filled the sub's tiny interior. Leslie looked young, but she was, I gathered, *Doctor* Chung-James, with flecks of grey in her black hair, and a stack of books and articles to her credit. She'd been in *National Geographic.*

"Call me Leslie," she said. "There's something I want you to do. Take your coat off, and your hoodie too. Do it fast. I'm going to ram this creature before it does any more harm. We may have to bail. If you end up in the water, a vest might not save you, if you're weighed down with all those clothes."

As fast as I could, I unbuckled myself, and removed a layer at a time, then re-buckled my vest and seat belt. I stuffed my coat and hoodie behind the seat as best I could. There wasn't a lot of extra space on board the submersible.

We'd descended a metre or so beneath the surface, so the bubbles were almost gone, but the view was still frustrating. All I could see was the green glow of the sunlit ocean. I heard the distant bang of the harpoon cannon.

"My god," Leslie said. "Your friends are good shots. That was a direct hit."

"They're highly motivated. I hope they don't get hurt." If

Magnus caught up with them, so close they couldn't use the cannon, Lovecraft and my grandfather would be toast.

A shadow fell over the submersible, and around us the water turned dark. My first thought was that Magnus had somehow become huge, had turned on the submersible and was about to eat us alive, like Jonah and the whale.

"What's going on?"

"I don't know," Leslie said. "A cloud bank? I can't tell. Here's my plan. On our bow there's a diamond-tipped rotary saw. It's what we used to –"

"Minnie," I said.

Leslie paused. "That's right."

"So are you going to attack Magnus with this saw?"

"Why do you call it Magnus?"

"It's a long story."

"Right." She pointed at the controls in front of her. "I've extended the arm as far as it will go and I'm revving to our highest speed."

Oh my god, I thought, don't tell me she's going to turn the whole sub into a giant . . .

"I'm turning the sub into a giant harpoon."

So we were going to ram the saw, and the sub attached to it, into a whale-sized marine alien at high speed.

"Are there airbags on this sub?"

"You're the one who was so eager to come along."

It suddenly occurred to me why the sky was so dark. My first impulse was to phone my mother, or Agnes, but my phone was stuffed behind the seat with my coat.

"Brace yourself," Leslie said. "If we get in trouble, pop the hatch and swim away."

"But Magnus . . ."

"If this works, the creature will be dead, or mortally wounded, and your friends will pick us up."

Clearly, Leslie was what Dad would call a "cockeyed optimist." From my point of view, my luck had run out.

"The thing has an armoured head," Leslie said. "There will be a soft spot right behind the carapace. That's what I'll aim for." In a quick sequence of short moves, she explained to me how to pop the hatch.

"We're almost at impact," Leslie said. "Ten. Nine. Eight – omigod, it's stopped! It's . . ."

I was thrown forward and my head bashed into the monitor. All the on-board lights blinked off. For a second all I could hear was the scream of the rotary saw as it tore into Magnus's flesh, and the sub was rocked to one side, then end to end. Suddenly we broke the surface. Water ran down the outside of the clear hatch bubble top. We were in the air . . . and kept going up.

"Omigod," Leslie cried. "Nate, you see that sleeve-framework on the right. Turn it on, switch the release and then put your arm into that framework until you can grip the handle. Quick!"

I found all the things she mentioned, and did everything she told me. Inside the rubbery accordion-fold sleeve, the cold metal handle vibrated under my touch.

"You're in control of the waldo-gripper, now, Nate."

"Mickey."

"You can see what you're doing on the monitor. Use Mickey to grab the creature's leg."

"Why?"

"Something's pulling us out of the water. Grab it as close to the body as you can, where it's thickest."

In fact, I could see that we were jammed right up against Magnus – pretty much embedded in it – and I waved Mickey around until I could see the metal arm enter the frame. Then I bumped it against the nearest leg, and grabbed on.

As I did this, the *Deep Range* turned tail-down. In a moment we spun around like a Tilt-a-Whirl, and beyond the bubble top was a spinning montage: ocean, mountains, ship, monster . . . The *Deep Range* was swaying back and forth drunkenly, alarms blinking and beeping all through the cabin, and outside the world still spun: ocean, mountains, ship . . .

"We're airborne," Leslie yelled. "What the hell is going on?"

"I'd keep my seat belt fastened, if I were you." I had an idea what was going on, but before I could explain, the *Deep Range* lurched forward, banged into something, swung into a horizontal position and flopped onto its side onto a hard floor.

CHAPTER 30
POSSESSION

I popped the hatch and Leslie, way ahead of me as usual, pulled herself out onto the floor of LOAD/EVAC. I slid out behind, to find her looking at Magnus, impaled on the *Deep Range*'s rotating saw, bleeding from the terrible wounds from my grandfather's harpoons, still quivering and dripping sea water and black blood, sprawling and sad as a drowned tyrannosaurus inside the closing loading door.

"Where are we?" Leslie looked around, reminding me of myself on my first entry into *Sorcerer*, just a few days before.

Eadric and another crew member were approaching, Eadric cautiously brandishing the flame-thrower. I thought this was a sensible precaution, even though Magnus looked deader than dead.

"Like a bad penny that always turns up," Eadric said. "Are you okay?" He frowned at Leslie. "Too many new faces on this old tub."

I introduced them. The loading door was not yet closed all the way; against the roar of the wind outside, and the growl of the winch machinery, we all had to yell.

"Get up to the bridge." Eadric gestured to the corridor door. "Tobias will want to know you're alive."

Outside of LOAD/EVAC, I crossed the corridor and opened the door of the pressure room. Surrounded by pipes and tanks of compressed gas, Offlife Access – what I now thought of as the vulsetchi hold – was quiet, its hatch still padlocked.

"Sorry," I said to Leslie. "Just had to check something here."

In fact, the vulsetchi made me nervous, and so did whatever was inside – that thing that had brushed my mind, writhing in agony within the vulsetchi's corrosive fungal colony. I'd felt it in my head as soon as the submersible had clattered over the airship's threshold. I closed the door, and on the way to the bridge, tried to keep things simple.

"We're on the airship R102 G-FAAX," I told her. "Also called *Sorcerer*. Commissioned by the British government in 1937, designed by a German engineer named Maxmillian Nordfeld."

We stopped in the lounge to take advantage of its windows – as much for my benefit as for Leslie's.

From up here, the *Pacific Odyssey* was a toy boat, far away on a bathtub sea. Closer to us, two smaller boats crept across the grey expanse of ocean, the white brush strokes of their wakes indicating they were heading for the ship.

"This is the shadow that fell over us," Leslie said. "This dirigible – airship. I didn't see it coming. It was just suddenly *there*."

"*Sorcerer* does that. Let's get up to the bridge." I was sure Tobias would be more than happy to explain everything about *Sorcerer*'s cloaking capability to Leslie but, more urgently, I needed to talk to Tobias myself. I was worried that even though Magnus/Nyarlathotep lay harpooned and apparently dead in LOAD/EVAC, we still might not be in control of the situation.

ON THE bridge, I introduced Leslie to Tobias and Margrit.

Twenty minutes later, I'd given up trying to get a word in edgewise and had retreated to a corner of the bridge, where I pulled out my phone to connect with the surface.

Just as I thought, my mother had reached the sound just as all hell was breaking loose. She had almost caught up with us when *Sorcerer* made its appearance and dropped Eadric in a bosun's chair to hastily reattach the lines from the harpoons and haul Magnus out of the ocean, with us and the submersible attached to it.

"I came around the point just in time to see that creature slide off the ship," she said. Minutes later, she pulled alongside the whaleboat and, with Lovecraft and my grandfather, helplessly watched as the struggling monstrosity, with the submersible tenuously swinging off one side, was towed into the sky and disappeared.

"I didn't know where you were, or what had happened to you," my mother said. "Now we're on our way back to the ship, to see if we can help."

"I don't know why *Sorcerer* showed up," I said. "Did you talk to Tobias?"

"No," said my mother, "and I'm not going to. I'd advise you to stay well away from him."

I looked up to where Tobias was showing Leslie the *Raumspalter*. He looked over at me and grinned.

"Mum, you've spent enough time on board this thing to know that's not practical."

"Nate, he's got an idea that having you on board somehow activates the *Raumspalter*. It's not an easy machine to get up and running. That's why he's not yet returned to R'lyhnygoth. *Sorcerer* hasn't been able to. Until now."

"That sounds like superstition to me."

"Not if you know R'lyhni technology. Practically all of it interfaces with living things. With organic matter. With nervous systems."

"Why would Tobias want to go back there anyway? It sounds . . ."

"Because Max is there. He's desperate to get Max back."

"That's like Meghan trying to get me back to Hamilton."

"I don't know who this Meghan is and I don't care. What's important, Nate, is that you get off *Sorcerer*. Don't let Tobias make that jump. If he talks about opening a threshold, you're not interested."

"We've got a deal on one condition. Mum, don't kill Howard. He's my friend."

"We're out here on the water together," she said. "I have to be negotiable. But if you knew the bigger picture . . ."

"At this point I just want to go home."

"Do whatever it takes. If we're lucky, even if he wants to make a jump, Tobias will probably want to go back to the hangar to prepare. Don't act as if you want off the ship. Make sure they let you move around the hangar. I'll come get you."

This sounded like the path of least resistance, so I agreed.

"Don't let happen to you what happened to me."

By the time I hung up, my mother had definitely given me food for thought. She was AWOL from *Sorcerer* and planned to stay that way. She was reunited with her father, and they were on their way to the *Pacific Odyssey* to see if they could help in the aftermath of Magnus's invasion of the ship. To get these tasks out of the way, and then make it back across the continent to pick up the threads of her past life, she was prepared even to make peace with Lovecraft, whom she still considered to be an alien demon in human form.

But her warning about Tobias had given me an idea. What

if, now that the *Raumspalter* device was working, the airship *could* open a threshold?

Rather than avoiding a crossing, I could use one to my advantage.

Tobias gave me a look as I left the bridge. Don't sweat it, dude, I thought. If you want to talk to me, make an effort. It would have to be a considerable effort, since Leslie was pumping him for information as ferociously as she'd pursued Magnus.

Then something caught his eye. He went to a panel on the dashboard and toggled a switch beneath a miniature old-fashioned CRT screen.

"What's going on? There's no LOAD/EVAC feed."

Margrit, Leslie and I looked over his shoulder at the black screen.

"I've looked at it every couple of minutes since we took you aboard," Tobias said. "The creature is clearly dead as a doornail. Eadric looked fascinated – he just stood staring for the longest time. But now the video feed is gone."

He turned to the three of us. "Margrit, Nate – can you go see what's going on down there?"

"I'll go too," Leslie said.

"No need, Dr. Chung-James. You're our guest here."

"Guest? There's so much work to do."

A FEW minutes later, Leslie and I stood beside Margrit as she peered in the window in the door of LOAD/EVAC.

"Why is he naked?" Margrit made a disgusted sound and leaned down hard on the metal handle. Inside LOAD/EVAC, things were a mess. For some reason, a row of parachutes had been removed and stacked haphazardly next to the arms locker, and Eadric had managed to remove the circular saw called Minnie from the creature's flesh. The harpoons, along with the spear from Leslie's gun, had been pulled out and thrown to one side. The monster, and the submersible lying next to it, lay in a growing pool of black blood. The loading door, which rolled from the ceiling like a garage door, was still not completely closed; there was a foot or so of space between it and the floor. Invading winds from the coastal atmosphere outside swirled around LOAD/EVAC, mingling the stench of death with the smells of mountain and ocean. In the middle of things Eadric stood facing us, naked and drenched in the creature's blood.

"What the hell happened?" Margrit asked.

Eadric looked toward Margrit, but his eyes were faraway and unfocused, as if he was only responding to the sound of her voice.

"It came . . ." His voice sounded hoarse and unmodulated, as if he was not only blind, but deaf. ". . . out of the water. It came out of the water."

"It sure did." Margrit moved closer but I could tell she didn't want to get too close. Not only was he covered with Magnus's blood, he was standing in a pool of it. "Are you hurt? Let's clean you up." She spoke slowly and clearly, the way people do to accident victims.

We were in kind of a standoff while Margrit figured out how to deal with Eadric. Obviously he'd been attacked, but all the carnage seemed to have happened to Magnus's huge corpse; it was hard to tell what kind of shape Eadric was in.

When Margrit said, "clean you up," I reflexively looked around for something to clean with. The place was a mess, but my eyes lit on a fragment of fabric right next to me, ripped and hanging off one of the vanes of the submersible. I grabbed it; a strip of beige cloth stippled not with the black ichor that was everywhere else in LOAD/EVAC, but with a spray of dark rust.

I looked up at Eadric.

"Just a second here," Leslie said to me. "When we came on board, didn't he have hair?"

"Don't touch him," I warned. "Something's happened to him."

"It came out of the water," Eadric repeated. "Out of the stars. *I* came out of the water. *I came . . .*"

Eadric fell to his knees. He was only a couple of metres from the loading door, and with it ajar I worried about him losing his balance and being swept outside by the gusts of wind. I left Leslie and circled the submersible, heading toward the wall control. I flipped the plastic cowling and hit Close. The motors started grinding and slowly the door started downwards.

Eadric awoke from his trance. With the door descending only a few feet away, he dropped onto his hands and started crawling toward it. Margrit cried out and we scrambled into action. As Eadric reached the door, I braced myself against the door jamb and grabbed his arm, slippery with Magnus's blood. The door hit Eadric's shoulders and stopped. I didn't know its mechanics; if it had a brake that would make it stop coming down, or if it would exert enough pressure to crush the breath out of Eadric. I tried all the harder to pull him back. Now Leslie reached the door, fitted her hands under it and pulled up. Margrit had grabbed Eadric's legs.

What had happened to him? The feel of Eadric's flesh under my fingers made me gag. Beneath the oily coating of the Magnus-thing's blood, his arm was cold and flaccid, and offered no friction. As his flesh surged under my ineffective grip, I couldn't see or feel any freckles, moles, skin tags, scars or even a single follicle of hair. But there were three determined people hanging onto him. We'll save him for sure, I thought, then Eadric twisted around, looked me in the eye and snarled. I recoiled; there was something the matter with the inside of his mouth. His teeth were the teeth of a fish, needle-sharp extensions of the ribbed tendons that lined his pale mouth. Wriggling like a crocodile, he forced himself farther out the door, freed one of his arms, and then grabbed onto my throat and pulled me with him.

Now we were both in danger. I made some kind of mangled cry for help and let go so I could grab on to the door, Leslie and Margrit both put out a hand to grab me, and with our grips loosened, Eadric pushed himself through.

Eadric slid out into the open air, vanishing from our sight as he fell beneath *Sorcerer* to the surface of the sound, hundreds of metres below.

"WHAT THE HELL is the matter with you people?" As I teetered on a pile of cardboard boxes and tried to reattach the wires from the disabled security camera, Tobias paced LOAD/EVAC, avoiding the tracks and spatters of blood that centred on the pool around the dead Magnus. There was no answering him. We'd already explained what had happened, time and time again, so Tobias was really asking the question no one could answer: *Why* had this happened?

Leslie was scooping blood from the floor into a Mason jar she'd found in the kitchen, keeping an eye on the huge corpse as she worked, and Margrit had gone up to the bridge.

"That thing gives me the creeps," Leslie said. "I feel like it's still alive."

I warily approached Magnus's corpse. Sure enough, the bleeding had stopped in the mashed, bleeding craters that my grandfather's harpoons had made in the huge carapace. Along the body, leathery expanses of pebbled flesh flexed into thorny exoskeleton, and then subsided, and I watched a limp tendril quiver microscopically.

"It just moved."

"If you ask me," Tobias said, "we should open the loading door, fly out over the Coast Mountains till we get to the hardest, rockiest mountaintop we can find and drop this thing from three thousand metres up." He pointed at the submersible, rocking on its side with *Sorcerer*'s every move and turn. "We've got to secure this thing too. Goddammit. The biggest room on the ship, and we've got no space to work."

"It moved, it really did," I said.

In the moments after Eadric had gone down, I shook my head to clear the shock, figured out how to pop the hatch on the submersible and retrieved the whaler's lance that I'd carried with me since I'd left the *Pacific Odyssey*. It made me feel better to have something, anything, to fend off Magnus with, if by any chance the monster stirred back to life.

I hadn't slept well on board *Sorcerer*, and now that I was back I could feel the restlessness returning. There was an uneasiness amid the sounds of the airship – the constant subwoofer hum of its huge electric engines, the rush of wind gusting over the gondola

Then I began to hear another sound above all the others. I heard a voice.

YIG SUN Y'IGIT YATH NYARLATHOTEP.

I shouted, "Guys – I think we should get out of here."

CHN'G R'LYHNGOTH RNG WRRYETKOSH. The voice in my head was as loud as ever. It was the voice from the ocean I'd heard on the deck of the pub in Egmont.

Magnus's great carapaced head moved. Its fanged mouth opened and closed hungrily, and the tendrils began to writhe, the rows of malignant eyes blinked and turned, furious that we'd escaped. Gingerly tightening the lid of her sample jar, Leslie jumped over the pool of blood and joined Tobias and me.

The long, sinuous corpse flexed, and I felt a painful heat hissing through the scars that crossed my right shoulder. I turned: Tobias was staring, fixated as the enormous creature breathed and expanded. Blood gushed from a wound and a black stream of it trickled toward us along the deck.

Suddenly the huge carcass exploded into life. With the blade of the lance, I batted away a tendril and ran to the exit. In a moment, Tobias was snapping a clip into a carbine he'd grabbed from the armoury but when Leslie grabbed his arm, he thought better of his plan and joined us at the door. We went through to the corridor and slammed the door behind us.

"WE ARE *screwed*!" Tobias said, back on the bridge.

"Eadric, for some reason, sabotaged the surveillance camera," I began, "but then –"

"I know, I know." Tobias stomped back and forth restlessly. "You got it working, by the way." He indicated the monitor on the dashboard. There, a low-res black and white Magnus threw

259

itself against the submersible, rattled against the loading door, snarled brainlessly.

"I should have realized something was wrong. I would have, if I hadn't been so busy with Little Miss Tom Swift here."

Leslie looked appalled. "Don't blame me for this."

I didn't know who Tom Swift was, but I had to speak up. We were running out of time. Then my phone rang.

"Meghan," I said. "I'm on it. I'll be home soon." Actually, this was looking less and less likely.

"Something's happening tonight. I have a very bad feeling about it. Maybe worse than before."

"Meghan, I'll get back as soon as I can. Have you contacted Howard's group?"

"The Underground? What can they do?"

"At least they're on our side," I told Meghan, "and last time, we more or less came out on top. Does Mr. Shirazi know about this?"

"I'm calling him next," Meghan said. "You picked a rotten time to go on holiday."

"It has *not* been . . ." But Meghan had already hung up.

Tobias and Agnes were in discussion with Gretchen and Margrit.

"Tobias, where are we going?" asked Margrit. "Back to the hangar? We can't circle Hotham Sound forever."

I pushed myself into the group and raised my voice. "Listen to me." Everyone looked.

Aside from my own needs, aside from these arguments, I was starting to sense that killing, and killing upon killing, would not make for a better, safer universe. I thought of my own scars, seared by immense heat, about the destruction and death at Ivor

Wynne Stadium, the Hounds and the death of Dana, and about the North End – once ponds and forest and marshland, now a Chernobyl-like wasteland of chain-link fences, pitted asphalt, leaky roofs and rusted steel sidings – and about how quick we are to reduce anything alive into smoke, ashes, silence. Why? Why do we do this? I looked up and saw the glow of the *Raumspalter.*

"If we crossed the threshold to R'lyhnygoth," I said, "and then crossed it again, right away, to return to Earth, where would we emerge?"

"We'd emerge where *Sorcerer* emerged last time," Tobias said. "In fact, where it's emerged the last two times we made the jump back and forth to Earth. In the absence of deliberate recalibration by the navigator, *Sorcerer* would head for the same arc transient of previous thresholds: just above that Hamilton stadium where, last fall, we emerged in the middle of your free-for-all with the Resurrection Church."

Just what an "arc transient" was, I could worry about later. What did my mother say was the time-duration difference between here and R'lyhnygoth? The hell with it.

"I propose that we open a continuum threshold now," I said. "And cross over to R'lyhnygoth."

CHAPTER 31
THE HAUNTED THRESHOLD

"I'm with you there," Tobias said.

"As soon as we arrive," I added, "dump the Magnus-creature, and head back right away. No delays."

"This would be terribly risky." Margrit looked up from the seats she and Gretchen had taken. "If the *Raumspalter* continues to operate at the consistently high level it's recently displayed, we could do both crossings easily. But it's never kept it up like this. It's as if the device is undergoing peaks in its internal metabolism that we've never seen before. It could be just a fluke."

"It's not a fluke. We've got an ace in the hole." Tobias pointed at me. "When we lost Nate to the thrals, that light starting blinking red again. And as soon as we winched him back on board, along with Leslie and the sub and that huge *thing* that just killed Eadric . . . well look at it." Tobias pointed at the *Raumspalter*. The light on the top was green. "We could cross over and be done in five minutes."

"You *would* say that." Gretchen and Margrit nodded at each other. "Tobias, we could see this coming."

I calculated – five minutes R'lyhnygoth time, times forty, equals two hundred minutes. If everything I'd been told was true, we could be back in Hamilton in a few hours. If Meghan needed me back there soon, I'd get back there soon – by crossing the galaxy and back.

"So, after Nyarlathotep's thousand-year journey through space, and according to you, his decades at the bottom of the Pacific Ocean, the bugger would find himself right back where he started." Tobias laughed. "Serves him right! I say it's worth trying."

"Plus, we can get Max," Margrit said. "Isn't that what this is all about?"

I looked out the side windows. We were over water; *Sorcerer* seemed to still be circling the sound. Beyond the green expanse of the coast, I could see the smog-haze of Vancouver and, far in the distance, the smouldering plume of Mount Baker.

Tobias said, "Of course it is. I've left Max on R'lyhnygoth. He could be dead for all I know. But if I don't go back and find him, I'll go out of my bloody mind. Plus, if we dump this creature on R'lyhnygoth, we won't have to worry if it's dead or not. It'll be someone else's problem."

"Well, all the work in the pressure room is more or less done," Gretchen said reluctantly, "and the tools have been secured."

"We've got a skeleton crew but it'll have to do," Tobias said. "You and Margrit: make sure everyone is secured for a crossing before I sound the alert. And look in on LOAD/EVAC. Right now, I don't trust the monitor. But under no circumstances go in there."

Gretchen started for the door, then stopped and faced Tobias. "We're coming back immediately, right? I mean, immediately?"

"We'll check in with our friends as soon as we land. If Max is there, we'll take him on board. If he's not there, the hihyaghi can take us to him. If they say he's dead, back we come."

"It's just that —"

"Gretchen, this will be a quick one. Cross my heart and hope to die."

"Everyone else, strap yourselves in." He indicated two chairs behind the navigators' table. With Margrit and Gretchen gone, Agnes and Tobias took the helm, adjusting waist and shoulder harnesses in their pilots' chairs.

"I'll be okay," I said. "I'll just stand here . . ."

This time, it was Agnes who barked orders at me. "Nate, you can't just stand there, or anyplace else. Threshold crossings are rough." She pointed at the navigator's chair nearest to me. "To say the least."

I sat down and strapped myself in. Tobias was already making the announcement through his headset. "Prepare for a threshold crossing . . ." He sounded like he was following a prepared text, reciting safety precautions and security priorities. Through the thinly padded chair, I felt a shudder pass through *Sorcerer*, as if the airship knew what was coming.

"We can see it moving," Margrit's voice came over the antique PA system.

"We'll land on R'lyhnygoth, open the loading door, and fricking Magnus / Nyarlathotep / whatever it is can scamper off and frolic with Yog-Sothoth and whoever the hell else. A family reunion – hugs all around." Tobias turned on the intercom again.

"Ten seconds," he announced, and I heard his voice booming through the system in the hall outside. "Everyone must be secured. Countdown starts now. Ten . . ."

Jeez, once he got going, Tobias moved fast. I looked out the window again. There was the ocean, the shore – a landscape I hoped I'd see again.

"Nine."

I felt cold sweat break out all over my body. After all, I told myself, if I could survive a fall from an airship by hanging on to a very angry winged extraterrestrial with lots of sharp teeth and claws, for sure this would be easy.

"Eight."

If I could go face to face with Nyarlathotep – Howard had called it the most frightening of the Great Old Ones – then I could survive this. Even though I was a passenger on an obsolete airship, entering an unpredictable transgalactic shift. A bottle cap tossed into an endless universe where everything could happen. If right this second, we fell into the ocean, passing boats would pick us all up in no time, wouldn't they? But if something goes wrong during a threshold crossing, who you gonna call?

"Seven."

Gripping the arms of the co-pilot's chair, Agnes looked over at me. Her face had gone pale.

"Six."

"Let's reconsider," I said aloud. "Maybe there *is* a less drastic way of handling this situation. Instead of crossing the galaxy."

"Five. Nate, it's fine. When you can create a continuum threshold, which is a kind of wormhole," Tobias said, hissing the words through clenched teeth, "an entire galaxy can seem like, well, only a few short light years."

"Call it off," I said. "Let's not do this."

"Four. Three. Two." Focused on the panel before him, looking out the front view window, occasionally glancing at the lights on the *Raumspalter*, Tobias totally ignored me.

"One."

The light outside brightened, as if suddenly the sky had been gifted a new sun, and then the view through the front window swivelled as if we were on a midway ride, or a plane flying a loop-the-loop. The horizon fell away, and *Sorcerer* tilted upward until it faced the sky, tail to the ground. Yet there was no sense of movement, no change in gravity. The airship looped into a surprising blackness outside (who knew it was so dark up there?).

"Oh my god," Leslie whispered. "It's like the dark in the Medusa Deep . . . I just glanced into the abyss, didn't get a good look. But Brad saw it full on. It affected him – so dark, he said, it blinds you . . ."

As she spoke, the blackness faded into indigo, then brightened to a universe of crimson. The colours outside gradually changed, as if we were somehow moving up through the colour spectrum. The red shaded gradually into a dull orange, and then yellow, then began to turn green. I felt a growing sense of nausea. I rubbed my eyes, and when I opened them, something was drifting toward me from across the room. It was long and pointed, and when I reached out and grabbed it, it bled blobs of black blood.

"Madre!" yelled Agnes. "Secure those papers."

With surprising agility Agnes unbuckled herself from her seat and pushed toward the navigation desk, where maps and charts were billowing out in a paper cloud. Agnes unsnapped a net and like a skilled housekeeper, snapped it back over the runaway papers and reeled them down to the desk's surface. Then she pushed away from the desk and flew back to her seat.

Weightless, I thought. Are we in outer space? I leaned back to avoid one of the black blobs – they were made of ink from the runaway rapidograph I'd snagged. The view outside was an expanse of green, with occasionally a wall of black flickering into existence, then out again.

Suddenly I had the feeling of a crowd of people swarming through *Sorcerer*'s control rooms and cabins and passageways.

"Who's this? In the room with us?"

I know you. I turned and with everything else floating, a figure stood there, firmly planted to the floor.

"Agnes?" I asked. "Tobias? Who the hell . . . ?" The figure coming toward me was human-shaped . . . roughly. It wasn't human in any other way. It was as if a creator had stuck together a ghost from a thousand creeping strands of living cloud. White tendrils, stained with flesh and blood, tendrils like long animate worms that trailed behind it, leaving a glistening silver path along the deck.

I know you. You know what I need. What I need from you.

"I can't give you anything," I said, "not death."

Death is precious. I need more death.

Agnes said, "Nate, what are you talking about? *Der Tod ist kostbar?* You're being morbid."

Around the figure blossomed a red haze shot with lightning bolts of green and gold and blinding white. It drifted toward me and I cringed at the needlepoints of light, throughout my body, that flashed and burned at its approach. The haze was pain; pain itself that had burst and blossomed and taken on some sort of awful life of its own. I cried out.

"Dammit, Agnes," Tobias barked. "Talk to the boy. Can't you see? He's having a visitation."

"Stupid of me," sighed Agnes. "Of course. Nate, I don't know what you're seeing . . ."

"What are you talking about? It's right there!" I stretched out my hand to point, careful not to get close enough to touch the thing.

"You're experiencing a visitation – a phenomenon of the continuum threshold that no one quite understands. Apparitions of friends and loved ones – sometimes hostile adversaries, hated enemies – can appear during a crossing. It's like a haunting but believe me, Nate, it only lasts as long as the crossing lasts. Or less. In a minute, it will dim and quiet and go away."

I stared at the apparition before me – the living embodiment of pain, of agony stretched out and prolonged forever, of suffering itself – and as I looked it began to fade. Leaving me in the physical sense – but behind it lingered the sense of its pain and rage against injustice, branded onto my memory.

"What is it?" Agnes asked. "What are you seeing?"

"It's not a what," I said. "It's a *he*. It's got a name. Gustav Kaindl – what Eadric called 'the thing in the hold.' He said it 'wants' me, and now I know why. It – he – wants me because he knows I can feel his suffering."

Outside the universe had turned indigo blue, and I began to get a sense of incredible speed.

"He wants me to help him die."

A crack of thunder shook the floor and walls around me.

"What was that?" Tobias said.

"The turnaround," said Agnes.

"It's never sounded like that before."

Objects clattered to the floor as our weight returned. A blob of ink fell, and a black stain appeared on my right pant leg.

"Everything's fine. We've reached the far limit of the threshold." Agnes craned her head toward me. "Nate, pay attention, because . . ."

Then *Sorcerer* began plummeting at incredible speed. Something's gone wrong, I thought. We're coming apart in the vacuum of space, or crashing onto the surface of a hostile planet. This is when I had that feeling, the feeling that nothing before had given me. The dritch, the Resurrection Church, the Hounds, the long plunge from *Sorcerer* into the coast forest, the blast of the harpoon cannon, facing off against a hissing monster. It's all over, I thought. I am dead now. Beyond the windshield, the universe had turned a deep unchanging purple. This is the colour of death, of eternity. Now, I'm . . .

I zipped my hoodie all the way to my neck, as if this would save me.

"Almost there," said Tobias. The purple faded to grey mist, shot through with the warm light of a yellow sun. He blinked. Unlike me, he was eager to face whatever would happen next. "Look at that!"

And then we were through.

ACKNOWLEDGEMENTS

Special thanks to Ashley Hisson for her expert, and enthusiastic, contributions to *The Medusa Deep* and its predecessor, *The Midnight Games*. With *Midnight Games,* Joe Stacey joined Ashley in going beyond the call of duty to make sure the book came in the best possible form. I am grateful for the enthusiasm of everyone at Wolsak and Wynn toward their books in general, and these books in particular.

For the present volume, my thanks for language advice goes to James Deaville (German), David Prentice (Spanish) and Diana Rae (Shashishalhem).

I also benefitted from funding from the Ontario Arts Council's Recommender Grants for Writers, through the recommendations of Kegedonce Press and Wolsak and Wynn. A Canada Council Explore and Create grant was also essential in helping to extend the imaginative world of *The Midnight Games* into this book, and the next.

Lastly, I thank Maureen Cochrane, whose love and support makes so much possible, and our sons, Malcolm and Simon, who have made so many efforts worthwhile.

David Neil Lee is the author of the novels *The Midnight Games* and *Commander Zero,* as well as the international bestseller *Chainsaws: A History,* and the acclaimed jazz books *The Battle of the Five Spot* and (with jazz pianist Paul Bley) *Stopping Time.* In 2016, the City of Hamilton awarded the Kerry Schooley award for "the book that best conveys the spirit of Hamilton" to David's Lovecraftian young adult novel, *The Midnight Games.* Originally from British Columbia, he has lived in BC and Ontario, and currently resides with his wife, Maureen, in Hamilton. His website is davidneillee.com.